It's all about that seco
The Way They Wer

Chance Series. (These are stand-alone books tied together by a common theme—belief in the beauty of that second chance.)

They promised to love one another forever, but tragedy tore them apart. Now, destiny just may bring them back together.

At eighteen, Rourke Flannigan and Kate Redmond thought they'd spend the rest of their lives together—until a family tragedy tore them apart. Fourteen years have passed, and they've both carved out separate lives hundreds of miles apart—hers as a wife and mother, his as a successful, driven businessman. But once a year, Kate pulls out a red velvet journal and writes a letter, which she'll never send, to the man who still owns her heart. Once a year, on the anniversary of the first and only night they made love, Rourke permits himself to read the annual investigative report detailing an ordinary day in Kate's life.

When a subcontractor at one of Rourke's holding companies is killed, Rourke decides to pay the widow a visit and offer condolences, never dreaming the widow will be Kate. As they embark on a cautious journey of rediscovery, one far greater than they could have imagined, secrets and lies threaten to destroy their newfound closeness—forever.

That Second Chance Series:

Book One: Pulling Home (Also prequel to A Family Affair: The Promise)

Copyright 2011 by Mary Campisi

ISBN: 978-1-942158-05-9

The Way They Were

That Second Chance Series, Book Two

by
Mary Campisi

Dedication:

To young love, true love, and the beauty of second chances

Chapter 1

"Once a year, I will pretend you are mine."—Kate Redmond Maden

Journal entry—May 4, 1997

It has been six hundred and thirty-three days since I last saw you. When you left, I destroyed all the pictures of us—everything—first out of anger, then despair, and finally, fear. I didn't want to remember the thick silkiness of your hair beneath my fingers, or the tiny chip in your bottom front tooth...I didn't want to remember there was ever an us, but your voice, your touch, everything about you, has consumed me for almost two years.

I've forced myself to wait until today to write. This has proved the hardest task of all. This is a special day—my daughter's first birthday. Her name is Julia. Her eyes are just like her father's—the color of a summer storm. She's the reason I have the strength to write this letter and not mail it. (Where would I mail it anyway?)

Where are you?

Do you ever think of me?

Do you ever wish things had been different?

Clay is good to me and I try to be a good wife to him. I try. He's an honest worker. A family man. He even changes Julia's diapers and reads her Good Night Moon *at bedtime. I pretend I don't see the hurt in his eyes when he touches me and I flinch—not so much anymore, just a little. He's always gentle, but he's not you. Nobody's you.*

How can I go on living like this—wanting you, thinking about you, wondering where you are and who you are with? And why you could not trust our love enough to get us through what happened? The pain is so deep I think sometimes it will ooze out of me and I won't be able to stop it. But I have to. For Julia's sake.

Where are you???? You promised me nothing would ever separate us. Were those words only to get me into bed? I won't believe that. I can't.

I chopped my hair off right after you left and dyed it red, but when I looked in the mirror, I still saw my mother's face. I am not my mother! What happened was not my fault but you blamed me, didn't you? And then you walked out of my life. I hate you—hate you—HATE YOU! That's not true. I love you. But you don't care, do you? I'll never love anyone else this way. Not even my husband. How sick is that? Clay saved me and all I had to give him was one tiny promise. Never mention your name again.

Not much. Unless your name was in every breath I took, every moment of my waking thoughts, every pore in my body.

My tears keep smudging the ink and I can hardly see what I'm writing. But I still see your face, right here in front of me, as though six hundred and thirty-three days had not passed, as though I could turn around and you would be standing there in your old faded jeans and Rolling Stones T-shirt—as though everything were normal.

No one talks much about what happened anymore unless someone new passes through. Then the gossips start whispering like scattered leaves. I'm sipping Chardonnay 1991, remember? I plan to save this bottle and toast us once a year when I open this book and write you letters I'll never send. I bought this book when Julia was six months old. I told Angie (remember her?) it was to keep track of Julia's milestones. But the way she looked at me, she knew it had something to do with you. Somehow, she always knew.

I waited six more months to write in it—six, long, tempting months. But there was Julia to think about. And what good would it have done anyway? So I hid the journal in the back of my closet, inside a shoebox, and spent the next several months devising a plan. I'd dig it out on Julia's first birthday while she was taking her afternoon nap, and the cake was in the oven, and the chicken was marinating for the dinner I'd planned for Clay's parents. I'd lock the bedroom door and pour myself a glass of Chardonnay from the bottle tucked away in the closet behind my dresses. Then I'd sprawl on the bed and ease open the first blank page. And dream about how life could have been. If you hadn't left me.

It's the only way I can survive the years to come. Once a year I'll permit myself to think of you, not in anger and hatred, but with the truth—with a love that cries for you, hurts for you, and a memory that stops with the last time we made love and erases the blood-stained sheet covering your mother's body. Once a year, I will pretend you are mine. And it will be enough. It will have to be.

***

Fourteen years later.

Kate Maden watched her husband rifle through the dresser drawer in search of his Syracuse T-shirt. He called it his lucky shirt, but Kate knew a tattered orange and blue T-shirt had nothing to do with Clay's success. Hard work and a will as strong as his twenty-two-inch biceps were what made Clay Calhoon Maden "lucky," but there was no use telling him that.

"Aha!" He yanked the T-shirt from the drawer and tossed it on the bed, then pulled open a second drawer.

"Looking for these?" Kate dangled a pair of thermal socks in her right hand.

Her husband's sunburned face broke into a grin as he snatched them up and said in a voice that held the tiniest hint of a drawl, "Babe, what would I do without you?"

That was Clay's way of saying *I love you*. Not a sophisticated proclamation or a grand gesture marked by diamonds and roses. Just a look that spoke of commitment as strong as the equipment he used to tear down the sturdiest building. Any woman would be honored to have such a man by her side.

"I'm thinking this job could get us carpeting *and* a new washer," he said as he sat on the edge of the flowered comforter and pulled on a sock. "How about a front loader?"

"You don't mind the drive?" He was a 5:00 a.m. rise-and-shiner, but an hour's drive on top of an early start time was a lot to ask.

"Nah. Every mile is that much closer to getting you that Berber carpeting." He grabbed her hand and pulled her onto his lap. "You just decide whether you want plain or one with those fancy designs."

"Clay." She ran a hand over the reddish stubble on his chin. "I have you. And Julia. I don't need carpeting to make me happy."

"You deserve more," he said, "but it's the best I can offer."

"Clay—"

"Gotta go." He gently set her on her feet and kissed the top of her head. "I'll call you after the interview."

When he'd gone, Kate straightened the comforter and picked up his work clothes—jeans, flannel shirts, thermal socks. The only suit he'd ever worn had been the department store pinstripe on their wedding day. She thought of her husband's callused hands, his weathered skin, his bad back. He was a hard worker who believed in honor and the strength of a man's word. He'd given her so much more than any other man—including the one who'd broken her heart.

***

Clay pulled up to the job site as the sun inched over the treetops. This was his sixth day and he'd decided to gain an hour on everybody so he could get home early. He pulled the gear from his truck, grabbed his thermos, and hopped out, whistling Bon Jovi's "It's My Life" as he made his way across the grassy lot. This job would net him the carpeting, the washer, and a hefty down payment on the eternity ring on hold at the jeweler's. Wouldn't Kate just croak? So, it wasn't Tiffany's; it was stamped with commitment and not even Tiffany's sold those.

As he made his way toward the building, a battered Ford pickup barreled down the side road, kicking up gravel and dust. It squealed to a stop beside him and Clay's foreman jumped out. "What the hell are you doing here at this hour?"

"Hey, Len." Clay raised a hand at the grizzled man in denim and flannel. "Thought I'd get a head start so I can make it home in time for Julia's choir recital. She's doing a solo."

Len Slewinski scratched his chin and spit on the ground. "You reckon to break union rules by starting here without the rest of the crew?"

Clay grinned. "Pretty much."

The older man shook his head and spit again. "Stubborn as your daddy. You know they say the owner of this here building is real persnickety about rules and regs."

"Well, he's not here, is he? There's just me and you, and we're not talking." Len had worked with the Madens for twenty-eight years in spite of a bum hip, a stiff knee, and last year's double bypass.

"I don't like it, boy. That pretty little wife of yours wouldn't like it either."

"That's why you're not going to tell her. What are you doing here two hours before starting time?"

Len kicked a clump of dirt and coughed. "Skip asked if I'd post watch for him seein' as he's taking Shirley to Niagara Falls this weekend."

"Let me guess. Another honeymoon?"

Len nodded. "You got it. Most women only get one honeymoon 'less they switch husbands. I told him he better not say a peep to Loretta 'cause I'm not leaving my own bed and I sure as hell ain't leaving my john for some foolish fanciness."

"Women like that sort of thing now and again." Maybe he should take Kate to Niagara Falls. They could ride *Maid of the Mist* and eat Chinese like they had on their honeymoon.

"Mostly they start squawking if they hear somebody else is doing it. That's why she can't find out."

"She won't hear it from me. Tell you what, why don't you go fetch yourself some of those fried eggs over easy at Sophie's? That way you can say you didn't see anybody breaking code and it'll be true."

Len jawed on the idea for all of three seconds. "You got yourself a deal. Be careful, boy. Just 'cause you done it your whole life don't make it safe. Them scaffolds is tricky. Fifty feet is still fifty feet."

"Got it." If Len didn't stop yakking, Clay would lose his early start.

"See you in a few." Len threw the truck into gear and bumped down the dirt road.

Clay headed toward the building, calculating the time he'd already lost. Damn, he'd have to work fast. He could secure the side section before Len got back. He entered the building through a side door and flipped the light switch. A stark expanse of beams, metal, and cement were all that remained of Jennings and Seward Faucet. Len said the new owner planned on putting some of those high-end condos in here.

A spark of anger surged through him as he thought of all the people who used to work in this building, people who had mortgages, tuition, and grocery bills. They'd lost out because China could make faucets cheaper than upstate New York. What kind of jobs could a high-end condo give to a machinist?

The rich kept stuffing their pockets and the poor fell deeper in debt. As a boy, Clay had never thought about which group he belonged to—his parents made sure he and his brother had a new jacket every winter and enough food on the table for seconds. Things changed the summer a rich kid from Chicago moved to Montpelier and taught Clay just how much he didn't have.

Clay sucked in a breath and pictured the first blow of the wrecking ball as it slammed into the building in a moving, swaying dance of destruction culminating in a rubble of steel and concrete. Len said Clay had the deadliest aim he'd ever seen. Maybe because he pictured the rich kid's pretty-boy face each time he swung.

Clay tossed his gear next to the scaffold and rummaged through his bag for his safety harness. Damn. He must have left it on the front seat of the truck. He glanced up the scaffolding to the top. In all the years he'd been demolishing, he'd only needed his harness twice. His Syracuse T-shirt and skill would keep him safe. He grasped the first rung of scaffold and heaved himself up.

***

Fifty minutes later, Len returned with a fried egg and bacon sandwich for Clay. "Clay? Where are you?" He scanned the beams and scaffolding in search of his boss. "You in the can?" Len made his way toward the back door and the three port-a-potties lined up like little blue boxes. "Clay?" He pulled open each port-a-potty door. Empty. Well, empty except for the smell of bad business. Dang, where the hell was he? Len stepped back into the building and scanned the area a second time.

It was then he spotted a crane hook swaying thirty feet away, just a slight sway, not enough to make a dent in a tin can. "Clay?" Len forgot his bum knee as he broke into an awkward run. "Clay!" He stopped short when he reached the crane. "Jesus, God Almighty." The boy lay sprawled on the concrete, arms and legs flung out, neck bent too far to be natural. A small pool of blood circled his head like a red halo.

Len knelt beside his friend, knowing before he touched him that he was dead. "Jesus, God, and all the saints." Len crossed himself and felt Clay's neck for a pulse. Nothing. He rocked back on his knees, swiping his eyes as he stared at the red-brown stubble on Clay's jaw.

How the hell had this happened? In all the years he'd been with the company, they'd never lost a person. And now this. Len's gaze flitted over Clay's back. A blue SYRACUSE splashed across it in bold letters. Where was his harness? A sliver of panic inched up his legs and landed in his gut. *Where the hell was his damn harness?*

Len pushed himself up and blew out a steadying breath as he made his way to Clay's truck and yanked out his safety harness. The boy was not going to be remembered as the reckless fool who got himself killed because he hadn't worn a damn safety harness. That would make him nothing more than a statistic for an insurance company, and Clay and his family deserved better than that.

Chapter 2

"Money is all those kinds of people want anyway."—
Diana Flannigan

"Mr. Flannigan? Excuse me, sir, but your niece just called again."

Rourke Flannigan glanced up from the financial reports spread out on his desk. Niece? Oh yes, Abigail. "What did she want this time, Maxine?"

Maxine Simmons cleared her throat. "It seems she's having a bit of a problem working your remote control."

"What?" The girl had been living with him for three weeks and was already driving him crazy.

"Your remote control, sir. To your television."

Rourke shook his head and forced the curse back down his throat. Maxine didn't appreciate "cuss" words, as she called them, and since she was the only secretary he'd ever hired who didn't want to marry him, he tried to honor her request and saved the swear words for when she was out of earshot. And right now, he'd saved up quite a few under the name of Abigail.

"Remind me again, Maxine, why I have not turned this child over to Child Services?"

"She's your niece, sir."

"She's also a tyrant, an abominable tyrant. Abigail the Abominable."

"Yes, sir."

Rourke leaned back in his chair and considered his current situation. "What am I supposed to do with her? I haven't been around a thirteen-year-old in," he paused and thought, "damn, oh, sorry, Maxine, in almost twenty years since *I* was thirteen."

"Yes, sir."

"What do I know about thirteen-year-olds? They're rude, slovenly, and self-centered. Why would anyone want one, can you tell me that, Maxine?"

"I suppose they grow on a person, Mr. Flannigan."

Spoken as the spinster Maxine was, as though she were referring to moss or barnacles. "I suppose, but good Lord, why would a person actually choose to be stuck with a child?"

"I'm sure I don't know, sir."

Rourke laughed. "Which is why we suit so very well." His laughter shrank to a half sigh. "But here I am, saddled with a niece I haven't seen in seven years and am now solely responsible for because my free-spirited sister and her idiotic friends decided to fly a prop plane across the Indian Ocean." Damn them. "How ridiculously irresponsible."

"Yes, sir."

"It's not like I can farm her out to Diana," he said, thinking of his aunt. "Can you picture her face if Abigail dropped the F-bomb?"

"No sir, I cannot picture it."

"You know, I'd pay Child Services a monthly fee for Abigail's food and clothing, and I'd rent a nice little apartment over on Crestwood—"

"They don't do that sort of work, sir." Maxine adjusted her cat-eye glasses and peered at him. "They handle children who are in danger. Abuse, abandonment, and the like, I believe."

"Well, if my niece continues to call me every five minutes, she will be in danger."

"Yes, sir."

He sighed again as the beginnings of a headache pinched his right temple. "Tell her I can't talk right now. She should go online and pick out her own television with her own remote, so she doesn't need to play with mine."

"Very well, sir."

"Do you think that will satisfy her?" He had no idea. If she were fifteen years older and not his niece, he'd send her flowers or jewelry—whatever a Centurion Black card could buy, which was anything. He stayed away from those who wanted non-monetary offerings. They were the ones who—

"It will help, sir."

"What? Oh, right. Tell her to order whatever she wants, make a list, and give it to you. DVDs, an iPod, whatever kids are into these days." Who knew what that was? "Something to keep her occupied."

"I'll see to it, sir."

"And make sure she practices the house code. I do not want the police department calling my office again today. Three times in three days is a bit much, don't you think?"

"It would appear a bit excessive."

"Do you think the child is slow?" He hadn't thought of that before. Perhaps she needed a psychological evaluation, IQ, and a battery of tests similar to the ones the company gave new employees to test their ability to mesh with the organization and calculate future success. Perhaps Abigail needed a test to measure her ability to mesh with *him*. Or perhaps she'd inherited her idiot father's genes, whoever that was. That was one thing about his sister; Gwendolyn had liked to keep the family guessing.

"I could contact the company psychologist, if you like."

Rourke waved the idea away. "No, we'll wait on that. Give it another week or so, though God knows how I'm going to last." He snatched his cell phone and checked his latest text message. Janice. Again. "I'll be taking a forced vow of celibacy if this continues much longer."

"Excuse me, sir?"

"Nothing. On second thought, take a poll of the women in the office who have teenage children. Be very discreet about it. See how they'd handle the situation. Whoever comes up with the winning solution will receive a ten-day trip to Hawaii—children not included."

Rourke spent the rest of his morning fielding requests for interviews with *Forbes* and *Money* magazines. The completion of his latest project brought both financial and entertainment icons swirling around him, anxious for a photo op and a cover story. *People, GQ, Newsweek.* The headlines read "Mr. Renovator of the Millennium." It was all so overdone, but if an occasional, well-placed smile and a penguin suit permitted him to forge his legacy, he'd tolerate the absurdities. His aunt said he had a face the public liked to look at, so he'd let them look if it helped the company. After all, it was all he had.

"Mr. Flannigan," Maxine buzzed him, "it's Mr. Gregory, sir. He says it's urgent."

"Send him in. And Maxine, check on my niece. She hasn't called in two hours and I want to make sure she hasn't blown up the house."

"Very good, sir."

Miles Gregory entered Rourke's office carrying a black portfolio and looking every bit the head legal counsel of RF Renovations, Ltd.—mid-fifties, trim, polished, and one of the few people Rourke didn't second-guess.

"We have a bit of a problem." Miles adjusted his bow tie and stroked his chin. The man had a habit of throwing out his concerns and if the issue were noteworthy, he offered a second, more forceful delivery.

Rourke waited to determine the level of concern.

"A potentially big problem."

Aha, it was indeed an issue.

"Rather huge, actually."

Three exponents. This *was* a problem. "What's the matter, Miles?"

His lawyer cleared his throat and eased open the portfolio. "It's regarding the property in New York. There's been an accident."

"An accident? How bad?" When Miles hesitated, Rourke's concern escalated. "How bad, Miles?"

"The man died."

"Died?" The word tumbled from Rourke's mouth in an unintelligible heap. People on his job sites suffered back strains or an occasional fracture. *They did not die.* He demanded safety precautions and instructions far past OSHA requirements, so much so that Miles dubbed him "man of a million precautions."

"Rourke?"

Dead. "What happened?"

Miles slid the portfolio across the desk. "He was a demolition subcontractor. Fell fifty feet onto concrete."

"Did his fall harness malfunction?" Rourke imagined the harness strap breaking and the unknown man's horror in the millisecond before he hit concrete.

Miles shook his head. "Not that the inspectors can tell."

"Christ." Rourke grabbed the portfolio and scanned the report. When he noticed the date of the incident, he cursed again. "Why am I just hearing about this if it happened almost five months ago?"

"We tried to insulate you. It's not good for the head of the company to get dragged down by something like this."

"Dragged down? The man died, for Christ's sake. I should have been told."

"I apologize. You were in the middle of the Chemstrol acquisition." Miles fiddled with his bow tie and added, "That's why we brought this to Diana."

"She knew about this?"

Miles nodded.

He'd deal with his aunt and her subterfuge once he handled this situation. "What problem could be larger than this man's life?"

"A lawsuit."

Of course. "I see."

"We've already begun preliminary work on our end and hired our own investigators."

"To prove what?" That, despite all the precautions, people still died?

"We're trying to determine if we might have some level of responsibility here." Miles cleared his throat—not a good sign—and added, "The man also had a wife and daughter."

Rourke stared at the file in front of him. Now there was a widow and a fatherless child involved. "I want to meet the widow. Express my sympathies. It's the least I can do." And then, "How old is the child?"

"I have no idea."

Nothing could replace a father, but he had to do something. "I'll set up a college fund."

"If you do that, you might as well wear a banner that says *Guilty.*"

"Do you know what it's like to lose a father?" Rourke knew. He knew what it was like to lose a mother, too. And inherit an aunt who—

"Thankfully, my father is alive, well, and the Dapper Dan of the senior center."

That provided an interesting picture and a welcome interruption. Dwelling on the past served no purpose. "Give me the woman's address and I'll have Maxine make flight reservations."

Miles hesitated. "Do you really think that's necessary?"

"Yes, I do."

"Very well." Miles turned the folder around and searched for an address. "Here it is. Montpelier, New York."

"Montpelier?" Dread wrapped itself around Rourke's gut and squeezed as a kernel of possibility exploded. How many demolition contractors were there in a town like Montpelier? He guessed no more than three.

"Yes, Montpelier," Miles repeated. "It's a small town west of Syracuse. Quaint. Backward. Less than a half dot on a map." He rose from his seat and picked up the portfolio Rourke had tossed aside. "Just a minute and I'll get you the woman's name." He rifled through the papers as Rourke's gut churned with disbelief and panic. "Ah, here it is. Name's Kathryn. Kathryn Redmond Maden."

Kate. Rourke pushed back his chair and moved to the set of windows overlooking Chicago. She was out there, hundreds of miles away, just as she'd always been. But one freak accident was about to erase that distance and demolish the walls between them. He could change his mind and send someone else to visit her. He wouldn't have to see her, wouldn't have to remember the taste of her...

"Would you like me to see what I can find out about this Mrs. Maden?" Miles asked. "I could do a bit of poking. Perhaps it would make your visit easier if you knew more about her."

Fourteen years ago I knew everything about her. "Thank you, Miles, but that won't be necessary. Let me look over the file and I'll get back to you." Such a calm delivery—as though they weren't speaking about *her*. Rourke waited for Miles to leave before phoning Diana. "Can you spare a few minutes? There's something we need to discuss."

"I'm on my way," she said with the casual self-assuredness that had become her trademark in the business world.

He'd thought about dealing with this over the phone so his aunt couldn't read his body language or the tiny nuances that might slip through when he referred to his old girlfriend. But if he did that, he wouldn't be able to study *her* body language. Had she kept this from him for business reasons or had she connected the family ties and discovered who the widow was?

***

"Rourke?" Diana Flannigan moved toward him, a dynamo of power and authority covered in a designer suit and pearls. The woman had demolished her share of businessmen who'd been fooled by her tiny stature and casual elegance. She'd never married, never expressed maternal desire or interest in anyone not connected to RF Renovations. "Do you have word from Gamitrond?" Diana asked as she slid into one of the wingback chairs opposite his desk.

Always the businesswoman. "Actually, Gamitrond's on hold right now." He ignored the raised brow and plowed on. "Why didn't you tell me we lost a man at the New York site?"

"You were in the middle of a major negotiation. Involving you would have proven too distracting."

"Since when is a man's death distracting?"

Her blue eyes flashed. "When you're in charge of a multimillion-dollar corporation, you can't concern yourself with every unfortunate incident that occurs. That's why you have people to take care of those things for you."

"Damn it, Diana, the man died."

"Yes, he did."

"He was from Montpelier." There. He'd said it.

She met his gaze head on. Even smiled. "Ah, yes. Montpelier. I'm surprised you remember that place."

How can I ever forget it? "I knew the man who died. Clay Maden. His family had a demolition business in town."

"I see."

"I'm going there to pay my respects to his widow." *Kate. Remember her?* That got her attention. So, she *did* remember. He doubted she'd bring it up. Memories of her eighteen-year-old nephew crying until he puked were better left alone.

"Do you really think that's necessary? Miles said there could be litigation. Aren't we risking exposure?" She must have seen the determination on his face because she softened her approach. "Can't you at least send a representative with a check instead of making a personal appearance? Money is all those kinds of people want anyway."

Doubtful, but he wasn't in the mood to debate the issue with his aunt who insisted everything started and ended with dollar signs. "I'm leaving as soon as Maxine can make arrangements." Had her complexion shifted from pale to paste? The change was so minute he couldn't tell but he'd swear it had.

"I see."

"Just so you know, I'm making provisions to care for the child."

This time her face downshifted to the color of soot. She coughed and sputtered. "What?"

"There's a daughter." *She probably has mud-brown eyes and red hair, just like the rest of the Madens.*

"Rourke—"

"It's time to make things right." He dreaded the thought of seeing Kate again, but maybe it was time to do that, too.

When Diana left, Rourke retrieved the key from his middle desk drawer and fit it in the credenza behind him. He opened the drawer and shuffled through several folders, searching for the most current, which he removed and laid on the desk in front of him. The file tab was marked with his own bold handwriting—Kate E. Redmond. He refused to think of Kate by her married name. There were eight such files, all reports dating back as many years. He drew in a deep breath and buzzed Maxine. "Hold all my calls for the next twenty minutes."

"Yes, Mr. Flannigan. Even your niece's?"

"*Especially* my niece's."

"Very good, sir."

Click.

Rourke ran his fingers along the tab, tracing the name on it twice before he slowly opened the folder and began to read.

Chapter 3

"We've got fourteen years of questions between us."—
Rourke Flannigan

"He's back."

Kate's brush slipped, smearing red paint onto the gray siding of the miniature dollhouse. *Damn.* She snatched a rag and began dabbing at the red spot.

"Kate?"

She dabbed harder as if she could blot out Angie's words. "I heard you."

"And?"

Kate glanced up, proud of the outward calm she displayed when her insides were a jumble of panic. "And what?"

"Oh for heaven's sake, it's me you're talking to here, the one who sat up with you for three nights straight after that jerk left." Angie swore under her breath and muttered, "He didn't even have the decency to say good-bye."

"It was a long time ago." Fourteen years in July.

"Sure."

Angie Sorrento was a pint-size dynamo with a giant-sized temper who swore in Italian and English and could carry a grudge longer than anyone Kate had ever known. The only grudge larger than the one Angie had for Rourke Flannigan was the one relegated to the ex-fiancé who skipped out on her three days before the wedding.

"Really, Angie. Fourteen years is ancient history."

Angie's dark eyes narrowed. "That's what I'm worried about, Kate. Your *history* with Mr. Jerk."

"There's no need to worry." Kate dipped her brush in red and filled in the trim along the roof. This house was a four-bedroom Cape Cod, designed for Rachel and Jared Hennessy and their seven-year-old twins, Jeffrey and Jason. The family had relocated from Richmond, Virginia, last year so Jared could teach sophomore English and coach basketball in Montpelier. Great family—devoted couple, beautiful kids, even a golden retriever named Jed.

Angie started up again. "Even if it weren't 'Mr. Holier than Thou, let me grace you with my presence in this Podunk town' and even if said man-boy weren't someone you'd been intimately involved with, I'd still be worried."

"Unnecessarily." Kate ignored the way her pulse skittered when Angie talked about *him*.

"You're vulnerable."

"Stop." Her pulse tripled.

"You buried Clay five months ago. That makes you a lonely widow. The perfect target."

"You watch too many movies." Had he heard about Clay? That was ridiculous, how could he have heard? She had no idea where he lived and now, suddenly, he was *here*. Why?

"Katie? Are you all right?"

No, she wasn't. She hadn't been all right since—Kate pushed the unwelcome truth away and glanced at her friend. "I'm fine."

"*Fine* is code word for *no*. Look, I know you don't want to talk about him, but there are some things you've got to know before this guy comes waltzing back into your life."

"He's hardly waltzing back into my life."

"Steamrolling then. You just wait and see."

"We haven't seen each other since we were eighteen." *A marriage and child ago.* "We're strangers."

"You were planning to marry the guy."

Kate set down her brush and plastered the same expression she'd worn when well-wishers patted her hand and offered prayers for strength to endure her newly widowed state. She'd never told Clay how much he meant to her, not really, and now one freakish accident had stolen her chances of ever telling him.

"They say he kicks people out of their homes to get a deal."

"That's crazy. He would never—" She stopped. How did she know what he would never do? He was a man now, not a teenager.

"They say he buys the buildings dirt cheap after he kicks the tenants out, and then renovates the places into posh apartments for his rich friends." Angie crossed her arms over her small chest and tilted her head to one side so several black springs of hair bounced off her shoulders. "While you were watching cartoons with Julia, I was watching *him* on E! and seeing his face plastered in *People.*"

Rourke had always hated media in any form, said they made it hard to find a nugget of truth in anything. Kate started to shake her head in denial and ended in a shrug. What did she really know about him anymore? The truth slipped out again. Nothing.

"He flew to Sweden to have dinner with some beauty queen. And spent Easter skiing in the Alps."

"Busy man." While Rourke was globe-trotting, she'd been burying her husband and trying to console her daughter.

"Still not married though plenty have tried to snag him."

So, there was no wife.

"Here." Angie slid a folder across the table. "Everything you need to arm yourself against Mr. Rourke Connor Flannigan."

Kate glanced at the manila folder in front of her. "You make him sound like a villain."

"If he gets to you again, you won't survive."

"Are there pictures in here?" Kate fingered the folder.

"Of course." Angie let out an indelicate snort. "Okay, he's drop-dead gorgeous, I will give him that, but not much else."

With a flip of the folder, she could satisfy fourteen years of wondering. "Maybe I'll just take a peek—"

"Damn! Close the folder. Quick."

"Why?"

"Because Mr. Jerk's standing right outside."

***

Rourke hesitated at the door of the little shop with scalloped pink and blue trim. *Dream Houses by Kate.* She was in there, the woman who had ripped his heart into tiny shreds, invisible to the human eye.

That was history. He was here to offer condolences, nothing more. But when he opened the door he realized two fatal errors: never engage on foreign ground and never underestimate the past.

She was more beautiful than the photo he obtained two weeks ago. A photograph couldn't capture the aura of femininity, vulnerability, and raw strength that emanated from her. If he weren't so good at masking his emotions, he'd be on the floor, sucking for air.

Not Kate. Other than a trimmed wariness flashing in the brilliance of her blue eyes and a slight flair of her delicate nostrils, she appeared unmoved. Where was the girl who had cried on his shoulder when her friend's dog died?

She spoke first. "Hello, Rourke."

Her voice swirled around him and threatened to pull him under. "Kate." He hadn't spoken her name since he was eighteen, and the raw unfamiliarity of it burned his lips.

She opened her mouth to speak, and Rourke zeroed in on her lips. Full, kissable.

"Well, if it isn't Rourke Flannigan."

He snapped his head up and glanced at Kate's best friend. He hadn't missed the censure or the distaste in her voice. Some things never changed. "Hello, Angie."

She dismissed him with a flounce of wild curls and turned to Kate. "I'll be in the back room if you need me."

"Thanks."

He waited until the she-witch disappeared and picked up a strip of miniature lattice, feigning great interest in the delicate wood, anything to keep from staring at Kate. "She never did like me."

"She's very protective."

"Of course." *She always said I'd hurt you.* He met Kate's gaze and the years chipped away. *Did I hurt you? Did I rip your insides apart? Did you think of me when you were lying in your husband's arms?*

"Why are you here?"

Was that a tremble in her voice? "Business. And my niece." He hadn't meant to mention Abbie, but two seconds with Kate and already his guard started slipping.

"Niece?"

There *was* a distinct tremble in her voice. Did he make her nervous?

"Rourke? What about your niece?"

"Gwendolyn was killed in a plane crash three months ago. I'm Abbie's guardian. She's having some adjustment issues and I thought Montpelier might be a nice break."

She looked away. "I see."

"I don't know anything about being a father." He slid into the chair opposite her workstation. "It's damned harder than when we were kids. I think. Hell, I don't know."

"It's never easy, being the child or the parent."

"I can see why people opt for the childless route."

Those huge eyes rimmed with emotion. "Some do."

"But not you."

"No."

She was pulling him in, one whispered word, one doe-eyed glance at a time. He was not a testosterone-crazed teenager anymore. He had been surrounded by far more beautiful, more sophisticated women than the one sitting across from him with red paint smeared on her fingers and a smudge of red on her chin. But none of them were Kate. That was the problem. That had always been the problem.

"I heard about Clay." He fidgeted with his keys but couldn't quite look at her when he said, "I'm sorry."

"Thank you."

She bowed her head and for one absolutely insane second, he wanted to pull her against him and inhale the scent of her chestnut hair. Would it still smell like coconut? What the hell was he doing here? This wasn't the Kate he remembered. This one was untouchable. What had he expected? That she'd gaze upon him with something akin to hero worship, like most other women did? He needed to get out. Now. He calculated his exit and just as he'd worked a strategy, he noticed his name in neat print on the tab of the folder lying in front of Kate.

"What's this?" He slid the folder forward.

"Nothing!" She made a quick lunge for it, but Rourke snatched it away.

"Nothing?" He eased the folder open. "Hmm." He stared back at magazine and newspaper clippings of himself in various locations, with various women, all beautiful, all supposedly in love with him. Rourke scanned the printed dates and captions, then closed the folder and slid it back to her.

"Angie—"

"Would never make it as a private eye. That wasn't just a Swedish beauty queen; she owned three businesses." He smiled and shrugged at her distress. "And the Alps," he leaned forward to whisper, "heir to a makeup dynasty."

"I see."

But none of them touched my heart the way you did. "Kate."

"Yes?"

"What happened to Clay?"

She looked away. "He fell fifty feet from a lift. He was always so careful." Her voice cracked. "I just don't understand."

Rourke cleared his throat and fiddled with a piece of lattice. How much could a person make painting dollhouses? Enough to support two people? "Have the investigators finished their reports yet?" When she shook her head, he said, "You should start receiving money once the investigations are complete."

She coughed as though embarrassed to be discussing such an indelicate subject as money with him when she so obviously had little and he so obviously had plenty. He thought of the night they planned their future together, the Victorian house they'd build, the lake, the workshop for her artwork, the four children they'd have…

"I've been talking to a few people. They say I have options."

That brought him around—fast. People meant lawyers, preyers of the weak and grief-stricken. Wasn't it his humanitarian duty to inquire before she got herself mixed up in a scam? "What kind of people?"

She shrugged. "What kind of people surface at a tragedy? Lawyers, of course."

"The cream of the crop, I'm sure." *Who? Give me their names.*

"They're not all bad." She looked down at her hands and picked at the red paint on her finger.

"You need to be careful. There are too many ambulance chasers out there trying to make a case where there is none." He laid a hand on the table, inches from hers. "If you want me to speak with them, I will."

Her head shot up. "Why would you do that?"

"To help you." It was such a smooth delivery, Miles would be proud. Was it true? The next words spilled out before he could yank them back. "I'm going to be here a few weeks, maybe several." *At least until I shut down these damn lawyers.* He flashed a smile that warped into a straight line when she merely continued to stare.

"Why are you really here, Rourke?"

He remembered the way she'd cried out his name the first and only night they made love. Another truth snuck past the subterfuge in his soul and aimed a steady path straight at her. "Who are we kidding, Kate? We've got fourteen years of questions between us, and I'm not leaving until every one of them is answered."

Chapter 4

"Somebody said he has a daughter or a niece or something."—Julia Maden

"So tell me about this new guy everybody's talking about. Rourke something or other."

Kate ignored her daughter and concentrated on slicing the red onion in front of her, glad she had an excuse if her eyes started tearing. Rourke Flannigan could do that to a woman. When she knew her voice wouldn't wobble, she said, "Flannigan. Rourke Flannigan."

Julia snatched a slice of cucumber. "That's the name. I knew it was something Irish."

"Yes, he's Irish."

"And didn't he use to live here?"

Julia was much too perceptive. "For a little while. Then he moved back to Chicago."

"Did Dad know him?"

Kate threw the onion in the salad bowl. Clay said a salad wasn't a salad without red onion and he was right. He'd been right about a lot of things. "Yes, we all knew him."

"Hmm." And then, "Mom, the onions. On the side, remember?"

"Oh, sorry." She concentrated on picking slices of red onion from the mound of lettuce and tomato in the salad bowl.

"So what's the big deal about this guy?"

Everything. Kate shrugged. "People talk, Julia. Don't listen to them." She flattened her hands on the countertop to keep them from shaking. How long would it take for someone to slip and string Kate's name with Rourke's? The nightmare they'd all tried to forget would resurface and leak into the present like poison. People would get hurt, lives would be ruined, and Kate would be right in the middle of it.

Julia plucked another cucumber from the salad bowl. "It's not like I've heard anything other than the guy's name and that he's staying at the Manor." She wrinkled her nose. "Why would anybody stay there?"

"Should he stay at Mrs. Crabtree's?" Kate asked, referring to the spinster who required guests join her for breakfast, lunch, *and* dinner.

"No, but the Manor is so," she shrugged, "boring."

"It's actually very historical. And it's all we have here. When people visit, they usually stay with family."

"So, he has no family here."

He did. Kate forced a tight smile and said, "No." She picked up a red pepper and sliced a thin strip.

"Somebody said he has a daughter or a niece or something."

The knife slipped and nicked the side of Kate's forefinger. "Damn!" She grabbed a napkin as blood gurgled from the cut.

"Sharp object in hand. Pay attention."

Kate dabbed at the cut, wrapped the napkin around her finger, and pressed tightly. "I'm just distracted, I guess."

Julia's voice dipped and shook around the edges. "It's Dad, isn't it?"

Oh God. Kate nodded.

"I know. I miss him, too. People are saying that company's responsible for his death. Liability or something like that."

That's what people had been telling Kate for months.

"We have to make those people pay. Dad shouldn't have died and that company has to pay."

Kate nodded again, not trusting herself to speak.

"It's the least we can do for him," Julia said.

"I know."

***

Georgeanne Redmond let the curtain fall into place and limped to the nearest chair. Rourke Flannigan was back in town. Good Lord, what a mess. She unscrewed the cap and poured vodka to the line she'd marked with a permanent pen. One-third cup, not a drop more. And one refill every three hours. Not a second before.

She sipped the drink, savoring the *pop* it sent to her lungs, her mouth, her brain. Vodka put her on the alert and helped her reason. In moderation, of course. She'd never go back to the way she was before, draining bottle after bottle of whatever she could get her hands on. In those days, she'd swallowed mouthwash when she couldn't get her fix.

This drinking was different but Katie wouldn't see it that way. She'd fuss and scold and frankly, Georgeanne had enough to deal with right now. Like Rourke Flannigan. She polished off the rest of the drink, perhaps a little more quickly than usual but still no sooner than eight minutes. Setting parameters would keep the drinking under control. One-third undiluted every three hours, not to exceed five times a day, and the drink must last at least eight minutes. Just like a doctor's order.

Georgeanne rubbed the outside of her right thigh, a slow massage that turned into a gradual kneading of the flesh beneath her cotton pants. It provided some relief to the damaged leg, but no amount of manipulation would ever make it normal again. The car accident that forced her into AA fourteen years ago also put a metal plate and screws in her hip. The pain served as a constant reminder of what she'd done to Rourke Flannigan.

Why was the man here, damn it? Surely not to prey on poor Katie whom he'd dallied with and dumped in the span of a summer. Georgeanne knew all about summer love—or lust, as it were. She'd succumbed just like her daughter but Katie had been lucky because Clay had adored her and looked beyond her mistakes to what could be.

It had all turned out just fine, better than Georgeanne could have imagined. All she'd had to do was steer her daughter in Clay Maden's direction and convince Katie that Rourke Flannigan was gone for good, which proved true.

But now Clay was dead and that damn man was back. Georgeanne lifted her glass and caught a few drops of vodka. The only question was why?

***

Rourke sipped his scotch and tried the Internet connection for the fifth time. This place was a technological disaster. Most visitors stayed with relatives or close friends. Since Rourke could claim neither, he'd opted for the historic elegance of Montpelier Manor. What he hadn't counted on was the antiquated ambiance that quickly shifted to annoyance. At eighteen, he'd admired the rustic setting that proved very different from anything he'd seen in Chicago. There was a lot Montpelier offered that he'd never experienced before—hospitality, fresh air, Kate.

"Rourke, this is ridiculous. How am I going to watch television?"

Abigail perched on the floor, pressing channels with her index finger. Two seconds after they moved in, she realized there was no remote to the television. Fifteen minutes of complaining netted her nothing from Rourke in the way of sympathy or understanding. She then resorted to manual channel surfing, but apparently three channels and no cable for longer than twenty-four hours was too much.

He supposed he'd have to do something about it.

"Rourke!"

"Admittedly, this does not hold the same character and charm it once did."

"Like in the prehistoric ages?"

"Keep it up and you won't have any channels, Abigail."

She made a face at him. "Abbie. My name's Abbie. Abbie, Abbie, Abbie."

"Keep it up and you won't have any channels, *Abbie*."

"We can't stay here."

He stared at her and waited. In a matter of seconds, she'd barrage him with an entire list of reasons they couldn't stay.

She didn't disappoint him when four seconds later, she lifted her fingers and began counting. "One, we have to share a community toilet. Two, a community shower, and that is just gross. Three, there's no fridge, so no orange juice, no yogurt, no ice cream. Four, there's no remote. Five, no cable. Six, no Internet connection in my room. You have the only one and that sucks. Seven—"

"Enough."

"I'm going to run out of fingers before I finish."

He'd rather haggle construction costs with his toughest opponent than sit here listening to this babble.

"Rourke, you are *not* listening."

"I heard you, *Abbie*." Damn his nomad sister for getting herself killed.

"I am so bored."

Rourke massaged his right temple. Why in the hell had he ever allowed Maxine to talk him into bringing Abigail—

Abbie—here? What did Maxine know? She was a spinster who'd never raised anything but a miniature terrier. "Where are all those DVDs you ordered?"

"How am I going to watch them? Maxine said the DVD player I picked is on back order."

"Books then. Read something." She could read, couldn't she?

She snorted. "Right."

Rourke studied his niece and wondered again why anyone would torture themselves with a child. They were messy, demanding creatures and he could see how they sucked the life out of a person.

Well, he was having none of it. She wasn't even his child, for Chrissake. If she had been, he'd never have let her get so out of hand and, dead parent or not, the kid was a bigger pain than the multi-unit luxury condos in Denver he'd just negotiated. He dug around in his briefcase and pulled out a handful of magazines. "Here." They skidded across the floor and landed a foot from her. "Learn something."

She snatched them up and rifled through them. "*Forbes? Money? Time?* I'm thirteen years old!"

He loosened his tie and smiled at her. "It's never too soon to learn about dollar cost averaging and leveraged buyouts."

"Are you for real?" She flung the magazines across the room and jerked to her feet. "I need to use your cell phone."

"Where's yours?"

She looked away and shrugged.

"Abiga—Abbie, where is it?"

"I'm not sure." At least she had the good grace to sound mildly apologetic. "It's either at home in my other purse..."

He raised a brow and waited.

"Or I lost it," she mumbled.

"I see."

"Yeah," she looked up and threw him a timid smile. "So I need your phone." He shook his head. "Why not? It's not like you can't spare the minutes." And then she zinged him with, "Or the money."

"That's not the point, is it?"

She ignored him. "Can you just let me use your phone?"

"No." She was a persistent creature, he'd give her that.

"Why not?"

"Because it's not my problem. It's yours." He pointed to the *Money* magazine sprawled face down on the hardwood floor. "There's a very interesting article in there on asset allocation."

"Arrghhh!"

He waited until her little outburst subsided. "Now go find something to do. Be back by five."

She glared at him. "This is so not fair."

He glared back. "Life isn't fair. Deal with it."

She mumbled under her breath but he ignored her and turned back to his computer. Apparently the tactic worked because seconds later the door slammed shut.

The next hour proved equally frustrating with no computer access. If he were going to stay at the Manor for a few weeks, he had to have Internet. He'd speak with the owner, Mrs. Gibson, and have her set up a service call with the cable company to upgrade this room, no later than tomorrow afternoon. Rourke closed his laptop and scooped up the magazines from the floor. When he opened his briefcase to dump them inside, he caught sight of the folder with Kate's name along the side tab.

Meeting her again certainly hadn't gone as planned. Not that there'd been any great plan, but he hadn't expected her to be so untouchable. And why had he opened his big mouth and said they had fourteen years of questions between them? He had no business getting anywhere near a woman who'd burned him so bad the scars still itched. Rourke picked up the folder and opened it. Kate's face stared back at him, lips slightly parted, eyes soft and alluring. He cursed and slammed the folder shut.

Chapter 5

"All I know is when I called her ten weeks later, she was married."—Rourke Flannigan

Journal entry—May 4, 1998

Julia is two today. Clay wants another child and it is only right and fair to give him one, though I have convinced him to wait until I finish college. (I'm taking classes at Montpelier Community College, majoring in art and design.) And you? Where are you??

Angie wanted to hire a private detective to find you—in Chicago? She wanted to get pictures of you with other women, I'm sure, so she could convince me what a worthless soul you are. I told her no. I've never mentioned you since the day you left, but there is something in my eyes when she says your name that tells her you still live in my heart.

Last week I took Julia to the lake and spread out a blanket in the very same spot where we made love two nights before you left. We ate peanut butter sandwiches stuffed with bananas and sipped juice boxes. She fell asleep on my lap as I stroked her hair and I remembered every single moment of that night with you—as precise and finite as a movie—the feel of your hands inching over my body, your mouth, your teeth, your tongue. The feel of you pressed so close to me, and then filling me, stretching me, loving me. Three times. Do you ever think of that night? The night we pledged our love and our lives to each other?

I choose to believe you do, even if only in your subconscious imaginings. There is strength in what remains

behind—remember William Wordsworth? Twelfth-grade Literature? That's what I'm doing, each minute, each day. I'm finding strength in what remains behind and I store it up for this day, once a year, when I can write freely about it. For myself. And for you.

***

By ten o'clock the next morning, Rourke had leased an office next to the post office. The idea struck him yesterday two seconds after Abbie stalked back in the door. He was not a man to be pinned in a room, especially one without a working computer, and it was impossible to conduct business with a thirteen-year-old manually flipping through channels and making snide comments under her breath.

Even if he only stayed in Montpelier a week, the office would provide a refuge for him. He was most comfortable in an office setting, among business associates who understood the protocol and didn't step outside those boundaries.

Thanks to Maxine's long-distance know-how, he'd assembled all the conveniences of a regular working environment. The place was a bit cramped and he'd had to settle for pressed wood rather than solid cherry, but it would suffice. He had his privacy and could begin his own investigation of Clay's accident. He already regretted offering Kate his services yesterday but she'd seemed so dejected he'd blurted out the first thing that came into his head. Again, proof she could still get to him.

How was he supposed to help her with a lawyer and remain objective? It couldn't be done. On the other hand, could he ignore potential information that might put the company at risk? What could it hurt to pry around the edges a little and get the names of the law firms that wanted to speak with her? Most of them were ambulance chasers anyway, slick talkers who preyed on the injured and grieving. Kate needed someone to look out for her interests. Didn't she?

By the time he finished his second cup of coffee, he'd convinced himself she needed his help. He refused to think of the way his pulse tripped when he thought of her blue eyes, her soft curves, her— The front door jangled and seconds later, Angie Sorrento beelined toward him with a pissed-off look on her face.

"Out with it," she said, gripping the edges of his new desk.

"Hey, easy on the furniture, it's only painted particle board." She'd probably like to rip the place to shreds, him included.

She threw him a cold stare and jammed both hands in her back pockets. "Why are you here?"

Same old pain in the ass. He leaned back in the leather chair and laced his fingers behind his head. "I see your disposition hasn't changed."

"Out with it."

He considered another sarcasm but settled on a different ploy. "My niece needs fresh air and this place has plenty of it."

"You mean that little paste-waif running around in a Jimi Hendrix T-shirt with earbuds stuffed in her ears? Fresh air? I doubt she's seen the outside of a room in six years."

He shrugged. "What do you want, Angie?"

"I want you to leave Kate alone."

"I hadn't realized I was bothering her."

"You are." Her nostrils flared, her dark eyes narrowing on him as though she might lunge across the desk and choke him with his tie. She would actually be attractive if she ever got over the perpetual PMS hump. Doubtful though. The woman had been a witch since the first time he laid eyes on her and she hadn't improved with age.

"How long are you planning to stay?"

"A few weeks, give or take."

"Why?" She worked her way around the desk and planted all five-feet-two of fury and force within arm's reach.

"I told you—"

"Oh, save it. I'm not a fool and I'm not the innocent Kate is. She just lost her husband a few months ago. She's grieving."

"I can appreciate that."

"She's vulnerable." She jabbed a finger at him, stopping just short of nailing his chin. "You, better than anyone, know how to exploit that."

"What the hell are you talking about?" Now she was annoying him.

Her voice dripped with accusation. "Who left her, huh? Who walked away without even saying good-bye?"

It wasn't supposed to be good-bye. He'd be damned if he'd admit that to her. "I had a lot to deal with, or have you conveniently forgotten what happened?"

"Of course not. But you could have been a man about it instead of pulling a disappearing act."

He didn't like to think about the early days without Kate, when he was filled with confusion and misery. Diana had guided him straight to Princeton and out of Kate's life.

Angie continued her little barrage. "Two months of nothing. No phone number, no address, nothing but silence."

Her words clogged his brain, jabbing him with memories of Kate. "I needed some distance."

"Right."

He didn't bother to respond. So what if she didn't believe him? She'd never believed a word he'd said, especially when it came to Kate.

The witch opened her mouth and blew him away like a nor'easter. "Kate was innocent and you deserted her."

"Damn you, I wanted to come back." *Like a fool.*

Angie Sorrento shook her head and a spray of dark curls fell across her forehead. "You are such a liar."

"I don't care what you believe." Anger festered in his gut and spiraled out in his next words. "All I know is when I called ten weeks later, Clay Maden answered the phone. Kate's phone. He said they'd gotten married." The words burned his tongue. "You tell me who got played."

"You bastard. You don't know anything."

"So enlighten me."

"Not on your life. Kate will get through this just like she did before, and the people who love her will be here to help her, just like they were before."

"Before what?"

But she was through sharing information. She turned on him and rattled off personal data about him as though they were a list of priors. "I know all about you, Rourke Flannigan. You traipse around the world in your little jet, wearing your fancy suits, bedding every woman who catches your eye, and you don't care about any of them. All you care about is money and power and your own ego, which is bigger than your whole bank account." Her dark eyes glittered with loathing. "Why don't you just go back to Chicago and your little uptown girlfriends and leave us peons alone?"

Rourke stared at the spitfire in front of him, half expecting her to blow flames from her nostrils. "What in the hell have I ever done to you?"

"Not me. Kate."

"She's the one who married somebody else." He could barely get the words out. "Got that?"

"Right." She let out a snort of disgust. "You ran back to Chicago and hid in your little rich life and then off you went to Princeton and a gazillion other conquests and I'll bet not once did you think about her."

"That's enough."

She actually had the gall to sneer at him. "Is the truth a little too real for your type? You just wash it all away with a disappearing act; that's your style, isn't it?"

"You don't know what the hell you're talking about." But a sick feeling gripped him as her words settled in his brain. Part of what she said had been true, at least in the beginning. He'd been hesitant to tell Diana about the girl from Montpelier whose mother had brought tragedy to his family, but when he came home from Princeton one weekend, she guessed and that made the telling so much easier. When he finished his heart-wrenching tale of undying love for Kate Redmond, Diana had kissed his cheek and, with an uncharacteristic show of sympathy, told him to follow his heart. All that honesty and it had been too damned late.

"Did she really love him?"

Angie must have seen something in his expression that softened her a little. "I'm not the person to ask."

"I need to know."

She lifted a shoulder and said, "What could it matter now? You live in different worlds; hell, you live in different *time periods*. She eats tuna melts while you snack on caviar."

"I've always had a fondness for tuna melts, especially with pickles."

Her lips twitched and flattened. "I don't like you, Rourke Flannigan. If you hurt Kate again, I'll pull out the rifle under my bed and I'll use it."

The gleam in the woman's eye told him she wasn't joking. "I'll keep that in mind." He stood and held out his hand which she accepted with about as much enthusiasm as a man on his way to a vasectomy. "And just so you know, I plan on seeing her tonight."

"Never happen."

"Yes, it will. Kate and I have a lot to talk about."

Chapter 6

"Some things should be left in the past."—Kate Redmond Maden

Kate locked the car and started across the street toward Sophie's Diner. When she was a young girl, her mother had brought her here after Sunday Mass for a grilled cheese sandwich and a cherry phosphate. Kate repeated the tradition with Julia, only the grilled cheese had morphed into chicken nuggets and the cherry phosphate into cherry Coke.

She spied the sleek black Mercedes outside and knew it was Rourke's. He must have gone two towns over to get it, unless it was his and his personal driver delivered it. *Did* he have a personal driver? The news clippings she'd devoured last night mentioned a limousine driver. They mentioned quite a bit actually, and what they didn't spell out, they alluded to with catchy phrases or photographs, such as the number of women he'd dated around the world, the price of his most recent Ferrari, and the value of his vacation home in Malibu.

In all the photographs, he was tanned, smiling, and oh so dazzling. A stranger. Kate took a deep breath and stepped inside the diner. Thankfully, Sophie was recovering from gall bladder surgery and wasn't present to descend upon Rourke with a list of reasons why he wasn't welcome in Montpelier, the main one being what he'd done to one of their own.

"Hey, Kate." Sophie's granddaughter, Melody, smiled at her and glanced shyly toward the back of the restaurant.

"Hi, Melody." Kate followed her gaze and spotted Rourke in a back booth where the lighting was dim and much too intimate. He wore a navy shirt of some thin material that molded and accentuated the muscles in his arms and chest. Why couldn't he have worn a sweatshirt and chosen a front table with clusters of bright lights and lively chatter?

She moved toward him, trapped by the aura that had always surrounded Rourke Flannigan like tentacles latching onto unsuspecting prey. Heat lapped over her, warming her arms, her legs, her breasts. The second she registered what a huge mistake this meeting was, Rourke looked up, his gray eyes shifting to liquid silver, just like they used to right before he—

"Kate."

The tentacles tightened around her waist and dragged her into the booth. She cleared her throat and focused on the bottom half of his face: chin, mouth, jaw. She did not want to look into those eyes. "Sorry I'm late."

"No problem. You never were the most punctual—" He cleared his throat and his lips pulled into a perfect, white smile. "No problem."

"Your tooth." She leaned in and stared at his mouth. "What happened to the chip?" She remembered exactly which one it was because she used to run her tongue along the irregular edge of it.

"Caps." He pointed to his bottom teeth. "I knocked three out sophomore year."

"Hockey?"

"Yep. Rough season."

"Do you still play?"

"No, I outgrew it a long time ago."

Like you outgrew me? Kate plucked a menu from behind the napkin holder and scanned the items. Sophie hadn't changed the menu in five years. Today was noodles and sirloin tips with cherry pie or apple cobbler. Kate and Rourke used to come here on Friday nights for burgers and fries. Then they'd drive down to the lake and—

She slammed the menu shut and said, "I'm really not hungry."

"Kate."

There it was again. That damn heat in his voice pouring over her like a trail of hot wax. Had she really thought she could have a civil conversation without remembering the way they were?

"Are you okay?"

He reached out and covered her hands with his. They were so much larger than she remembered, his fingers covered with a light smattering of dark hair. He stroked the back of her hand…slow, casual, so very sensual. Her breath skittered through her lungs and fell out in a long sigh.

"Did you love him?"

"What?" His touch pulsed through her, blotting out fourteen years of marriage to another man.

"Did you love him?"

She yanked her hands away and buried them in her lap. "That's an inappropriate question."

His gaze slid across her face and paused on her lips. "It's only inappropriate if the answer is no."

"This was a bad idea." She gathered her purse and scooted toward the edge of the booth.

"Please don't go."

It was the obvious pain in his voice that stopped her.

"I've been waiting fourteen years for this. I was coming back, Kate. I wasn't going to leave you."

Of course he could say that now. She closed her eyes against his words. "It was a long time ago. It doesn't matter."

"Damn it, it *does* matter. After the accident, I wanted to blame somebody."

"Rourke, please." Why was he doing this? She did not want to relive the pain all over again. "Some things should remain in the past."

"If you can keep them in the past. That's the hell of it, I can't seem to do that. I refused to believe your mother hadn't been drinking. Why else would she wait eight hours to go to the emergency room? She must have been in horrible pain, and yet she waited."

"If it's any consolation, she hasn't walked right since."

"It's not. My mother never recovered, though the doctors said there was no reason she wouldn't walk again. She just gave up." He paused. "And gave in to her pills. She died thirteen years ago."

"I'm sorry."

"I couldn't accept that my mother was 'luded out on tranquilizers when she got hit even after I found the open bottle by her bedside." The tormented honesty in his voice reminded her of the old Rourke. "Who walks down the middle of an unlit road at midnight unless they're on something? Guilt messed me up. I told myself if we hadn't been together that night, I could have stopped her from leaving the house. It took me a long time to come to terms with everything, especially you."

She kept her head bent. If she looked in his eyes and saw the pain there, she'd start crying, and she might not be able to stop.

He cleared his throat. Twice. "I figured you'd be angry, maybe not talk to me, even make me beg forgiveness—"

"Rourke, please."

"All I wanted to do was apologize and get back to the way we were."

She could not dig up the old pains. It would be unbearable. "It's done. There's nothing we can do about it now."

"I was too late, Kate." He traced the plain gold band on her ring finger. "When I called, Clay told me the two of you had taken off and gotten married."

She jerked her head up. She could not have heard him correctly. "You called?"

"November twenty-second. At 4:17 in the afternoon. You weren't home."

Her brain pinched. "You called my house?"

"Your house but Clay answered." Bitterness coated his next words. "Imagine my surprise."

She couldn't breathe. "I don't believe you." Her voice shook when she said, "Clay would have told me."

"You think so?" The steel in his voice sliced her resolve. "He hated me for stealing his chances with you. Ring or not, he didn't trust you to stay with him if I was back in the picture."

She wouldn't have trusted herself. "If what you're saying is true..." She stared at him, unable to finish the thought.

Rourke clasped her hand. "It's true."

Kate pulled her hand away, trying to break the tingling sensations shooting through her body. "Clay was a good man and you will not desecrate his name."

"He was still just a man and a damn jealous one at that. I would have done the same thing."

"Stop."

"Why *did* you marry him?"

She forced calm into her voice. "That's a ridiculous question."

He must not have thought so. His eyes narrowed and he grew still. "How old is your daughter?"

Fear tripped through her like shock waves. She'd learned to answer this question without a tremble in her voice. "She's thirteen."

He picked up a salt shaker and traced the "S". "When's her birthday?"

The calm in his voice matched hers but she didn't miss the tensing of his neck muscles or the way his shoulders straightened, as though on heightened alert. A man like Rourke would not let it go. She told him and added, "Julia was a premie."

His head shot up and the burn in his eyes scared her. "Is she mine?"

"No."

"And I should believe you, why?" His voice grew harder, his gaze hotter.

She could see why the articles she'd read last night referred to him with words like strong-willed, compelling, and determined. Well, she would not fall apart under his interrogation. This was Julia they were talking about. *Her child.* Kate met his gaze and thought of Julia's laughter as it bubbled through the house, filling the emptiness inside. "You should believe me because I'm telling you the truth."

The left side of his jaw twitched. "Which truth is that? The one where you married Clay and had his child less than nine months later? Or the one where you got pregnant with my child and married Clay?"

"No!" Her heart slammed against her ribs with a force that bruised.

"No? No what?"

48

Rourke watched her like a lion about to devour its prey. He was waiting for a misstep. Kate shrugged and folded her hands in her lap. Julia was *her* child and Rourke Flannigan had no rights to her. "As disappointed as you may or may not be to hear every woman isn't waiting to have your child, it's the truth. You're not Julia's father. Clay is." Bitterness flashed across his face and she knew what she had to do. "Why did I marry him? Because he didn't leave and he vowed to love me until the second he drew his last breath." She leaned forward and gripped the edge of the table. "You think you have a right to question me because my baby was born a month early? Well, you don't."

Rourke Flannigan, the entrepreneur with a quote for every magazine from *People* to *Newsweek*, was speechless. Kate cleared her throat and let out a quiet breath. "Now that we've settled that, I would appreciate it if you didn't bring it up again." He nodded, a quick jerk of his head that almost didn't qualify as acknowledgment. His face had paled beneath the tan but his eyes had taken on a stony opaqueness that disturbed her. "If that's all, I think I'll be going." Kate grabbed her purse and eased toward the edge of the booth.

"One more question."

She met the opaque gaze and wondered how she'd ever thought him warm and tender. "Yes?"

"Did you love him?"

She hadn't expected that. The man certainly had an arsenal of ammunition in ready supply, but why?

"Did you love him?" he asked again when she didn't spit out a quick response.

Why did it matter to him so much? She'd seen the hurt on his face after she'd blown him away with her little speech about not living and breathing to carry his child.

Angie would have been proud of the delivery, given with such conviction, contempt even, as to be convincing—if one didn't know better. The man was obviously used to asking questions without regard to the sensitivity of the subject matter. He wanted a response? She'd give him one—sort of. "Everyone loved Clay," she said, forcing a half smile. "He was just that kind of person."

He actually huffed his irritation. "I know that, but did *you* love him?"

A left jaw twitch. A clenched mouth. Now he was irritated *and* angry. Good. Let him think ten times before asking such personal questions again. She had fourteen years of rage stored up for him and given the opportunity, she'd dole it out a teaspoon at a time. "You mean as much as I loved you?" Oh, he didn't like that. "That's really what you want to know, isn't it?" His lips flattened but he said nothing, so Kate continued. "Of course, it is. That's exactly what you want to know. Next you'll be asking me to make comparisons about more, ah, intimate situations."

"Just answer the damn question."

Kate flung her purse over her shoulder and scooted out of the booth. "I did answer it, just not to your satisfaction." Rourke squeezed his eyes shut and massaged his temples as though he were in real pain. She'd gotten to him, no doubt about that. Why then didn't she feel vindicated? Why did she feel small and petty and sorry that she'd hurt him with her cruel words? She reached out to touch his shoulder. Why at this moment did she want to press his head against her breasts and comfort him?

She yanked her hand away. Good Lord, where had that come from? She stepped back, anxious to put distance between herself and the subject of that horrible thought. Kate pressed her hands together to keep from doing something stupid, like touch him, and said, "Are you okay?"

He opened his eyes and stared at her. "Headache. Tension, I'm sure."

"Look, I'm sorry. I didn't mean to cause you physical pain."

His lips twitched. "You've been causing me physical pain since the first time I saw you."

Her insides quivered. That was something the old Rourke would say.

"I'm sorry, that was out of line." He rubbed his left temple and said, "I never used to have to think about what I said to you. It just came out and you always understood."

Maybe that was the problem; she understood what he was saying and wished she didn't. Kate shrugged and tried to ignore the confusion in his voice. "That was a long time ago."

"I want to get to know you," Rourke blurted out. The opaqueness in his eyes cleared and turned silver. "There's fourteen years of mystery between us. Can't you just share a little of that with me?"

"Why?" *So you'll leave again?*

"I don't know, call it gut instinct, but right now it's all I can think about."

He'd almost destroyed her once with words like those. She couldn't let it happen again, no matter how tempting. "Don't do this to me, Rourke. I'm not as sophisticated as your socialite girlfriends. I don't do well with empty words and emptier promises."

"They're not empty words. They're the truth. And I haven't made any promises. Yet."

He sounded sincere. He looked sincere, with his eyes glittering a silver honesty. She thought she knew him once, but he turned out to be someone she hadn't known at all. "I don't know. I'll think about it," she said. It was the best she could do.

Chapter 7

"Did he call you before he built his house, because this room's in his house."—Abbie Flannigan

Miles Gregory left Rourke two messages while he was at Sophie's Diner with Kate. Rourke punched in Mile's home number as he drove back to Montpelier Manor and waited for his lawyer to pick up.

"Miles Gregory speaking."

"Working late?"

"Rourke. Where've you been?"

"Out. What's wrong?"

"Mrs. Maden. Some well-credentialed attorney from New York has contacted her about representation in a wrongful death case. Rourke, we're talking millions here."

"I read the insurance and OSHA reports at least five times." *To be certain there was nothing the company could have done to prevent the fall.* "They list Maden's death as an accident."

"I read the same reports, but there's always room for a lawsuit, especially when a widow and a child are left behind."

"I see."

"How are you coming along with Mrs. Maden?"

Kate. "Actually, it's a slow go. I'm still laying the groundwork."

"For what?"

Good question. "I've got to build her trust before I can get information from her."

"Well, do it fast. The meeting is set for next week. You need to get in her head before that."

"Say she doesn't budge and they sue. What's our liability?"

"He's a big hitter; he'll go for millions. Then there's the publicity. And you can forget the deal with Megatron and Logistics. That's based on your overall safety rate."

"So we take a hit for a while." This was Kate they were discussing. "It's not as though we'd be out of business. Hell, isn't that why we pay insurance premiums?"

"When they're warranted, yes. And you can expect the premium to skyrocket or they might even drop us. The man's death was an accident. Why would we pay on it?"

"I'm not saying we would. I just want the information so I can figure out our options."

"If they sue, there's only one option. We do what we always do when somebody tries to take a piece of something that's not theirs. We eliminate them."

Rourke hung up and stepped out of his car. What a mess. Kate didn't trust him, which was obvious from the way she'd attacked him when he'd asked about her daughter. And inquiring about her feelings for Clay had been about the most asinine thing he'd ever done. Now he had to go prowling around and try to find out about some lawyer who was trying to convince her to sue him. Only she didn't know it was him. Yet. She couldn't find out he was Reese Construction. If she did, she'd never trust him, and right now, it was very important she did.

He fitted his key in the lock and stepped inside. The Manor was starting to grow on him, especially Mrs. Gibson who was the niece of the couple who had owned the place when he'd lived in Montpelier. All he needed was a little more time with Kate and maybe—

"Where the hell have you been?"

Abbie leapt at him, arms crossed, jaw clenched, eyes narrowed.

"Excuse me?"

"It's 10:45. Where have you been?"

Rourke didn't know whether to laugh or brush her aside. What would a father do? He had no idea. He opted for the boardroom approach. "Abiga—Abbie, I am the CEO of a Fortune 500 corporation, am I not?"

"Yeah." She started tapping her right foot. "So?"

Three-quarters of the other Fortune 500 companies would bow in his presence if he let them, but apparently his thirteen-year-old niece did not understand her role here. Fine, he'd enlighten her. "Well, the CEO makes the rules, like the captain of a football team."

"Lame."

"And you are like Maxine."

"That old gizzard."

"That old gizzard is very important to me, but she doesn't boss me around or even suggest I do something."

"So?"

"So, in this relationship right here," he pointed to himself and Abbie, "I give the orders, I make the rules, and you follow them. Period." There.

"That is such bull."

"Who pays your cell phone bill?"

She shrugged.

"And buys your clothes, and gives you a place to stay, and DVDs, and—"

"Okay, I get it."

"Good." He hid a smile. This parent business wasn't so bad. All a person had to do was employ reason and levels of expectation.

"So where were you? 'Cause I've been sitting here for hours, wondering if you got killed and I'd be stuck in this rat hole forever."

Then again, maybe a person really did have to be certifiably insane to want a child.

"I was just getting ready to walk to Julia's house," she said. "She invited me to hang out tonight, but you'd already left and I couldn't remember your cell number and I thought you'd blow a gasket if I just took off."

"Julia?"

"Yeah, she's really cool. Her dad died a few months ago. Some kind of accident. She's an only child, too, just like me, so we've got this instant bond thing going. Her mom makes these dollhouses. Kind of weird, but Julia says they're cool. I guess they're miniatures of people's houses, like with the same exact furniture and everything. Maybe you should have her make a copy of your house." She giggled. "I'd like to see her put twelve flat screens in a dollhouse. Rourke? You didn't hear a word I said."

Julia Maden. Kate's daughter.

"Rourke?"

"I heard you, Abbie. I heard every word."

***

July 23, 1995

Huntington Lake

"What do you think of a Victorian house with the back windows overlooking the lake so the children can watch the geese?"

"I think it sounds perfect."

"How many children?"

"Three?"

"Four."

"Okay."

They were lying underneath a sliver of moon as the mid-July heat rose and fell from the lake in a misty gurgle of hope and longing. Rourke had his arm flung around Kate's waist. His shirt was half-unbuttoned. Her silk panties lay jumbled next to one of her sandals.

"How many bedrooms?"

"Five." She stroked Rourke's jaw and placed a soft kiss along his neck, trailing her tongue behind his ear until he groaned. "Our bedroom will have a king-size bed and a sunken tub shaped like a heart." She reached her hand inside his shirt. "Big enough for two."

"Stop. You're killing me." She let out a laugh that spilled over his body like warm honey and made him hard all over again.

"But what a happy death it would be."

He groaned. "Worth every second."

"And I'd like a workshop where I could paint."

"If we have enough land, I could build you a barn and you could fill it up with your little dollhouses."

She swatted him on the stomach. "Don't make fun."

He laughed and pulled her hand down to feel his hardness. "Does this feel like I'm making fun?"

Kate wriggled her slender body against him. "Hmm." She leaned over and placed a kiss on his lips, her tongue teasing his mouth open. "Let me inside," she whispered. He opened his mouth and she thrust her tongue against his teeth, greedy, needful. Then she straddled him and reached for his belt buckle.

"Kate. Stop."

"I can't." She unzipped his jeans.

He squeezed his eyes shut and groaned. "Kate, you really are killing me. I only had two condoms. I never thought...damn, I never imagined..."

"We'll be careful," she murmured against his mouth. "Very, very careful." And then she slid her hands inside his jeans and he was lost.

***

"And all these little pieces of wood are what my mom uses to make the balconies and the stairs, and all that stuff."

Rourke's niece seemed genuinely impressed. She was a short, petite thing with spiky auburn hair and sorrowful, brown eyes set deep in a pale, narrow face. She had Rourke's nose and his jaw. When she smiled, which wasn't often, Kate thought she saw a bit of Rourke in that, too. She should have known Julia and Abbie would meet. After all, how often did a new person arrive in Montpelier? Abbie's uncle was the reason Kate had a headache today. She'd slept a total of two hours last night because memories of him, past and present, bombarded her attempts to sleep.

"This looks like my uncle's place," Abbie said, pointing to the Victorian house Kate used as a display.

Julia gave her an odd look. "He has *this* house?"

"Yeah. Kind of." Abbie walked around the dollhouse and peered inside. "Five bedrooms. Pond in the back." She scrunched up her nose and whispered, "But he has this dorky heart tub in his bathroom."

"Gross."

Kate gripped the coffee mug in her hands. "A heart tub?"

"Yeah. It's pretty dumb, but he likes it, I guess." She lifted a thin shoulder. "I told him he should have you make a miniature of his house because I wanted to see how you'd put all the flat screens in there."

Kate was still puzzling over the tub. "I'm sure I'd figure out a way to add a few flat screens."

Abbie looked at her the way Rourke used to when he thought she was in over her head. "He's got twelve of them."

"I see."

But Abbie was already poking around inside the dollhouse, touching couches, spindles, wallpaper. When she reached the fifth bedroom, she stopped. "You knew Rourke when he lived here, right?"

Kate forced the word out. "Yes."

"Did he call you before he built his house, because this room is in *his* house." She squinted and leaned closer, a frown creasing her pale face.

He'd built the house they talked about? "Lots of Victorian homes have turrets. It's very common actually."

"But are they all this purple color? I mean, this *exact* shade? And this fireplace in the bedroom? He has this."

Julia leaned over, too, and peeked inside. "I can't believe somebody actually built that." She straightened and eyed Kate. "Is he an architect or something?"

Before Kate could answer, Abbie piped in. "No, he's like a developer or something."

"So maybe he and my mom talked about a house like this when he lived here."

Abbie shrugged. "I guess."

"I want to meet this guy," Julia said, her voice pitched with excitement. "He sounds kind of cool."

Abbie rolled her eyes. "He is so totally clueless."

"Really? Why?"

"He has no idea what to do with a kid. He lets me stay up as late as I want, doesn't care what I watch on TV, and he even told me to go online and get stuff I needed. With his credit card."

"So, what'd you get?" Julia whispered, her eyes wide with hero worship.

Abbie rattled off a list in a bored voice and finished with, "It's not so great, though. We have to eat out almost every night because he doesn't cook and he won't let me answer the phone. Ever."

"Why not?"

"He has all these women calling him and he has to screen everything."

"Really."

"Yeah, there's like superstars calling him, too, and he acts like it's no big deal."

Julia had forgotten her mother was less than three feet away. "Do any of his girlfriends ever stay over?" she whispered.

"Not since I've been there, but I found a bunch of fancy underwear in one of his drawers."

"Really?"

"I know you're not supposed to snoop, but you have no idea how boring it is to sit in this monster house all day with nobody to talk to except a German cleaning lady who speaks two words of English and the plant man, who never talks."

"Your uncle has a plant man?"

"He has everything," Abbie nodded with a glowing satisfaction. "Maybe your mom will let you come visit sometime. We could have a blast."

Julia shot a look in Kate's direction and turned scarlet. "Mom! Were you listening?"

"Of course not."

Both girls flashed suspicious glances Kate's way but when she turned to her workbench, they went right back to chattering, only this time their voices didn't resonate past the perimeter of the model dollhouse.

Kate sank into her chair and reached for the stack of mail. Some envelopes were addressed to Kate Redmond, others to Kate Maden, still others to Kate Redmond Maden. She'd been all of those names at one time or another; she just wished she knew who she was now.

Clay had been gone less than five months and already his voice had started to fade, the loud belly laughter so characteristic of him growing dim. She'd pulled out several pictures last week and placed them throughout the house. So she wouldn't forget. Some voices stayed with a person forever, some smiles, some touches, lived just below the surface. She sliced through an envelope with the letter opener. Damn Rourke Flannigan. Why did he have to come back now?

There were three letters from attorneys informing her she could have a multi-million dollar negligence case in front of her. Before the week was out, she'd have six or seven more. Even after all these months, the letters continued. She'd meet with the lawyer from New York, listen to him, consider the options, and then make her decision whether to press forward or let the case rest. The enormity of the task made her head ache. If only she had an objective listener, someone who had nothing to gain from her decision but who would be able to consider the ramifications of her choice in a purely analytical manner. She thought of Rourke. Perhaps he could help.

Chapter 8

"We're going to have to finish this thing between us, you realize that don't you?"—Rourke Flannigan

To file:
Client: Rourke Flannigan
Subject: Kate E. Redmond
Date: July 23, 1999

Ms. Redmond was observed entering Tops grocery where she purchased the following items: four Rome apples, one head of lettuce, three bananas, and a loaf of whole wheat bread. She picked up a prescription from the pharmacy for amoxicillin (for daughter, Julia). She later traveled to Hannah's Greenhouse where she purchased one bunch of forget-me-knots, two bags of topsoil, and a spade. She returned to her residence and left twenty minutes later with a small satchel and a blanket. Ms. Redmond traveled north four miles on Indian Road, entered Huntington Lake where she proceeded to park her silver 1997 Toyota Corolla and walk toward the lake. She spread a blue and red plaid blanket on the ground and sat down.

Ms. Redmond removed the forget-me-knots from her satchel and placed them on the blanket beside her. She sat for approximately thirty-five minutes, after which time she rose and tossed the flowers in the lake.

Dinner reservations at The Granery with Mr. Maden. Ms. Redmond wore a black low-cut dress with black high heels. Mr. Maden wore tan slacks and a navy sport coat. Couple returned at approximately 8:45 p.m. and retired to bedroom.

***

"I need you, Maxine."

"Sir?"

Rourke scanned the stacks of papers and folders on his desk and wondered how he'd made such a mess in two short days. "I've got Higgins calling me from London looking for reports, Evans from Seattle wondering about the Caintrano projects we promised him, and Sedurilli in Boston demanding to know why I didn't show for their annual meeting. Did you not inform him I wouldn't be attending?"

"Yes, sir. Three weeks ago."

"Well, he's ticked. And I've been working on a proposal for the Grendall project which I promised to send in Thursday's mail but I've misplaced it in this mess."

"I'll be on the next flight to Montpelier, Mr. Flannigan."

Rourke closed his eyes and rubbed his right temple. "Thank you."

"Ms. Prentiss left three messages this morning."

Probably because he hadn't answered his cell phone. "What did she want?"

"She's looking for you, sir. Something about a charity ball."

"Call her and tell her I can't make it. Then send her flowers or something. You decide."

"Yes, sir."

"And don't tell her you spoke with me." Janice was beautiful and witty, with the longest legs he'd ever seen, but damn she required effort. There wasn't a congenial cell in her genetic makeup. Not like Kate.

"Will there be anything else, Mr. Flannigan?"

Here goes. "Actually, yes. I'm going to need you to do a little babysitting while you're here."

"Sir?"

He heard her sipping air. "Relax, it's not as bad as it sounds." Actually, it was, but Maxine could figure that out once she was here. "I need you to keep an eye on Abbie."

"But, sir, I know nothing about children."

"Which is ten times more than I know. I've got real business to tend to here and I can't have her running loose and driving me crazy. No wonder Cresten looks so old. How many daughters does he have?"

"Five, sir."

"Give the man a raise. He's earned it."

"Yes, sir."

"Okay, I'll see you tomorrow. Dress casual. You don't need those tweed suits and plaid jackets. Jeans are fine."

"Jeans, sir?"

"Yes, Maxine. Blue, black, gray. Jeans."

"Yes, sir." Pause. "Mr. Flannigan?"

Just once, he'd like her to call him Rourke. "Yes?"

"I really am not familiar with children, though I will endeavor to do my very best."

"You'll do fine."

By noon Rourke had a two page list for Maxine and a ten-point strategy to bridge the fourteen year gap with Kate. He'd once been called a brilliant strategist by *Forbes*, and *Money* said he had the brains to lead the next industrial revolution. But this was Kate and suddenly, uncertainty plagued him. Kate, the woman, wasn't as easily swayed by him as Kate, the girl, had been.

When the front door tinkled someone's arrival, Rourke reached for his wallet. "How much do you need now, Abigail?"

"It's Abbie, isn't it?"

He jerked his head up. "Kate. Hello." She wore jeans that molded her hips and a semi-fitted pink T-shirt. Years had passed, but he still remembered every inch of skin underneath those clothes.

"I met your niece this morning." She moved toward him, a half smile skittering across her lips.

He'd tasted those lips. Full. Inviting. Rourke cleared his throat and stuffed his wallet in his back pocket. "She's interesting, isn't she?" For once he was grateful he could talk about his niece, the instant libido blaster. "Not that I understand a damn thing she says or does."

"She's a typical teenager." Kate stood across the desk, less than two feet away, the scent of her perfume teasing his senses. At eighteen, it had been hyacinth. He'd never heard of the flower before but she'd shown him one in the neighbor's garden. The next night, he'd picked every one and brought them to her. "Hyacinth?" he asked.

"What?"

"Your perfume. Hyacinth?"

She blushed. "Yes."

They stared at one another a second too long and he knew she'd never forgotten him. It was in the blue of her eyes, the flush of her cheeks, the wetness of her parted lips. Did she realize they weren't finished, that maybe they'd never be finished, no matter how much they fought it?

"Rourke?" It was a soft plea of uncertainty.

"Yes?"

"Don't do this. Please." Her eyes glittered with tears and a hint of fear.

"I can't help it," he said softly. "Neither can you."

She stepped back and clutched her middle. "We can't do this."

"It's too late, Kate." He kept his voice gentle. "It's always been too late. We're going to have to finish this thing between us; you realize that, don't you?"

"Maybe if you just leave…"

He shook his head and stood. "It won't work. You know that."

"Clay—"

"You were never his." He moved toward her. "Not since that night at the lake. I want to get to know you again." He closed the distance between them, lifted a hand and traced her jaw with his fingers.

"We live in different worlds now. Perhaps we always did." She blinked hard and leaned her face into his hand. "You've been all over the world. I've never even been to Disneyland."

"I'll take you there."

"You know what I mean."

He cupped her chin and tilted her face to his. "All I know is that traveling the world can't erase what we shared." He lowered his mouth to hers and murmured, "It can't even dim the memory."

When their mouths met, she whimpered. Rourke eased his arms around her waist, careful not to frighten her, but it was Kate who urged his mouth open, Kate who plunged her tongue inside with desperate need. She was the one who thrust her arms around his neck, pressed her breasts and hips against him.

"Rourke," she breathed into his mouth.

He wanted her with the ferocity of the young man he'd been at eighteen. Without reserve. Without a past. Without a dead husband between them. This was what he'd been waiting for all these years. He slid his hand along her spine. This—

The jingle of his office door slashed through the intimate moment. "Rourke?" Abbie's voice drifted to them. "You here?"

Kate tried to jerk away but Rourke grabbed her wrist. "Nothing happened. Understand? Pull yourself together." The pain of regret splashed across her face as she opened her mouth to speak. "Nothing," he repeated under his breath. Then he released her and moved to the other side of the desk where he sank into a chair just as Abbie bounced in the doorway. "Hey! Hi, Mrs. Maden. What are you doing here?"

"I—"

"She had some documents she wanted me to look over," Rourke interjected, flipping over a clipped pack of papers. Damn Kate, she wouldn't even look at him.

Abbie scrunched her nose and glanced from one to the other. "Didn't you two know each other in high school or something?"

"Yes, we did." *Look at me, Kate.*

"Long time ago, huh?" Abbie let out a squeak of laughter and added, "Very long time."

"Funny." He dug in his wallet and fished out a ten-dollar bill. "Here. Go get lunch."

Abbie snatched the bill and stuffed it in her shorts pocket. "Thanks." She turned to Kate. "Julia said she had some chores to do, but do you think she could go to the sub store with me?"

"If her work's done, she's welcome to go. I'll walk with you." Kate darted a glance in the direction of Rourke's forehead. "Nice to see you again. Thanks for looking at the papers."

"Right." If Abbie hadn't intruded, he'd have been looking at a lot more than her papers. And he still would. Soon.

Chapter 9

"You know that was a very bad time in my life, Katie, and I would just as soon not dredge up the past."— *Georgeanne Redmond*

Journal entry—May 4, 2000
I wish you had never come to Montpelier.
I wish you had never looked at me.
I wish you had never touched me.
I wish you did not have eyes the color of a storm slicing the lake.
I wish you did not have a chip in your bottom front tooth that makes me want to kiss you.
I wish you did not have a laugh that pulls my insides like warm taffy.
I wish you were not tall and strong and tanned.
I wish you did not know how to make me smile.
I wish I had not touched you.
I wish I could forget your face, your taste, your scent, your touch.
I wish you had loved me enough to come back before it was too late.

***

"What is he doing here?" Georgeanne Redmond tried to hide the agitation in her voice but it clung to her like cigarette smoke.

Kate shrugged and placed a tuna on rye alongside a kosher spear and a scoop of potato salad. "He said he's here for his niece." She handed her mother the plate and sat down.

"You spoke to him?" Oxygen seeped from the room in big gusts, rendering speech and thought nearly impossible.

"He came to the shop. I really had no choice."

Georgeanne forked a hunk of potato salad and said, "He's after something, I know it. That man's never done anything for the pure sake of doing. There's always been a motive."

Kate looked up from her sandwich and frowned. "Mom, you don't even know him."

"I know what I read." *And what I remember.*

"He'll be gone soon."

He better be. "Don't forget the pain he brought you, Katie. If Clay hadn't been there for you, what would have happened? Can you imagine the disgrace?" She didn't mention how or why Clay happened to be waiting with a proposal or her part in it.

"Mom, how could it have been any worse than having you almost thrown in prison for running over his mother?"

There it was again, slapped right back in her face. "That woman lunged into the road, I swear on a stack of bibles before Our Lord Jesus Christ. Judge Conroy believed me, too, you know he did."

"But they flew Mrs. Flannigan back to Chicago, which left the town talking about you."

Georgeanne rubbed her leg and scrunched her eyes shut. "You know that was a very bad time in my life, Katie, and I would just as soon not dredge up the past." Oh how she wished she'd timed her drink so she could have had it before Katie showed up. A good jolt of vodka would have done the trick.

"You brought it up, Mom. I'm just saying Rourke Flannigan is here to give his niece a slice of fresh air. That's all."

Now why did Katie look away when she said that?
Something was up; she could feel it in the flesh between
her screws and plate. The man bore watching and
Georgeanne Redmond was just the woman to do it. She'd
gotten rid of him once before; she could do it again.
Nobody was going to hurt her Katie.

***

"You are not to go near that guy again, do you hear
me?"

Kate didn't respond. She fingered the stone on the
fireplace in the bedroom of the model and said, "His niece
says he has a floor-to-ceiling fireplace in his fifth
bedroom."

"So?"

"We talked about building one." She didn't mention the
heart-shaped tub.

"Teenagers say a lot of things they don't mean. If the
world cried over every misspent emotion of a teenager,
we'd have another ocean."

Kate couldn't expect someone whose fiancé skipped out
on her three days before the ceremony to understand about
love. Angie had been hurt once, and she'd vowed never to
let anyone get close again. "It was real, Angie. It wasn't
melodrama."

"Okay, so it was real. It was also fourteen years ago.
What do you think Mr. GQ has been doing all this time?
I'll clue you in. He hasn't been sitting home Saturday
nights mooning over the fireplace you were planning to
build together or getting the exact shade of purple for his
turret."

"I know."

"The guy's a player and he's hell-bent on playing you
again."

"It won't happen."

"Good." Angie put her arm around Kate's shoulder. "He'll leave, you know. Just like before."

"He told me he was coming back."

"Of course he'd say that now."

"And the phone call—"

"Kate. Stop it. The guy disappears for months and then supposedly calls you? I'm glad Clay answered, if Rourke even called. He wasn't calling to propose; he just wanted to get laid again."

"Angie, don't."

"Sorry. The truth isn't always gentle." She softened her voice and asked, "What do you think Mr. Princeton would have said if you'd told him you were carrying his baby?"

"I don't know." The wondering had plagued her for years.

"I do. He would have vaporized. Men like Rourke Flannigan do not get caught in traps. They set them."

"You're probably right."

"And what about Clay? Not many men would feed their wife ice chips while she delivered another man's baby."

"I know." Guilt ripped through her. "He always deserved better than I could give him."

"You had a good life together." Angie touched her arm. "You were happy. Weren't you?"

Kate looked away. "Of course."

"Then don't upset your whole world for this guy. He isn't worth it."

Kate nodded as a slow ache seeped through her. Angie was right. Rourke would only hurt her again and then he'd leave.

"Kate? Are you listening?"

The ache shifted to a burn as the truth surfaced. There was no protection from Rourke Flannigan. "The only time I really felt alive was when I was with him."

"Are you willing to risk Julia for that feeling?"

"Of course not."

"Then you'd better come up with a way to control yourself because he doesn't strike me as a man who likes to lose, even if he doesn't want the prize."

Kate thought about Angie's words the rest of the day as she cut strips of carpeting for the house she was working on. It was a rich, wheat-flecked Berber. Did Rourke have Berber like this in his home? And why *did* he have a heart-shaped tub in his bathroom?

***

Maxine Simmons did not arrive a moment too soon. Rourke wasn't used to a child, let alone a teenager who questioned every time he breathed. Not that Maxine had any idea how to respond to a thirteen-year-old, but the woman had estrogen pumping through her body, and that was a start.

Besides, he missed Maxine's stingy smiles and superior organizational skills. The woman could give lectures on maximizing time and minimizing waste. How would she parlay that into looking after his niece?

"I got you a desk," he said, eager to get her situated so she could work her organizational voodoo. "Try out this chair, not our usual, but I think it will do."

She pushed her cat-eye glasses up her thin nose and perused the entire room. "Thank you, sir." It was hardly the penthouse of RF Renovations but she didn't seem to mind. "I'm very anxious to get to work, Mr. Flannigan." She set her suitcase behind the desk and turned toward the computer.

"Don't you want to go to the Manor first, freshen up maybe?" *See the second half of your job?*

She touched her cheeks, patted her curly hair in place, and smoothed her skirt. "No, sir. I rested on the plane."

"Oh. Well then." Abbie was probably running around with Julia Maden. He'd yet to meet the girl and wasn't looking forward to the product of Kate and Clay's union smacking him in the face.

He was almost grateful when the front door jingled open, signaling another disruption to an already unproductive morning. He was even more pleased to see the disruption was Kate. "Hi," he said, trying to keep his voice noncommittal. Maxine followed his gaze and tilted her head just so as she processed Kate's entry.

"Rourke," Kate began, "I need—" her gaze swung to Maxine. "I'm sorry, I didn't realize you were busy."

"Kate, this is Maxine, my secretary."

Kate forced a smile and extended her hand. "Pleased to meet you, Maxine."

"Likewise." Maxine hesitated a second, preparing to formalize the introduction with a Miss or Mrs., but Rourke had conveniently left it off, leaving Maxine no choice but to finish with a feeble, "Kate."

"Maxine flew in from Chicago to help me."

"Oh?" Kate cleared her throat and turned to him. "How long *are* you staying?"

He shrugged, avoiding both women's curious stares. "I haven't decided."

This made Maxine cough and sputter like a tea kettle. For God's sake, what did she have in Chicago anyway? A cat? A fish? The dog she had died last year and Rourke only knew about that because she'd come to work with bloodshot eyes. It wasn't as though she had a family there.

Not even a mother or father. Did she? He made a note to find out.

"How can I help you, Kate?" *You look wonderful.*

She lifted a large packet of papers from a shopping bag. "I met with a lawyer yesterday, and I don't really understand all the ramifications, but he thinks we have a strong case."

"I'll help you."

She gave him a hesitant smile. "Thank you. Do you want me to leave these with you?"

"That would be fine." He felt like a fifth grader with a cheat sheet. He was *helping* Kate, he reminded himself. There were too many swindlers out there and she was too innocent to tell one from the other.

Kate pushed back a tangle of dark hair and said, "He's going to call me tomorrow to discuss how I want to proceed."

"I'll review this today and get back with you. You'll be home tonight?" A chance to see where she'd spent her days and nights with another man.

"Yes." She licked her bottom lip. "Seven-thirty?"

He nodded, but he was thinking of those lips and what they could do to him. Delicious, wicked, wonderful things.

"Thank you. Nice meeting you, Maxine." Her gaze shifted back to Rourke and she said in a half-shy, uncertain voice, "I'll see you tonight."

He watched her leave, the sway of her hips pulling him back years to hot nights of unfulfilled passion and desperate promises.

"Would you like me to organize that file?"

Maxine stripped his fantasies with her clipped efficiency. "What? Oh, sure. Get this in order and then let me see it."

Kate had the softest skin he'd ever felt. He wanted to touch her again, worship her naked body...

"Mr. Flannigan?"

Bury himself deep inside her ...

"Sir?"

Make her forget there was ever anybody else...

"Sir!"

He swung around to find Maxine staring at him, a confused look pinching her face. "What is it? You look like you're about to be sick."

She held the file out to him. "This—this—"

"Yes?"

"This is you." She pointed to the name of his holding company.

"Kate doesn't know that."

"You're going to give her advice on how to go about suing you?"

"I'm going to look over the documents and see what the lawyer has told her," he corrected. "Then, I'm going to advise her to settle."

"But, Mr. Flannigan—"

"It was an accident, Maxine. The lawyer is probably some ambulance chaser looking to take advantage of a widow with a child. I won't let that happen," he paused, then added, "to Kate, or to me."

Her small mouth pinched together like a crepe.

"You disapprove." Maxine had a way of making her opinion known without saying a word.

"It's not my business to approve or disapprove, sir." She slid into the secretary chair and swiveled around to face the computer.

"I'm not going to take advantage of her." He scratched the back of his neck and spoke to her ramrod tweed back.

Hadn't he told her to dress casual? "We knew each other years ago." What a pathetic understatement.

She opened the folder and began perusing its contents. "I gathered that, sir."

"You did?" He moved to the side of the desk so he could see her face. "How?"

She turned her birdlike neck toward him and said matter-of-factly, "It was the way you said her name."

"Kate? What did I say?"

She shifted in her chair, clearly uncomfortable with the line of questioning. "Your voice shifted a few decibels lower. Soft. Gentle." She shot him a quick look. "There's nothing soft or gentle about you, Mr. Flannigan."

"So, I didn't bellow. That doesn't mean anything."

"No, sir."

"There's nothing wrong with being civil and concerned, especially with a woman who's skittish to begin with."

"Of course, sir."

"I was being a gentleman."

"You were."

"And I saw no need to establish my usual aggressive demeanor when the woman posed no threat." *Except to my peace of mind. And possibly, my heart.*

"Exactly." She powered up the computer, clicked on the mouse, and waited.

"Right." Rourke shoved his hands in his pockets and studied his assistant. Maxine was a strange character but she was an honest one. "You're thinking I'm full of it, aren't you?"

Her fingers faltered on the keyboard. "It's not for me to say."

"Truth, Maxine."

She nodded her grayish-brown head. "I'm sorry, sir."

"For what? Being right?"

"For telling you what you don't want to admit to yourself."

Chapter 10

"You think they'll wear a big G for Guilty on their foreheads?"—Rourke Flannigan

"For God's sake, Rourke, why is Maxine there?"

"She's a very capable assistant, Diana. I depend on her."

"Why would you need an assistant?" And then, "Exactly how long do you plan to stay?"

He hesitated, just an extra breath, but he knew his aunt noticed. "Did you call to lecture or talk about Megatron's financials?"

"I never lecture, Rourke. If I did, you wouldn't listen."

He laughed. "You make a horrible victim. Leave the antics to the weaker sex."

"What are you doing there and why is it taking so long?"

"Tying up loose ends." What an understatement.

She sighed her impatience. "You're opening yourself up to tremendous exposure every day you stay in that town. You do realize that, don't you?"

"I've got it handled."

"What if the widow finds out you own Reese Construction?"

"Her name is Kate."

She ignored him. "Miles agrees with me."

"So, the two of you have been discussing me? I thought you were negotiating a huge deal."

"We are. We're also trying to protect our biggest asset." She paused, then added, "You."

***

Kate changed her shirt three times. The first revealed cleavage, the second was too tight, and the third had a paint stain on the sleeve. She yanked a fourth from the hanger as the doorbell rang, signaling Rourke's arrival. She hastily buttoned the lavender cotton, smoothed her hair, and raced down the steps.

When she opened the door, Rourke stood there, looking cool and handsome in slacks and a navy silk shirt. She doubted he'd ever suffered clothing indecision, or any indecision for that matter. His gaze swept over her and a smile slid across his lips. "In a hurry?"

She glanced down and spotted a scrap of skin and pink lace where she'd missed a button. She jerked around and rushed toward the bathroom, propelled forward by the low rumble of Rourke's laughter. Once inside, she buttoned her shirt and sucked in several breaths. *He's just a man. Stay calm.*

Kate found him standing in the living room by the fireplace mantel. The silk shirt pulled across the muscles of his back and she wondered what he'd look like minus the shirt. She cleared her throat. "Would you like something to drink?"

"Chardonnay?"

Kate blinked. "I haven't had any in years." So what if it was a lie? She wasn't about to dig it out of her closet and offer him a glass.

His eyes glittered with feigned innocence. "Neither have I, but I find that since I've returned to Montpelier, I have a sudden desire," his gaze narrowed on her lips, "to taste it again."

Damn him, he knew it was the wine they'd shared the night they'd— "No," she shook her head, "I don't care for it anymore." *Another lie.*

"Really?" He settled on her couch and crossed his long legs.

Rourke looked so different than Clay had sitting in that same spot. Clay preferred to hunch over a crossword puzzle or toy train magazine, hands fisted under his chin. When he'd exhausted his mind, he'd slide back onto the couch and stretch his compact frame flat out.

In contrast, Rourke sat like a king, chest expanding, head high. If he deigned to lie down, his feet would dangle over the edge. They wouldn't be double cotton, moisture-wicked stocking feet either but silk-clad, Italian woven. She'd never be able to sit on the couch again without the image of Rourke Flannigan attacking her brain. And if she considered him stretched out on the plaid print—

"Kate?"

…with her body on top of his…

"Kate?"

Dear Lord. "Yes?"

"Water's fine."

"Oh. Yes. Water."

This seemed to be a night where she was bound to make a fool of herself. At least Julia wasn't here to witness her mother's rapid brain cell deterioration. Rourke's secretary had taken both girls, under protest of course, to the movies, though Kate wasn't sure who'd been more uncomfortable.

She'd been able to postpone the inevitable one more day—but soon, Rourke *would* meet Julia.

Kate returned from the kitchen with two waters and sat on the chair opposite him. He took a sip and flipped open the folder resting in his lap. "Clay was contracted by Reese Construction to head up the demolition crew for the renovation at," he glanced down, "4528 Harvest Glen in Syracuse, New York. On the morning of the accident, he was working alone, presumably before starting time. The accident report theorizes he slipped and fell fifty feet."

Her heart still ached when she thought of the fall. The coroner assured her Clay's death had been quick and painless, but what about the second or two before he hit concrete? Had he known he was a dead man?

"Kate?"

She met Rourke's gaze and willed him to understand the sacrifices Clay had made for her and Julia. "He was so excited to get this job. He said even though it was almost an hour away, there would be top pay and lots of overtime. He wanted to buy me new carpeting and a washer. We'd hit some rough spots financially. Julia was hospitalized last year with pneumonia and Clay's insurance wasn't the best."

"I'm sorry you've had a tough time."

"Clay used to say tough times built character. He never complained, just went to work, day after day, bad back and all." She shrugged. "He'd just taken out loans to buy more equipment so he could bid on bigger jobs like the Harvest Glen one. Lot of good that did him." She sniffed and said, "Know anyone who needs a crane and a dump truck?"

"I might."

"I've got to move forward and do what's best for Julia. It's what Clay would want."

"Money."

"Only if it's money that's due us," she corrected.

His gaze narrowed. "According to whom?"

"The lawyer. People in town. Everybody."

Rourke set his glass on the mug rug Julia had made in technology class last year. His whole demeanor shifted and it was easy to picture him in a boardroom negotiating multimillion-dollar deals. "I've reviewed the reports from OSHA and the insurance company. They've both determined Clay's death was an accident. I'm sorry, but nothing I've read indicates negligence on the company's part."

"Mr. Dupree said they're still responsible because it happened on their property."

"Do you believe that?"

"I don't know. Clay's dead. They should be responsible for something, shouldn't they?"

"Because he chose to enter the property unsupervised?"

"He was only trying to finish faster," she blurted out. "For the company, and..." she could hardly get the words out "...for me."

"Of course you wouldn't want him gone from home," he said in a tight voice.

Kate looked away. "Of course not." Clay thought if he worked bigger jobs, he'd buy her a bigger house, a fancier car. He thought it would make a difference. "I don't want to take advantage of a company just because they have the assets to make my life more comfortable. Nothing will bring Clay back, but maybe I can get what he wanted us to have, especially for Julia."

"Didn't he have life insurance?"

"Some. Clay was old school. He believed hard work and honesty would carry him through rough times. We'll get social security and worker's comp, but that's it. I hate to think that's all Clay was worth."

"I'm sorry, Kate, but he was a fool for not taking care of his family."

"He took care of us, Rourke, more than most men would." *He didn't leave us behind.*

"How much is the lawyer asking?"

She hesitated. "He thinks we should ask for four million and settle for two."

"Have you ever been cross-examined?"

"Mr. Dupree said it would never go to trial. He said the company would settle out of court."

"He's guessing. What if the owner believes your Mr. Dupree is just trying to bilk money from him? What if he believes it's his duty to do right and fight the case?"

"He probably doesn't even know somebody on his site was killed. Unless it's going to get him bad press, then he'll be trying to execute damage control. Or he'll send his publicity minions to shore up any leaks. I'm actually surprised no one's come snooping around here. Mr. Dupree said they might."

"Hmm."

"But no one's come here except you."

"So your lawyer's theory may not be exactly accurate."

"It could still happen. Don't you think?"

His gray gaze darkened. "It could."

"I'd spot them in a minute."

"You think they'll wear a big *G* for Guilty on their foreheads? They could look just like you or me."

"No." She shook her head with newfound certainty. "I would absolutely know."

Chapter 11

"You knew my mother."—Julia Maden

Journal entry—May 4, 2001

I graduated from Montpelier Community College last Saturday. Magna Cum Laude. Not bad for a mother with a five-year-old. Not Princeton, of course, but still, not bad. Julia was there, sitting in the third row with Clay and his family. Clay's father has emphysema and has to wear one of those oxygen masks and carry that little cart around with him everywhere he goes. They don't expect him to be here next Christmas.

You must have graduated by now, too. Princeton? Or did you change your mind and opt for Dartmouth? I have absolutely no clue where you are or what you are doing, other than making a huge success of yourself. I always knew you were going places, but there was a time I thought I'd be going there with you.

Angie Sorrento (you remember, the girl with the frizzy hair and bandanas?) and I are talking about starting a business. Since my degree is in Art and Design and hers is in Marketing, and since we both LOVE dollhouses, we thought we'd make our own dollhouses. What's the high concept? We'll model them after the customer's house, right down to the ceramic tile in the bathroom. Great idea, huh?

Angie will do the initial interviews, take pictures, etc., and then if I have to, I'll travel to the customer's home and get a more detailed assessment. Of course, I wouldn't be traveling any more than a twenty-mile radius since most of our clients will be friends, relatives, and referrals, but maybe one day, I'll actually get to travel.

Maybe I'll come to Chicago. Bad idea. Very bad idea.

Clay thinks Angie and I are crazy, but he says whatever makes me happy is fine by him. And I think I am happy. Finally. Maybe. Or at least I'm on my way to becoming happy.

Happy Graduation, wherever you are. I love you.

***

Kate Redmond's bedroom

July 24, 1995—early morning

Kate huddled in the corner of her bedroom, hugging a pillow to her chest. Faint strips of daylight poked through the blinds, falling in silvery-pink strands into the blackened room. She still wore the same shirt and shorts from last night—the same ones Rourke had gently eased off moments before he covered her body with his. Her underwear felt itchy and stiff from spots of dried blood. Virgin blood.

While she and Rourke were cocooned in their own world of erotic discovery last night, Rourke's mother had been plowed over by a hit-and-run driver on Indian Road. She was in the hospital, barely alive. Kate lowered her head to her knees. There were no tears left. Her throat was parched, like her insides.

She didn't know how long she sat hunched in the corner—one hour, two, five. The police told Rourke not to speak with anyone about the accident, but they didn't understand. Kate wasn't just anyone. She waited for him to come to her.

"This is a small town," Sergeant Kilney had said. "We'll catch him. Or her."

When Rourke found Kate, the sun had pierced the blinds and shot across the bed. She hadn't noticed.

"Kate? Are you okay?" His voice drifted to her, a godsend pulling her from murky water.

She blinked. Twice. He crouched before her, a thick lock of dark hair falling over his forehead, concern stretched across his tanned face. He was so handsome and so perfect. And she was so in love with him. Kate reached out and touched his cheek. "Didn't the police tell you not to talk to anyone?"

"To hell with them." He sat down next to her and stroked her hand. "Have you been in this corner all night?"

She nodded. "I couldn't stop thinking about you. I wanted to call and I almost came over—"

"Oh, baby." He pulled her into his arms and whispered, "It's going to be okay."

"Is it?" She kept her voice low so she didn't wake her mother. Georgeanne Redmond in a gin stupor was not a pleasant woman.

"Of course it is."

"What's going to happen now?" She could hardly get the words out.

"My aunt's coming from Chicago. She'll handle everything."

"The rich one?" Rich people did not live in Montpelier.

He shrugged "I guess. She's my mother's older sister. I hardly know her."

A tiny trickle of fear pulsed along the edges of her brain. "Is she going to take you away?"

"Of course not." He pulled her against his chest and stroked her hair. "I love you, Kate. Nobody's going to come between us."

She turned her face into his shirt and let the conviction in his voice soothe her. "Don't ever leave me."

"Never." His grip tightened. "We're bound together for life."

Two days later he was gone.

***

He'd been watching the girl for ten minutes, captivated by her tumble of black hair and the intense concentration blanketing her small face as she bent over a sketch pad. Aside from the obligatory christenings and random birthday parties of his clients' offspring, Rourke avoided children. Abbie was the first one he'd actually conversed with and only out of necessity, if one could call her monosyllabic responses peppered with sighs a conversation.

The girl with the black hair appeared to be about the same age as Abbie, but taller, thinner, quieter. He'd come upon her during a morning jog when he'd stopped at the stone fountain for a drink of water. He'd spotted her hunched against a monstrous oak, oblivious to the passing cars and shrieking children on the nearby swings. He'd behaved the same way at her age. His mother once said the whole world could collapse around him when he was sketching his buildings and he'd never notice.

As he studied her, an ambulance whizzed past, its siren and horns blasting through the morning din, but the girl with the black hair didn't flinch. Rourke jogged toward her and stopped a few feet away. "What are you drawing?" The girl didn't respond, not even a change of expression. Was she deaf? Is that why a siren screaming down the street didn't bother her? He moved closer until his shadow passed over her tennis shoes. She jerked her head up and her slate-gray eyes sent a jolt through him. He managed to find his voice and rasp out, "Who are you?"

The gray eyes widened as the girl clutched her sketchpad and inched away. "Get away," she snarled, "or I'll scream."

"I'm not going to hurt you." He stepped back, repeated in what he thought was a calmer voice, "What's your name?" She didn't answer. Clearly, she thought he was some psycho-sexual pervert come to attack her. "Look, I'm new in town. I used to sketch all the time when I was a kid. I just wanted to see what you were drawing. That's all. Really."

She wasn't impressed. No doubt she'd pinned him for a serial rapist and this was his standard line. "Why are you looking at me like that?"

"Like what?"

Those gray eyes narrowed to silver slits. "Like you're some kind of psycho," she bit out.

Now he was getting annoyed. No female had ever accused him of behaving as less than a gentleman, unless of course, they asked him *not* to behave as such.

"Get away, right now, or I swear I'll scream and I know the police chief personally."

"Look, just relax, okay?" She opened her mouth. Rourke hesitated. Children were like hieroglyphics—he'd never understand them. And teenagers? They were worse than interpreting a Rorschach test.

"Julia!" His niece's voice blasted him from behind. Rourke turned to see Abbie running toward them, her usually pale face red and sweaty. "Rourke?" she panted when she reached him. "What are *you* doing here?"

"Julia?" He looked at the girl who'd pegged him for a rapist.

"Rourke?" The girl stared back at him.

"You're Kate's daughter." He continued to stare at those eyes.

She relaxed a little. "*You're* Abbie's uncle?"

Damn those eyes. Slate. He wondered if any of the Maden clan could lay claim to those eyes. The Madens he'd known had eyes the color of wet mud and Kate's were blue.

"You knew my mother."

A true understatement. "I did."

Her expression turned curious, then hopeful. "Did you know my father, too?"

Rourke yanked the towel from his neck and wiped his face, avoiding her eyes. "I knew your dad. He was a good guy." *But he didn't have your eyes. Where did that little aberration come from?* A slow queasiness filled his gut as he considered the possibilities.

"My dad was a *great* guy." Julia's voice wobbled. "Really great."

He continued to stare at her. Kate had some serious explaining to do, starting with photo albums of the Redmond and Maden family tree. And they better damn well be in full-blown color.

***

July 23, 1995
Huntington Lake—later that night
"What names do you like?" She lay with her head on his bare stomach and breathed in the scent of night and his lovemaking.

"Agatha. Brunhilda. Prudence—"

She nipped the flesh above his navel and said, "Be serious."

"Gabrielle. It reminds me of a princess."

"Gabrielle," Kate murmured against his skin.

***

Kate grabbed a shirt from the closet and stuffed one arm through it. If she hurried, she could get back to the shop and finish the second coat of stain for the Peabodys' roof and still make it home in time to fix dinner. Where on earth were her sandals? She spotted one poking out from the dust ruffle of the queen-size bed. She snatched it up and knelt to search under the bed for its mate. She spotted the errant sandal on the other side of the bed, well past reaching distance. One of these days, she'd have to clean the bedroom, maybe box up Clay's shirts and pants and the Syracuse T-shirt she kept under his pillow... She straightened, took two steps, and let out a shriek. Rourke Flannigan loomed in the doorway of her bedroom in workout shorts and a sweat-stained T-shirt, his dark hair plastered to his head.

"We need to talk."

"What are you doing? Get out of my bedroom!"

He advanced on her in three quick, dangerous strides. "Not until I have answers."

She glared at him and yanked her shirt together.

"Don't play prim on my account," he said. "I've seen you without your shirt on."

Stay calm. He doesn't know anything. But when she met his gaze again, she saw a flash of outrage coupled with disbelief, warning her he might know more than she thought. "This is highly inappropriate."

"Noted. Now stop playing cute. I want the truth and I want it now."

He rounded on her and she was reminded once again he was no longer a boy but a powerful, intimidating man. Her voice wobbled the tiniest bit but she forced out an "Okay."

He scanned her face for seeds of truth or lies. "I met Julia this morning."

She clutched her shirt tighter. "Really?"

"Is she mine?"

Look him straight in the eye and tell him. For Julia's sake. Kate opened her mouth and delivered the most convincing lie of her life. "Of course she's not your child. I told you that the other night."

"No one in your family has eyes that shade of gray—my shade."

"You are not the only person on this universe with eyes that color."

"But I was the only person you slept with who had eyes that color." And then as if his words weren't painful enough, he added, "Wasn't I?"

She ignored the jab. This man had a cruel streak the younger Rourke had never possessed. Was she responsible for that? Or had it always been there and she'd been so lovesick, she'd refused to notice it?

"Answer me, Kate." He closed in on her, forcing her against the bed. "Were there others after I left? Once you had it, did you crave it, no matter who it was?"

She slapped his face. "How dare you!"

He grabbed her wrists and backed her up until her calves cut into the edge of the bed. "Is she mine?"

"No."

"I think we'll let a blood test decide that."

"She's not your daughter." *Not in any way that counts.*

"We'll see."

"Please. Don't subject her to that."

He leaned in close, his gaze slipping to her lips. "I just want the truth, Kate." His voice dipped. "All of it."

"There's nothing else."

He let out a low rumble of laughter that gripped her insides. "Oh yes, there's a lot of truth that hasn't come out." He released one of her wrists and traced her lips with his fingers. "So many truths that need to be unearthed."

She blinked, trying to deny the rush of pleasure surging through her. Oh, but she did not want to remember how good it had been with him.

"Did you ever think of me in all those years? Ever wonder where I was, what I was doing?" He eased a finger between her lips. "Wonder if you'd hurt me, maybe broken my heart?"

She closed her eyes and flicked her tongue over his finger. *Does the right hand ever forget the left? The mouth forget the tongue?*

"Did you ever wish he were me beside you?" He slid his finger from her mouth. "Wish it were me inside you?" he whispered seconds before his lips found hers.

Kate whimpered. She wanted to get away from him, away from this truth, but her body betrayed her as Rourke coaxed her mouth open, stroked her tongue until she cried out and grabbed fistfuls of his T-shirt.

He buried his hands in her hair and muttered, "There's never been anyone like you." The kiss deepened, tongue to tongue, teeth to teeth, deeper and deeper until she could think of nothing but the years of longing and emptiness away from him. His hands stroked her back, molded her butt, and pulled her against his arousal.

"I've never stopped wanting you, Kate."

I've never stopped loving you, Rourke.

"All those years, I never forgot how good we were together." He ground against her, slow and easy, his breath ragged inside her mouth.

She slid her hands under his shirt, along the tight muscles of his back, up to his shoulders and then lower to the waistband of his shorts. There might be years and secrets between them, but the passion hadn't died; one tiny spark and they were both on fire. And *that* was not something Kate could lie about.

"I want you," Rourke murmured, his large hand pushing her shirt aside to cup her breast. "I've imagined this too many times." He eased her onto the bed and lay beside her.

Don't think. Just feel. Kate lifted his shirt and helped him out of it. His body glistened with sweat and muscle and she could think of nothing but the feel of him against her. Inside her. He reached around and unclasped her bra with an expertise she chose not to think about.

"Tell me you want me, Kate. Tell me you haven't forgotten."

She couldn't. If she uttered one word, he would hear the need pulsing there and know life without him had been lonely. She couldn't betray Clay, who had been a faithful, loving husband and deserved so much more than a woman who could not give her whole heart.

Rourke clasped her chin between his fingers and stared at her. "Tell me. I can see it on your face. You want me. Say it."

Kate bit her lower lip to keep from blurting out the words. *I can't. Don't you understand?*

"Damn you," he muttered before he kissed her again with a fierceness that left her both shaken and exhilarated. His hands found their way to the zipper on her jeans, and he inched it open until his fingers skimmed the silk of her panties. "Tell me to stop now, Kate, or I swear to God, I'm not going to."

In answer, she pulled his tongue into her mouth and sucked. He let out a muffled curse and went wild. She was naked in ten seconds and five swift jerks of his practiced hand. He was naked in three, buried deep inside in four, with her legs hiked high over his back as he pumped into her with the strength of ten Olympians. They both shattered in less than sixty seconds.

Late afternoon summer noises drifted through the window—a lawnmower, the ice cream truck, a dog barking. Kate had heard none of these moments ago, yet now they swirled around the bed, tormenting her with their ordinariness. They had a right to be here, in her neighborhood, in her bed. In her life. Rourke Flannigan did not.

He moved first, easing from her with an awkwardness that was at odds with the superman agility he'd exhibited seconds before. He didn't look at her as he pulled on his shorts and snagged his shirt from the bedpost. "I didn't hurt you, did I?" His voice sounded raspy and uncertain.

"No."

He blew out a long breath and ran a hand through his hair, which still bore the marks of her fingers. "I'm not usually so..." He paused and cleared his throat. "I'm usually much more..." He faltered again.

Kate pulled her shirt closed and thrust the edge of the comforter over her waist. This was what it felt like to have sex with a stranger.

"Look," finally he met her gaze, "I've never hurt a woman, forced a woman, or been rough with a woman." He cursed under his breath. "And I've certainly never embarrassed myself with a millisecond performance like what just happened. I'm sorry."

"For what? Losing control?"

He flashed a dark, angry look at her and yanked his shirt over his head. "Yeah, pretty much."

"Then consider us even." She looked away and concentrated on the hydrangea pattern of the comforter. "I've never been one to lose control either."

"You're okay?"

She nodded, her eyes burrowed into a lavender bloom. "I'm fine."

"This shouldn't have happened. Not now. Not when there's too much unfinished business between us."

"I know." *I will remember every second of it.*

"It's going to confuse everything."

"Probably." *I would do it all over again.*

"Is that all you have to say?"

"What else is there to say?" *I love you, Rourke Flannigan. I never stopped loving you.*

Kate watched him out of the corner of her eye as he bent to retrieve his tennis shoes. He hesitated, waiting for her to say more, and when she didn't, his lips flattened into a hard line and he said, "I still want a blood test. If Julia's mine, we're going to have a lot to talk about."

And then he was gone.

Chapter 12

"One year or three, when a person feels as though they've known someone a lifetime, what does it matter?—Janice Prentiss

Journal entry—May 4, 2002
I'm pregnant. The baby is due at Thanksgiving and Clay is delirious with excitement. I am happy—and hopeful this baby will make me forget you, once and for all. Some days I really do hate you for leaving me with a hole in my heart that keeps me from loving another man completely.

What would happen if we had never known one another and then met on the street one day? Would there be this instant attraction? This obsessive need to be together? Would you even notice me?

My stomach isn't flat like it used to be. Even when I'm not pregnant, there's a tiny pooch that won't go away no matter how many sit-ups I do. I have stretch marks on my belly—faint and silvery, but I know they're there. Would you? Would you care?

I am sad today and tired. Clay's family is coming for dinner and then we're celebrating Julia's 6th birthday.

***

It was close to 4:30 by the time Rourke jogged back to the Manor, showered, and made it to the office. He was in no mood to talk to anyone and hoped Maxine had left for the day.

Damn, how could he have made such a mess of things? He'd had no business touching Kate, not yet, and certainly not like a starved lecher. She said he hadn't hurt her but how could that be true when he'd half attacked her?

And then what had he gone and done? He did not even want to consider it, but the truth tortured him with remembering. Premature ejaculation. Just thinking the words made him queasy. He'd never had that problem before, why now? Had she even climaxed?

He certainly hadn't given her much pleasure; no wonder she couldn't look him in the eye. Had she done so, he'd have seen disappointment, or worse, pity. *Damn.* She probably thought he always behaved that way. Next time would be different. Next time she'd moan with pleasure and an earth-shattering climax that would not make him wonder if she enjoyed it. *Next time.* He grew hard at the thought of Kate stripped and spread on his bed like a sumptuous dessert.

"Mr. Flannigan?"

Wide open and inviting…a tantalizing feast.

"Excuse me, sir?"

Rourke turned to find a semi-frantic Maxine wringing her hands against her tweed-clad middle. "Maxine?" Her pale skin looked transparent and brittle. "What's wrong?"

"I tried to call you, sir." The hand wringing grew more urgent. "But I was unable to reach you."

"Yes, well," he rubbed the back of his neck and tried to push images of Kate's naked skin from his brain. "I was detained."

She merely nodded. The woman had seen him through more than one sticky situation, usually involving women who did not know when the relationship was over, and whether or not she thought his current detainment had anything to do with Kate, well, Maxine was too discreet to mention it. Besides, it appeared she was too caught up in her current dilemma to wonder at his whereabouts.

"What is it, Maxine?" Now her face had switched from pale to paste.

She inched toward him in her respectable black pumps and said in a low voice, "You have a visitor, sir."

"Oh?" Perhaps Kate had called Angie Sorrento and now the Wicked Witch of the West was waiting for him with a hatchet, ready to neuter him.

"It's Ms. Prentiss, sir." She motioned toward the restroom. "She arrived ten minutes ago."

"Janice? How did she find out I was here?"

"It was the temporary assistant filling in for me. Apparently, Ms. Prentiss persuaded her to give up the information as to your whereabouts."

"What possible method of persuasion could convince someone to disclose information they were expressly warned *not* to disclose?"

Maxine's hand wringing started up again. Her gaze darted toward the bathroom door and she whispered, "She said she was your fiancée, sir."

"What?"

"She said she was—"

"I heard you the first time. Where did she get that idea?"

"I'm sure I don't know. Perhaps it was the recent trip to the jeweler's you took with her?"

Rourke shoved his hands in his pockets and muttered, "A mere ploy to *avoid* an engagement."

"Sir?"

"I bought her a bracelet, not a ring. I never said a damn thing about a ring. Why would she think I wanted to marry her?" A trip to Switzerland was one thing, but marriage?

Hardly. He hadn't thought of marriage for years. Fourteen to be exact.

His ruminations were disturbed by the *click-clacking* of stilettos and a loud, presumptuous "Darling, where have you been?"

"Hello, Janice," Rourke said, removing his hands from his pockets to greet her. She fell against him in a half swoon, draped her arms around his neck, and sighed.

"I have missed you so, my darling."

"It's only been three days."

Her eyes glittered with tears as she gazed up at him and murmured, "It's felt like three years."

Janice was an actress. Small-time stuff, a few hand commercials, a fill-in on a bath soap, and a room deodorizer. She descended from a long line of blue bloods and had attended Vanderbilt for economics. A brilliant woman who preferred to play the "helpless female with two brain cells" routine, even though her father had promised to pass along 51 percent controlling interest in his investment firm if she would give up acting and join the firm. Janice refused.

Rourke disengaged himself from her willowy frame and forced a smile. "We haven't even known each other three years."

She stuck out her Botox-injected lip and wrinkled her nose at him. "One year or three, when a person feels as though they've known someone a lifetime, what does it matter?"

Rourke worked a hand over his face and vowed to fire the whole damn temp agency. But first he had to deal with Janice. "Maxine and I have been very busy. We really aren't going to have time to socialize."

"That's perfectly fine." She smiled up at him and *click-clacked* over to the side of Maxine's desk, where she lifted a designer tote and said, "I've got loads of magazines to get through."

Loads. Great.

"I'll just sit right here," she perched on the edge of one of his chairs, "and mind my own business." She reached a slender hand inside the bag and retrieved a magazine. "Hair, the perfect accessory. Hmm." She toyed with a straight lock of black hair.

Rourke rolled his eyes at Maxine and shook his head. Janice was beautiful and entertaining, and when she wasn't putting on a show, a keen intelligence flowed from her that captivated him. And then there was the bedroom. And the living room. And the car. Front *and* back seat. She was a creative, enticing lover. But she was not Kate. The reality of this truth struck him. She was nothing like Kate. None of his women were. Perhaps that's why he'd chosen them.

"Did you know they're coming out with a lime and salsa conditioner?" Janice pointed a perfect red nail at the page. "Maybe they'll make a cilantro shampoo to go with it."

Rourke glanced at Maxine whose small lips puckered just enough to make him think she was imagining the lime between her lips. "How long are you staying?"

He didn't realize he'd spoken aloud until she looked up and cooed, "As long as you need me, Rourke."

Just one time, he wished she'd lose the stage voice and say something real. But she wouldn't, or maybe she couldn't verbalize, unlike some people he knew who had no problem saying exactly what was on their minds. "I've got a lot going on, Janice, and I wouldn't be able to spend any time with you."

She stroked her red nails from knee to thigh and threw him a sultry smile. "We'd have the nights."

Rourke cleared his throat. "My niece is staying with me."

"Which is why I've booked the room across the hall from you."

Damn that temporary agency for sending him a blabbermouth. Maybe he'd sue the agency for breach of confidentiality. What the hell was wrong with him? What man wouldn't want Janice in his bed? The answer stung his brain—*he* didn't want her in his bed. All because of Kate and this afternoon.

"...so we can grab dinner and once you put Annie to bed, you can come visit me." She sat up straighter so her boobs pushed against her tight black knit sweater—for his express benefit since he was the only male in the room.

"Abbie," he corrected. "Her name's Abbie. Short for Abigail."

"Oh, well, Abbie then. Put Abbie to bed," she lowered her voice, fingered the opening of her sweater, "and then I'll put you to bed."

Chapter 13

"The owner of the parent company is a celebrity of sorts; handsome, charismatic, well-connected, with a pristine record in the industry that has prospective partners begging him to do a deal."—Edmund Dupree III

Sophie's Diner boasted the best burgers and fries in Montpelier. It was the only reason Kate agreed to forgo the waffle and egg dinner she'd planned. At least that's what Julia thought. The real reason had nothing to do with Sophie's French fries. The real reason had to do with Rourke Flannigan.

What they'd done in her bedroom earlier had stolen Kate's desire to cook, or eat, or do anything other than berate herself for such weakness. When she wasn't remembering the feel of his arms around her, the thrust of his hips, the power of his—

"Mom? Can I get a milkshake, too?"

Kate tried to refocus. "What?"

"Wake up, Mom. Can I get a milkshake, too?"

"Sure." Julia had the same high cheekbones as her father.

"You want one?"

"No, I'll stick with my water." The same small earlobes, too. And of course, the same slate eyes. She was not going to lose Julia, no matter what she had to do.

"Hey, there's Abbie and Maxine!" Julia waved to them as they waited for a booth. "Can they eat with us?"

Kate was surrounded by Rourke: his secretary…his niece…his daughter…his scent still clinging to her. "Sure," she let out a long sigh.

"Over here!" Julia waved her hand at Abbie. "Wanna join us?"

The secretary looked uncomfortable with the offer, which made Kate wonder what she knew. Abbie ignored the woman and plopped down in the booth next to Julia, leaving Maxine no choice but to follow.

They'd barely had time to glance at their menus when Abbie burst out giggling. "You should see who's come to visit Rourke. Her name is Janice. She's a trip, isn't she, Maxine?"

Janice?

"Abigail, Mr. Flannigan's private business is not our concern."

Abbie scrunched her nose. "Come on, Maxine, Janice is a piece of plastic wrapped in designer clothes. What's he see in her anyway, other than the big boobs?"

"Abigail!"

Abbie ignored her. "She's some kind of model or something." She paused and her lips curved into a sly smile. "I think she's his girlfriend."

Girlfriend?

"Abigail!"

Abbie merely waved a hand at Maxine and continued. "She's got some great clothes, though."

Kate smoothed the wrinkles out of her khaki skirt. *Girlfriend?*

"He doesn't even act like he likes her. Does he, Maxine?"

"I'm sure I have no idea how Mr. Flannigan acts or does not act toward Ms. Prentiss."

Abbie's brows inched together as she took in Maxine's white cotton blouse. "I'm sure you don't."

"I think he's kind of cute."

They all turned to Julia, who merely shrugged and smiled. "For an older guy."

"I guess." Abbie scratched her chin and opened a menu. "But he's still a pain."

The conversation shifted to Sophie's burgers and fries. Kate tried to think of different ways to inch the subject back to Rourke and his girlfriend, but aside from asking outright, which would make her as transparent as cellophane, she could think of no other way.

No man with a girlfriend should have been doing what she and Rourke were a few hours ago. Kate pushed down a rush of nausea as she recalled exactly what they'd been doing. He ignited a burn in her that Clay had never been able to accomplish, no matter the skill or technique, and for that she despised Rourke, almost as much as she despised herself.

"...wants to marry him, don't you think, Maxine? He won't, though, not unless he's into self-torture." Abbie leaned in, lowered her voice. "You should see the stuff women send him. Flowers, sweaters, ties," she giggled, "underwear."

"Abigail, that is absolutely enough."

"What's he do with it?" Julia's voice quivered in anticipation.

Abbie shrugged. "Gives it to the cleaning lady for her kids and her husband. Not sure about the underwear, though. They were those silky boxer kind."

"Abigail—"

Julia giggled before Maxine could finish. "I thought they were *women's* underwear."

"No, but I told you he has a drawer of those in his bedroom, remember? I think they're *Janice's*."

"Abigail, if you do not cease this conversation this instant, I will call your uncle and insist he return you to the Manor." Maxine's thin nostrils flared in unison, her pale complexion flushed crimson as she added, "And see how you'll explain *that* to him."

Abbie rolled her eyes and made a face. "Fine. I'm done."

When the food arrived, Kate picked at her fries and forced three bites of burger. There was no getting around it. She'd have to convince Rourke that Julia wasn't his child and then she'd have to confront him about the other matter. What had happened between them this afternoon was a mistake that could *not* be repeated. And then there was the matter of protection. They hadn't used any. But neither had she and Clay and other than one pregnancy that ended in a miscarriage, she'd never even missed a period. She nibbled on a fry. What were the chances she'd be pregnant with Rourke's child again? Doubtful, considering her cycle. But what if she'd contracted an STD? Rourke had probably slept with dozens of women. The half-chewed fry threatened to explode in her stomach. *Damn*, she'd have to ask him about his sexual history.

"Hey!" Abbie stifled a squeal. "Look who just walked in! *It's them!*"

Kate turned just as Rourke spotted her. Even in the dim glow of the diner's lighting, she could see the dull red splashed across his cheeks. Her gaze flickered from his face to the woman clinging to his arm, a willowy brunette in three-inch heels and diamonds. Janice. The girlfriend.

Kate turned around and picked up a French fry. *That* was the woman he slept with on a regular basis. *In a bed.*

She was the one who had fancy underwear stashed in Rourke's bottom drawer. *She* sent him flowers and bought him ties, even if he did give them away.

"Here they come," Julia whispered.

"Watch the way she flips her hair over her shoulder when she talks," Abbie said. "Just watch."

Rourke's voice covered Kate as he spoke to the hostess. Seconds later he was facing her with Janice still clutching his arm, her waist glued to his. *Rourke had a girlfriend and this afternoon had been nothing more than a diversion.*

"Well, I see you're all enjoying Montpelier's finest cuisine." He smiled at them but his tone sounded forced. "Janice, this is Kate Maden and her daughter, Julia. Kate, Julia, this is Janice Prentiss."

Abbie had definitely made a major error in her description. Janice Prentiss was Hollywood beautiful with jet-black hair, hazel eyes, and long, long legs. Whether she had the help of silicone or Botox, she was still beautiful. But then she would be, because *this* was the kind of woman a man like Rourke Flannigan would align himself with in life, not a woman in jeans and cotton with paint creased into her fingertips and stretch marks on her belly. Janice extended a hand and smiled. Perfect teeth, too.

"How wonderful to meet you, Kate." She turned to Julia. The brilliant smile faltered a half second and then she recovered, clasping Julia's hand. "And you, too, Julia."

Maxine darted a glance at Kate, cleared her throat twice, and sipped her iced tea.

"Well, we won't interrupt your dinner any longer," Rourke said, his voice more forced than before. "Enjoy."

"Yes, enjoy," Janice echoed, her hazel eyes sweeping over Julia one last time before she smiled up at Rourke and they moved on toward their table in a dark corner of the diner.

"Told you," Abbie whispered. "She is such a pain."

"I thought she was beautiful," Julia commented. "Like a movie star."

"She is, sort of, isn't she Maxine?"

Rourke's secretary pierced a green bean and said, "I believe she's involved in the entertainment industry in some capacity."

Abbie nodded in a knowing manner. "That means yes."

"Do you think he'll marry her?" Julia whispered.

"Julia!" Kate lashed out. "That's none of your business."

"I was just wondering."

Abbie pointed a French fry toward the booth in the corner where Janice sat cozied up to Rourke. "She's trying. She's even got a *Bride* magazine stuffed in her bag. Rourke would flip if he knew that."

"Doesn't he want to get married?" Julia snaked a quick glance in his direction. "He's really pretty hot for an older guy. How old is he anyway?"

Three months shy of thirty-three.

Abbie shrugged. "At least thirty-eight. As for not wanting to get married, I haven't been around long enough to investigate, but give me another month and I'll be able to tell you."

"Mr. Flannigan would not like being the subject of dinner conversation between two thirteen-year-olds." Maxine dabbed at the corner of her thin lips with a paper napkin. "You would be best served to change the subject."

"Oh, Maxie, loosen up. Rourke's not going to fire you. Heck, you're the only woman he trusts."

Why doesn't Rourke trust women?

"Your uncle trusts those who deserve to be trusted."

"Right." Abbie snatched a fry and pointed it at Janice. "And that woman is definitely not to be trusted."

***

Edmund Dupree III sat on the same couch that Rourke had occupied less than twenty-four hours ago. As the third partner of Angston, Jefferson & Dupree, he was a small, wiry man with sharp blue eyes, a silver crew cut, and a presence that belied his diminutive stature. When Mr. Dupree spoke, his voice resonated with perfect pitch and diction as though he were on stage. He'd just informed Kate that her advisor had underestimated Angston, Jefferson & Dupree and had neglected to factor in the most important issue—reasonable doubt.

"Your source has not considered all available options, Mrs. Maden. Perhaps he is not well-informed in the areas of law?"

Kate poured Mr. Dupree coffee from a porcelain pot that had belonged to Clay's great-grandmother. "I only turned to this gentleman as another opinion. Certainly, I don't consider him an expert."

Edmund Dupree studied her over the rim of his coffee cup and murmured, "Exactly."

"I would never take money that didn't belong to me, no matter how badly I needed it."

He nodded. "A very noble gesture."

She clasped her hands together to keep from fidgeting. There'd been so many lawyers calling after her mother's accident, twisting and contriving Kate's words until they hadn't even sounded like her own. "I don't want to sit in a courtroom and listen to a judge tell me Clay was negligent."

"I understand, Mrs. Maden. I'm not about to put you in a position such as that."

"You're sure?"

His blue eyes pierced her with cool calculation. "This case will never go to court." A small smile crept over Edmund Dupree's thin face. "We'll threaten a media blitz; photos of you and your husband, your daughter, maybe even talk shows and newspaper articles citing the devastation your husband's loss has wrought on you and your daughter. The economic loss, the physical loss, the emotional loss." His words sparked with certainty. "Reese Construction won't want the publicity. They'll be glad to pay you to keep quiet."

"So basically, I'd be bribing them?"

Edmund Dupree's expression remained placid. "Think of it as forcing them to do right. If it takes polite, friendly persuasion, so be it."

Kate relaxed her hands. She was doing this for Clay, and for Julia. Maybe Rourke was wrong. Maybe Reese Construction was ultimately responsible, accident or not.

"Now, I'd like to talk numbers." Edmund Dupree flipped a page on his legal pad and began writing. "I know we've bandied a few figures about, but let's try to find something concrete. What do you think of four million?"

"Four million?" They'd talked about a number that large but still, to actually ask for *four million dollars?*

"This is only a holding company, Mrs. Maden. We go for the parent company and we've hit the mother lode."

She owed it to Clay and Julia. "Okay."

"I would advise you against sharing any further information with your friend. One can never be too careful, especially where millions of dollars are concerned."

She wanted to tell him that Rourke Flannigan was a fourteen-year aberration who landed in Montpelier last week and would be gone before the case was settled. The thought of him leaving started a sharp twinge in her stomach, which she blamed on too many cups of coffee. But later that night, when the twinge became a dull ache throbbing through her, she knew Rourke was behind the pain. Just like he'd always been.

Chapter 14

"It doesn't thrill me to admit it any more than it thrills you to hear it."—Rourke Flannigan

July 24, 1995
Montpelier, New York

"I wish you didn't have to go." Kate buried her head against his chest and closed her eyes. She inhaled his scent like a dose of oxygen. He was the only one who could make everything right and now he was leaving.

Rourke tightened his arms around her back and buried his face in her hair. "I'll be back in a week."

His mother was being transported to a Chicago hospital and, of course, he had to go with her. But he was coming back. "I'm sorry for acting like such a ridiculous baby." She lifted her head so she could see his eyes. "It's just that everything is happening so fast. The other night at the lake..."

"I love you." He brushed his knuckles across her cheek and gently turned her face toward him. "I want to spend the rest of my life with you." He leaned down and touched his lips to hers. "Always."

"I'm scared. What if your aunt won't let you come back?"

His laugh rolled over her, making her insides burn. "I'm eighteen. What can she do? Force me?"

"I don't know what she can do. You don't even know her."

"I don't have to know her. She's merely a means to help get my mother settled and see that my tuition at Princeton *is paid." He smiled down at her, a lazy, seductive smile that made her want to touch him. "Relax, baby. Nothing's going to happen to us. I won't let it."*

***

Rourke found Kate at Sophie's Diner the next morning, attacking a plate of waffles mounded with strawberries and swirls of whipped cream. "I guess you plan on rolling out of here, huh?" She stopped chewing and looked up. A flush of pink smeared her face and a syrupy sheen coated her lips. Right now he'd sign over controlling interest of the company for one taste. He slid into the booth opposite her and gestured toward her plate. "Don't stop on my account."

She set down her fork and pushed the plate away. "I'm full."

Rourke snatched up the fork and slid the plate closer. "Good, because I'm starved." He pierced a hunk of waffle and strawberry and plunked it in his mouth. Her lips had touched this fork. He speared another chunk of waffle. Her tongue had slid over the tines.

"Rourke? What are you doing?"

"Hmm?"

"Take a breath. Nobody's going to steal your food."

He glanced down at the near-empty plate that seconds ago had been smothered with waffles and strawberries. He threw her a haphazard grin. "I guess I *was* hungry." *Hungry with thoughts of your mouth and your tongue.*

She looked away. "Actually, I'm glad I ran into you. There's something I need to tell you."

Damn, he *had* hurt her yesterday. He set down the fork and steadied his voice. "What's wrong?"

"It's about Julia…and what you thought."

"You mean that I might be her father?"

She shot him a mortified look. "Quiet. If you speak any louder you'll be reading about it in next week's *Gazette*."

He lowered his voice. "Is that what you're referring to?"

She nodded.

"Go on." *Here it comes. Julia's your daughter.* The thought had him gasping for air. He had a child. With Kate. No wonder he'd never been able to let her go. They belonged together...

"Julia's not your child."

The words clogged his brain. "Julia's not my child." Was that disappointment in his voice? Or disbelief? Right now, he couldn't say.

"No, she's not. I know I told you this yesterday, but you deserved more of an explanation." She licked her lips. "Apparently, my biological father had black hair and gray eyes."

He merely stared at her, trying to discern the truth.

"As you know, my mother was not always very forthcoming with information."

"I seem to recall she had a penchant for that sort of thing." He did not even want to think about Georgeanne Redmond and her vodka-soaked brain.

"After the accident, she finally told me his identity." Kate's eyes misted. "His name was Carter. She met him the summer she waitressed at Lake Chautauqua. His family owned a cottage there." Her voice wobbled. "She said they wanted to get married but his parents had other plans. When summer ended, he went back to law school and she came home. Eight months later I was born."

"Let me guess; she never heard from him again."

"Pretty much. The first time she saw you, she said you reminded her of someone. It had to be him."

If this were a business deal, he'd have his attorneys confirm the facts and check the timeline. But this was Kate and she was so much more than a business deal. When the first tear fell, he forgot about doubting her story. When the second followed, he could think of nothing but making the tears stop. He reached across the table and clutched her hand. She didn't pull away when he turned her palm upward and stroked her soft flesh. Instead, she shivered.

"Where's your girlfriend?"

Ahhh. Was that a speck of jealousy? "She's not my girlfriend and she's on her way back to Chicago." Of course she'd tried to coo and fawn her way into an invitation to stay, but the attempts had been futile.

"I see."

"What does that mean?" Code talk for *I've already analyzed the situation.*

"I saw the way she looked at you. Who is she, Rourke?"

"She's just a friend."

Her blue eyes pierced him. "I see, a friend with benefits."

"Oh, for Chrissake." At least the tears were gone. Where was the sweet, young Kate who had once watched him with reverent awe? She shook her dark head and despite his annoyance, he wanted to bury his hands in the swirl of silky hair.

"Just the truth, Rourke. Can you give me that?"

He met her gaze and everything else fell away. She was so damn beautiful and she didn't even know it. Maybe that's what added to her beauty, the unaffectedness with which she moved and spoke and lived her life. Hollywood could take lessons from Kate, but they'd never match her.

"I'll tell you the truth." He'd spent years trying to forget her, only to realize he never would. He had to speak before the words disappeared from consciousness.

"Janice is a beautiful woman, but she's not you." Her eyes glittered and he thought the tears would start again.

"Please don't say that."

"Why, because it's the truth? Isn't that what you asked for? Well, there it is, uncoated and, I'm sure, unwanted. It doesn't thrill me to admit it any more than it thrills you to hear it."

"You've been with dozens of women. Surely, one of them—"

"Mere distractions."

"Beautiful distractions."

"But none with that breathy laugh and eyes the color of a Montpelier sky. None of them you, Kate."

She gave him a helpless, confused look. "What do you want?"

"You," he said simply. "Spread out on my bed, naked, under me…on top of me." He stroked the fleshy part of her palm. "All over me."

She eased her hand from his. "It's not that simple. We can't let yesterday happen again."

"If yesterday happens again, I'm contacting a doctor." He cleared his throat. "I went from zero to blastoff in two seconds and that's never happened before."

Pink stained her cheeks. "That's not what I meant."

"What *did* you mean?" He liked the way she fidgeted when he talked sex with her, as though she didn't want to remember but couldn't forget.

"Just that we can't," she faltered, started again, "we can't do that. Again." Her gaze flitted across the table and landed on the napkin holder. "It would only end badly."

Rourke leaned forward and pressed his hands flat on the table. "You can't believe that. We're not kids this time, Kate. It can only end the way we want it to."

The blush deepened and she dragged her gaze to his. "I don't think straight when I'm around you. We didn't use any protection. How ridiculously stupid is that?"

"Very. I'm sorry." And then, "Is there a reason to be concerned?"

Her blue eyes turned dark. "Damn right there's a reason to worry. I don't want to end up with an STD or HIV."

"I meant pregnancy." *What the hell kind of traveling disease fest did she think he was?*

"There's no need to worry about that."

"What does that mean?"

"It's not a concern."

"For whom?"

She blew out a frustrated sigh. "Either of us."

"How do you know?"

"I know."

"Are you on the pill?"

"No."

"Tubes tied?"

"No."

"Then how do you know you're not pregnant?" The thought of her belly filling with his child sucked the breath from him.

"Lower your voice." She leaned across the table and hissed with the ferocity of a she-cat. "I just finished my period and I'm not ovulating. Now do you understand?"

"In great detail."

She straightened her shoulders and eyed him. "So do I have to get tested?"

"For what?"

Her nostrils flared and he thought she might spring across the table and go for his throat—or another part of his anatomy. "A sexually transmitted disease, you big oaf."

Rourke cocked his head to one side, considering her question. She really was adorable when she played feisty witch. What would she look like angry *and* naked? "It's not a concern."

"What does that mean?"

"It means you don't need to be worried about it." *Angry, naked, and panting beneath him.*

"Not good enough. With all the women you've been with, I'll have to get tested for everything."

"Hold it." Now she was annoying him. "I'm not a man-whore, for Chrissake. And I always use a condom."

"Not always," she bit out.

"You are truly trying my patience. Let me rephrase that. I always use a condom *unless* I'm with you. *Then* I seem to lose my senses." She looked pleased with that confession.

"Really?"

Oh, what the hell, he'd already said too much. "Unfortunately, yes."

Her lips tugged at the corners. "Then I guess we're even." She held out her hand.

"You've got to be kidding."

"I've never been more serious."

Rourke shook her hand but when she tried to release her grip, he held firm. "Come to my bed, Kate. Let me show you how good it can be." She licked her lips. Twice. He remembered the taste of those lips.

"You've got to be kidding."

He smiled. "I've never been more serious."

Chapter 15

"There's never been another you, Kate. Ever. And God knows I've tried."—Rourke Flannigan

Rourke turned the key in the lock of the Montpelier Manor and opened the door. Kate followed him inside, inhaling the scent that clung to the room. If she were blindfolded and placed next to three hundred men, she'd still be able to sniff out Rourke Flannigan. He threw his keys on the desk and turned toward her. She could tell from his guarded expression and the stiffness in his posture that she would have to take the next step. She offered him a hesitant smile. "Make love to me."

His jaw twitched the tiniest bit. "You're sure?" When she nodded, he drew her to him and searched her face. "No regrets, right?"

She could barely breathe, let alone think. He was so close, so real, and she'd dreamed of this for so long. The truth seeped through her desire. "Of course I'll have regrets, but that isn't going to stop me."

"I don't want you to live with regret. There's been enough of that between us." He trailed his lips along her temple and murmured, "I want us to get to know one another again."

Kate squeezed her eyes shut to block his words, but she'd dreamed them too many times to pretend she wasn't desperate for them.

"I've never forgotten you, Kate." His broad hand rested at the base of her neck, fingers splayed to touch her skin. He met her gaze and eased his hand down the front of her shirt until he found the opening. He undid the first button, then the next, and the next, slowly, painfully, until her shirt fell open, leaving her vulnerable and wanting. "Even when I wanted to hate you for what you'd done, I couldn't." His gaze dropped to her breasts. "Pink lace. My favorite."

"I remember." She'd worn a pink lace bra the first time he unbuttoned her shirt. They were in the backseat of his Malibu, supposedly on their way to the movies. He'd traced every swirl and dip of frothy material, first with his hands and then his tongue...

"Do you ever wear any other colors?" His fingers outlined the scallop of fabric covering her right breast. "Black? Red?"

She swallowed. His fingers were so close to her nipple, if she moved the tiniest bit, he'd touch it. Just a hint closer...

"Kate?"

"Black. Sometimes I wear black."

He flicked his thumb over her nipple and smiled when she stifled a whimper. "I'd like to see you in black. Black bra, black panties, black garter belt."

"Hmm." Right now, she'd paint her whole body black if he asked. He cupped both breasts, stroking them as his thumbs worked her nipples. "Rourke." She closed her eyes and arched her back. "Please."

"Please what? Please stop?" His fingers stilled. "Please don't stop?" The stroking started again. "Or, please do this?" His tongue poked through the lacy fabric to lick the rigid peak of a nipple. When he began to gently suck, she gasped and clutched his shoulders.

"You're driving me crazy."

"I'm trying for certifiably insane." He reached behind and unfastened her bra. "But I think I'll beat you to it." He let out a muffled groan as he eased her bra off and buried his face between her breasts. "You were always perfect."

She stroked his back, tugging at his shirt until she reached bare skin. "I want to feel you inside again," she murmured into his tangle of hair. "Deep inside."

He groaned. "Stop. We're taking it slow this time. I've waited too long for this and I'll be damned if it's going to be over in fourteen minutes."

A smile escaped her lips as she eased open the top button of his shirt to expose a dark sprinkle of hair. She flipped open another button and then another. Rourke was here, and he was hers, at least for this moment. "Unless a lot has changed, the first time was only a warm-up for the second and *third* time."

"That sounds like a challenge." His fingers slid to the zipper of her jeans.

She leaned forward, brushed her breasts against his chest, and whispered, "I like to think of it as a wish."

He squeezed his eyes shut. "You know how to bring a man to the edge with a single sentence."

"Are you saying I have a big mouth?" She nipped his earlobe and glided her tongue along the cord of muscle on his neck.

"I'm saying you have the perfect mouth." He clasped her face between his hands and drove his tongue between her lips. "Playtime's over."

She stepped between his legs and pressed her body against his. "Thank God."

Rourke's slow, methodical lovemaking switched to urgent, out-of-control need as his hands roamed her body and slipped inside her jeans, searching for a swatch of lace panty. Kate yanked his shirt from his shoulders and reached for his belt buckle.

"Wait." He leaned over, pulled a condom from the nightstand, and tossed it on the bed. Then he pulled her on top of him. "I don't want to stop once we get started."

"Awful sure of yourself, weren't you? Or did Mrs. Gibson provide these instead of the standard mint on a pillow?"

His expression hardened. "I bought them this morning. Call it wishful hoping."

The box wasn't opened, which meant maybe he really hadn't been with Janice.

"I want to see you naked. I want to memorize every curve."

"I'm not eighteen anymore." *Not model-perfect like Janice either.* "I've had a child—"

"You're beautiful." He inched her jeans over her hips and murmured, "Perfectly beautiful."

His gaze flashed with a heat that said she was the only one he wanted. Kate pushed a lock of hair from his forehead and kissed him softly on the mouth. Her heart had always belonged to him even though she'd married Clay, and maybe that was a sin she'd carry with her forever. But right now, didn't she deserve this tiny slice of happiness, no matter how fleeting?

Rourke drew in deep, uneven breaths as she worked his zipper over the very obvious bulge in his pants. "Let yourself go, Rourke." She inched her fingers inside his jeans. "Let's be eighteen again." Two fingers slid inside his navy boxers to stroke the tip of his penis.

"Witch," he muttered, tearing at the scrap of lace panties, yanking them off to expose her nakedness. He scooped her up and flipped her onto the bed, covering her with his large body. "You want to be eighteen again, hmm? I remember you at eighteen. Every delicious detail." His eyes glittered as he stroked her breasts. "And I remember everything about that night at the lake."

"So do I." She wrapped her arms around him, licked his bottom lip.

"Damn." He reached for the pack of condoms and tore one open. "You really do make me lose my head."

"Let me." She took the packet from him, ripped it open, and with painfully slow strokes, eased it over his penis. Sweat peppered his forehead by the time she finished. "All done."

"Hardly." He laced his fingers with hers and pinned her hands above her head. "Look at me, Kate. I want you to look at me when I bury myself inside you." Then he dove into her, hard and fast, his silver gaze burning her soul.

She cried out and wrapped her legs around his waist, trying to pull him deeper into her. He took her with a need that erased fourteen years. It had never been like this with Clay, no matter how much she pretended.

"Kate," he groaned, thrusting into her, long and hard. "Kate," he said again, gripping her fingers tighter.

He was hers, a magnificent blend of heart and soul and flesh. Her climax burst from her, tearing a zillion tiny shreds of ecstasy from deep inside her soul. Rourke followed, arching and pumping one final time before he cried out her name and collapsed against her. It was the aftermath that almost made her cry. He didn't roll off and fall into a deep, immediate sleep as Clay had always done. Rourke remained wedged inside as he lifted his head and placed a soft kiss on her lips, her forehead, and her chin.

"Thank you."

She ran a finger along his jaw. "Thank you."

"Do you have any idea how many times I've dreamed of this?"

"Tell me."

He kissed her lips. "Every night since our first night together."

"I seriously doubt it was every night. Some nights I'm sure you were otherwise occupied." The thought of him making love to another woman squeezed her insides until they hurt.

His smiled slipped. "There's never been another you, Kate. Ever. And God knows I've tried."

She did cry then.

"Don't be sad." He swiped her cheeks with his forefinger. "Be happy. We've found each other again."

More tears slipped down her cheeks. Easy to say when he wasn't distracted with his Hollywood life and women like Janice Prentiss. And what if he found out she'd lied about Julia?

Rourke kissed her mouth, gently at first and then with more urgency. "There's only one way I know to get you to stop crying," he said on a sigh. "And I'm just the man to do it."

They made love again, with hearts and hands and bodies. There were no words this time, only sensation and the power of their need flowing between them. After, Rourke pulled her into his arms and they slept. An insistent buzzing woke her minutes or maybe hours later. "Rourke?"

"Hmm?"

Kate opened her eyes and tried to locate the sound. "It's your phone."

"Ignore it."

"What if it's Abbie? She and Maxine may have finished up early and are on their way back."

"They'll leave a message." The buzzing stopped.

"*Rourke*, what if they're on their way here?" Kate jerked up in bed and scanned the room for her clothes. She threw back the sheet and was about to step out of bed when he grabbed her wrist.

"Don't go."

He lay against the pillow, tousled and sleepy, all male and much too handsome. "Kate—" The phone buzzed again. "Hold on." He reached down and grabbed his jeans, fishing around in the pocket until he located his cell phone. He flipped it open and said, "Hello?"

What if Abbie and Maxine were on their way here right now? Maybe Abbie had grown bored of the movies and convinced Maxine to call it quits early. What if—

"I told you, Miles, everything is under control. No. Not yet. I know. When? Are you sure?" Rourke glanced at Kate. "I'll take care of it. I don't know. Damn it, don't push me. Okay. I'll get back to you." He hung up the phone and tossed it on the floor.

"Bad news?"

"No, just something I need to take care of." He lay back down and dragged her on top of him. "Phones should be banned from bedrooms." He trailed a hand along her hip and stroked the outside of her thigh.

"I should go." She glanced at the clock on the nightstand and saw it was almost eleven.

"I'm not letting you out of my bed yet. Besides, Abbie won't be home until three."

Kate pressed her lips against his chest and inhaled his scent. "Well, in that case…"

She woke some time later, sore and exhausted from their third round of lovemaking. Rourke proved a thorough and demanding lover who reveled in her enthusiastic responses. She pushed back a nibble of guilt when she thought of Clay and his honest, even attempts at lovemaking. It wasn't as though he'd ever disappointed her. He just wasn't Rourke. Kate untangled herself from Rourke's arm and eased off the bed. Apparently, she wasn't the only exhausted one. He slept on his belly, one hand under his pillow, the other flung out where he'd held her. As much as she wanted to crawl back into bed for another hour, she had to get to work. Angie would be looking for her and Julia would be finished babysitting in another hour. Kate picked her clothes out of the pile on the floor and slid into them.

She wanted to leave Rourke a note and tell him—what exactly? *This was great. Let's do it again sometimes soon? Thanks for the sex, it was super?* What kind of note did one leave an ex-boyfriend after sleeping with him? Kate decided on *Off to work. See you later.* There was no notepaper on the desk and nothing inside the drawer. Darn Mrs. Gibson and her campaign to remove distractions from her guests' lives. Kate spotted Rourke's briefcase next to a chair. What businessman didn't carry a notepad of some sort? Would it be pressing boundaries if she opened the briefcase and took a piece of paper? Her desire that he find something besides an empty bed outweighed her concern over invading his personal space.

Kate flipped the locks and opened his briefcase. She lifted the manila folder resting on top and tore a piece of paper from the notepad beneath. She scribbled a few lines, then tiptoed to the bed where she laid the note on the pillow next to Rourke. As she watched him sleep, a tiny part of her heart opened and she began to believe in second chances.

Chapter 16

"This big bad wolf, what's his name?"—Kate Redmond Maden

August 15, 1995
Montpelier, New York
"When is he coming back?"
"Soon." Please, Rourke, please come back soon.
"Didn't he tell you he'd be back in a week?"
"Maybe his mother had complications."
"But three weeks? What if he doesn't come back?"
"He will." Please, Rourke.
"Maybe the aunt won't let him come back. She looked like a tough one. Did you see the Cadillac she was driving?"
"Everyone saw it, Angie. It was the only one in Montpelier."
"You didn't tell me he was loaded."
"I didn't know."
"He should have told you."
"It wouldn't have mattered."
"Kate, money or lack of it, always matters." Pause. "Maybe the aunt's convinced him to stay in Chicago. She might, you know, especially if she's a rich bitch. They don't like mingling with us common folk. And with him going to Princeton and all, hmm, she might not think Kate Redmond from Montpelier, New York, is good enough for her blue-blood nephew."
"Shut up, Angie."
"I'm just saying."

"Don't. Rourke's coming back." Her voice wobbled. *"He has to."*

"What does that mean? Kate? Ah shit, are you pregnant?"

The words fell out in tiny, half-spoken syllables. *"I don't know."*

***

Rourke fastened his watch and slipped his keys in his pocket. He had a few more minutes of quiet before Abbie got back and started yammering in his ear. He'd concede there were moments these past few days when he'd wondered what it would have been like if he and Kate had been together and Julia was their child. Damn Georgeanne Redmond for ruining that possibility. A twinge of disappointment pinched his gut as he acknowledged Julia was Clay's daughter. There would be no need for a blood test because Kate was incapable of subterfuge. He'd realized that a few hours ago when she gave herself to him—openly, honestly, and completely.

He'd made the bed, fluffed the pillows, and emptied the trash can with the thoroughness of the cleaning woman who visited each morning. There were no signs that Kate had ever been in this room. Even the last traces of her hyacinth scent had evaporated into the yellowing pores of the wallpaper. He wished she'd woken him before she left. They needed to talk, the sooner the better. They belonged together, and if Kate belonged with him, so did Julia.

He pulled out his briefcase and flipped it open. The plain manila envelope that held the investigative report for Clay Maden stared back at him, an unwelcome reminder that the man threatened to once again keep Rourke and Kate apart.

***

To file:
Client: Rourke Flannigan
Subject: Kate E. Redmond
Date: July 23, 2004

Ms. Redmond, Mr. Maden, and daughter packed up Ms. Redmond's Toyota Corolla and drove to Huntington Lake where they proceeded to picnic on a red and blue plaid blanket.

How could you eat on the same blanket we made love on, Kate? Was it the same one? Did you think about that night while you were feeding your husband watermelon balls?

Mr. Maden and his daughter walked to the edge of the lake and spent approximately twenty minutes attempting to catch tadpoles. Attempt successful. Ms. Redmond remained on the blanket.

Ms. Redmond, not Mrs. Maden. Good job, Graves. How much extra do I pay you to remember that tidbit?

Ms. Redmond gathered up picnic basket and blanket at 3:25 p.m. and returned home with Mr. Maden and their daughter.

10:35 p.m.—Ms. Redmond left residence and returned to Huntington Lake where she spread out the same blanket and sat down, facing the lake. She was alone and remained there until 11:30 p.m., at which time she returned home. Downstairs light remained on until 2:10 a.m.

What were you doing, Kate? And why? Why, why, WHY?

***

Kate punched in Edmund Dupree's number as she drove home from the Manor. He'd called her cell phone four times in the past two hours but she'd left it in the car. She'd been so consumed with Rourke that the phone could have been on her pillow and she would have ignored it.

"Dupree speaking."

"Mr. Dupree? This is Kate Maden. Is something wrong?"

"Thank God I found you." His voice skittered through the line with excitement. "I need to speak with you immediately. I can be at your house in ten minutes."

"Okay. I'm on my way home right now. Is everything all right?"

"Oh, yes indeed. Couldn't be better." He let out a high, giddy laugh. "Go straight home and wait for me. Do not speak with anyone."

"Okay." *Click.* The next few miles proved a struggle to negotiate the road she'd traveled for years. Had Edmund Dupree discovered proof that found Reese Construction at fault for Clay's death? Rourke had been so adamant against this possibility she'd begun to think there would be no case. She couldn't wait to hear what Mr. Dupree had to say so she could tell Rourke and get his opinion. Her insides warmed and she wondered if she'd see him tonight. She could invite him to dinner, fix linguine with clam sauce, and introduce him to Julia. Her brain froze. She wasn't ready for Rourke to spend time with Julia. He might recognize the way she tilted her head just so when she was thinking or how the shape of her earlobes resembled his. No, it was definitely too soon to introduce him to Julia. Right now she had to concentrate on Edmund Dupree.

She had just enough time to get home and splash cold water on her face before the doorbell rang. Kate grabbed a hand towel and made her way to the front door where Edmund Dupree III stood in a seersucker suit and baby blue tie. "Hello, Mr. Dupree. Come in. What on earth has happened?"

A smile stretched over his face as he stepped inside. "I should have known. I don't know how I could *not* have known. Talk about the proverbial fox in the henhouse." He shook his head once more and chuckled. "Clever. He's very clever. I'd heard that about him."

"What are you talking about? And whom?"

"Our mystery man. Do you remember when I told you Reese Construction was merely a holding company for a much larger conglomeration?"

"Yes. You thought we would file a case against both, once you determined the parent company."

"Exactly. Well," he rubbed his small hands together and slid onto the couch, "I've discovered it and, my dear, it is a gold mine."

Kate smiled, partly from the news but also because the couch swallowed Mr. Dupree's fragile frame, giving him the appearance of a child in a time-out chair, a much different visual than Rourke had cast when he'd sat there a few days ago.

"The man behind the company is well-connected, well-known, and well-bred. He won't want the publicity, at least not this kind. I must say, he is something of a celebrity in his own circles." He sighed and added, "And quite a handsome, charismatic man."

It was obvious Mr. Dupree was enamored with the mystery man. "Tell me more."

"He's unmarried, lives in—"

"I mean business information."

"Oh, yes, well, there is a good deal of that as well. He's known among his peers as a fearless, tough negotiator. Not one to be crossed, but fair."

"So how do we approach him?" Kate perched on the edge of the ottoman and clasped her knees. Social security and worker's compensation were not enough to support Julia, even if they were extremely frugal for the next several years. But most importantly, no amount of money would bring Clay back. This big-shot owner should take better care of his subcontractors and learn that money didn't buy him a free pass.

"I've been working on a plan. It's going to be fairly high profile, Kate, no way around that."

"I don't know." She chewed on her bottom lip and wondered what Rourke would say. "I want to protect Julia, and I don't want Clay's name splashed on some newspaper headlines."

Edmund Dupree shrugged. "It's the nature of this business. The bigger the buzz, the bigger the payout. It's corporate America against Mrs. Everybody. We can't get the public to care about you if they don't know you."

She was certain Rourke would disagree with this strategy. "I'll have to think about it." And consult with Rourke.

"Now's not the time to go soft. You need to think of your daughter. This man and his company must share in the blame. We'll capitalize on the fact that your husband left behind a wife and child." His smile spread with confidence and anticipation. "That alone will net you an extra million."

And you a hefty percent of that. "If this man is as powerful as you say, he's going to fight me, isn't he?"

"Of course he will. He'll call in his lawyers and try to make a case for negligence against your husband. I'm sure he'll spin it to the newspapers and maybe even a few tabloids. He's quite the looker and not afraid to squash those who get in his way."

She bet he wouldn't squash Rourke. Maybe she'd go see him after Mr. Dupree left and get his opinion. "I have right on my side, Mr. Dupree. As long as I have that, I'm not afraid."

"That's a good attitude." He nodded and rubbed his chin. "Keep it and we'll do just fine. Now, give me a day or two to complete our strategy and then we'll file the suit."

"Okay." She should be nervous but the thought of Rourke guiding her increased her resolve. "Let's do this."

Mr. Dupree stood and brushed his wide pin-striped slacks. "I'll be in touch."

"Thank you. Mr. Dupree?"

"Yes?"

"This big bad wolf, what's his name?" Maybe Rourke had heard of him.

"Flannigan. Rourke Flannigan."

Chapter 17

"You killed my father."—Julia Maden

Journal Entry—May 4, 2003

I saw a man in People Magazine *who looked like you. I don't read* People *unless I'm at the dentist's, which is only twice a year. There was a copy in the waiting room, eight months old. Go figure. You popped out on page 13, staring back at me in a black tux with those silver eyes. A beautiful woman clung to your arm. She wore a green sequined dress, low cut, and white-blond hair piled eight inches high. You were surrounded by Hollywood-type people. I never pictured you in California, I guess because you loved the snow so much, but then I never thought you liked blondes either.*

I ripped the page out of the magazine and folded it neatly, careful not to crease your face. I'll bet the other people in the waiting room thought I was stealing a recipe for pot roast. I stuffed it in my jeans pocket and vowed I would only look at it once a year, when I wrote in my journal. I broke the promise two seconds after I left the doctor's office. I carried your picture in my back pocket and I swear, pulled it out at least once an hour. That sounds crazy, doesn't it?

I memorized the smile, the eyes, the hair. Okay, I memorized everything about that picture and I hoped it was you because if it wasn't, I'd become obsessed with a stranger. But you are *a stranger, aren't you?*

Of course, you are, but there's a tiny piece of me that says, NO, you are still the same person who said he loved me, who still loves me.

Angie caught me staring at the picture and made me rip it up—right in front of her. She was right, of course, but I still wish I had it. By the way, she said it WAS you.

***

Len Slewinski hopped out of his pickup and scurried up the front steps of the Montpelier Manor as fast as his bum leg would carry him. Damn that son of a bitch and all the saints in hell, he'd pay if he hurt Katie again. Len spat out a slew of curses and yanked open the Manor door. The place was dead quiet, which wasn't surprising, seeing as most visitors flooded Montpelier in the winter to witness what they called a wonderland. Len cursed again. He'd show that son of a devil what happened when an outsider took advantage of someone else's wife.

He clambered up the first flight of stairs and looked around. The bastard was in one of these rooms. Len massaged his right hand and clenched it into a fist. Times like these, he wished he'd lived in the Wild West so he could draw a gun first and work out the details later. He thought he heard a noise behind the second door and tiptoed toward it. Sure enough, there were drawers closing, footsteps, and what the hell, humming? Len knocked and waited. When the door opened, he shook a fist at his target and snarled, "If shootin' were legal, you'd be dead."

Rourke Flannigan stared at him as though Len had just escaped from the Syracuse Mental Institution. "Who are you?"

Most men cringed when Len gave them his evil-eye once-over. Not this one. He stared back with his own silver devil glare. "Len Slewinski," Len spat out, then added, "I worked with Clay. He was a good friend."

The man tensed. "I'm sorry. Clay was a good man."

There was something unnatural about his words, like they didn't fit his expression. "Save it," Len said. "You're about as sorry as a bear caught in a honey pot and unless you want to read about this in tomorrow's paper, you'll let me inside to finish what I come to say."

Rourke Flannigan didn't budge. "I don't know you and I'm not interested in what you have to say." He started to shut the door but Len stuck his foot out to stop it.

"Not even if it has to do with Katie?" That comment stole the tan right off the man's face.

"You've got five minutes."

"I only need two." Len entered the room and stuffed his hands in his pockets so he wouldn't do something stupid like try to cold-cock him. "I remember you. Came here with your ma. Big city boy. You and Katie got thick fast. Poor Clay acted like a puppy with a bellyache, he was so heartbroken. Downright sad. Then the accident happened and before anybody could say wedding bells, you flew the coop. You hear me, boy? Clay was the one who stuck around." Len paused and tried to get a bead on him but Rourke Flannigan was as unreadable as cement. "Now he's dead and you come dancing back in your fancy car and your shiny shoes. You think you can pick up where you left off? I saw the two of you coming here this morning. How many other people you think saw?"

"I care about Kate. I'm not going to hurt her."

"Hah! That's what everybody says, right before they pull the trigger." Len eyeballed Rourke Flannigan one last time. "Leave her alone. She's a good girl and she don't need to mess around with the likes of you."

***

"Where have you been? I told Mrs. Peabody we'd send her a picture of the crown molding and it's not even painted yet."

Kate avoided Angie's gaze. "Give me twenty minutes and I'll have it ready." She pulled out a can of Amber Mist and popped the lid off with the opener.

"Glynnis Peabody has already brought us three new customers. We can't afford to alienate her."

"I know." Kate busied herself selecting a brush. "Sorry."

"That's it? You're sorry?"

Kate stirred the paint, anxious to lose herself in Glynnis Peabody's crown molding. "I was detained."

"Hmm."

"Julia wasn't feeling well."

"Is that why she called looking for you twenty minutes ago?"

Kate's head shot up. "She called here?"

Angie's dark eyes burrowed into Kate. "She called from the Andersens', where she'd been babysitting since eight this morning."

Kate looked away and slowly removed the paint stirrer, wiping the paint against the edge of the can. Amber Mist was such a fancy name for brown but it suited Glynnis Peabody. Who named paints, anyway?

"Kate? What's going on?"

I trusted him and he did it to me again.

"Talk to me. I know this has to do with Rourke Flannigan, so just tell me."

A tiny cry escaped Kate's lips. She tried to hold it inside but the betrayal was too great. It wasn't just his betrayal—

she'd betrayed Clay. Her shoulders slumped forward and she let the ache slip out. "I can't even say it."

"You have to, Kate. It's the only way I can help you. Remember how it was last time?"

Painfully, yes. Kate studied the paint on the tip of her brush and said, "I'm okay. Let me get this done so Mrs. Peabody doesn't pull this project and all of her Martha's Vineyard friends with it."

Angie clutched Kate's wrist and eased the brush from her fingers. "It can wait," she said in an uncharacteristically gentle voice. "Besides, the crown molding called for Ambient Mist, not Amber."

"I knew better, Angie." Her voice slipped. "But I couldn't help myself."

"Tell me what that bastard did now."

Tears slipped down Kate's cheeks and onto her chin. "*He's* Reese Construction. That's why he came to Montpelier."

"What?"

It hurt to say the truth out loud. "Reese Construction is Rourke's holding company. He came here because of Clay." Everything out of his mouth had been a lie.

"How did you find out?"

"Mr. Dupree called this afternoon and said he'd made a huge discovery and had to see me right away." She waited for Angie's rage and disappointment, but neither came, which was actually worse. "Just say it. Tell me what a screw-up I am, how I dishonored my husband and my marriage. Tell me how I should have kicked Rourke Flannigan out the second he walked through this door."

"Why should I? You already know that."

"I slept with him."

"I know."

"What's wrong with me?"

Angie shrugged and clutched Kate's hand. "You love him and that gives him the power, because he doesn't feel that way about you." Her voice turned brittle. "Oh, he'll tell you he does and right when he's got you believing it, he'll use you, just like he did last time."

The truth in Angie's words sliced through Kate's pain. "I can't let him do this again."

"Oh? How do you plan to stop him?"

"I'm going to sue him."

"He's not going to play nice."

"Neither am I."

***

"Is your mother here?" Maybe he should have called first, but he hadn't wanted to risk Kate telling him it wasn't a good idea, because of Julia, or the town, or who knew what. He needed to see her tonight, needed to push Len Slewinski's words out of his head.

"She's out back in the garden." Julia peeked behind him and frowned. "Where's Abbie?"

"Watching a movie with Maxine."

She wrinkled her nose and made a face. "Abbie likes that?"

Rourke shrugged. "No, but I didn't give her a choice."

"Oh." Her face brightened. "Can she come over?"

He glanced at his watch and said, "If she can get here in the next ten minutes and not change clothes fifteen times, then yes. It's going to be dark soon and I don't want her out on the streets." Damn, he sounded like a father.

"Thanks! Go through the kitchen." She pointed behind her and took off up the stairs.

"Thanks." Rourke glanced around the living room, a cozy, suburban family nest, and nothing like his house in

Chicago with twelve-foot vaulted ceilings and Surround Sound. Given the right occupants, his place could house a family and that's what he'd come here to work on.

When he reached the kitchen, he took in the tiny windows over the sink and wall-to-wall appliances—gas range, refrigerator, dishwasher, built-in microwave. The entire kitchen would fit in his pantry. What would Kate say to an imported stove from Italy and a Sub-Zero refrigerator? The thought of her in his life again made him restless. He'd never been one to sit back and let things happen in due course. That strategy belonged to laggers and losers, and he was neither. Rourke believed in action but he didn't want to scare her, so for now, he'd wait and hope nature would move quickly and Kate would realize just how much she wanted him in her life. He glanced out the back door and spotted her mounding dirt at the base of a rosebush. He had his hand on the knob when she grabbed a pair of red-handled trimmers and hacked at the bush with sharp, uncontrolled whacks, chopping until nothing was left but a stump with jagged clusters of green. When she finished, she heaved the trimmers across the lawn and slumped forward.

What the hell? Rourke yanked open the kitchen door and ran across the lawn. "Kate?" He wanted to scoop her in his arms and comfort her but Julia was too close to chance it. "Kate? What's wrong?"

Slowly, she lifted her head but made no effort to turn toward him. He could tell she was crying by the way her breath quivered when she inhaled. Obviously, she didn't want him to see her crying. Didn't she know she didn't need to hide from him? That the sooner they both owned up to their feelings, the better for all of them, even Julia?

"Look at me, Kate." When she didn't turn, he walked around to face her. In the pinkish light of passing dusk, she formed the perfect backdrop of beauty and pain, her face splattered with tears, her lips and eyes swollen, a streak of dirt smearing her cheek. Rourke knelt beside her and smoothed a piece of hair from her face. "What's wrong?"

"Why did you come back here?"

"I told you, Abbie needed a place to—"

"Stop. You're lying."

What had gotten into her? "I'm not lying. Abbie needed a place to regroup and get away from the city."

Her swollen eyes narrowed to puffy slits. "That's all? No other possible reason?"

He didn't like the accusation in her voice. "What are you getting at?"

"Abbie wasn't the only reason you came back here."

This wasn't quite the way he'd planned it. He'd hoped for dinner and flowers, maybe a candle or two, not hunks of soggy earth clinging to his shoes and half the neighborhood within eavesdropping distance.

"Okay. You're right. Abbie wasn't my only reason for coming to Montpelier." The faint gleam in her eyes unsettled him but he plowed forward. "I came to see you." His voice dipped but when he leaned forward to touch her cheek, she jerked away. "I needed to see you again," he continued, "needed to find out if the magic was still there all these years later." She stared at him as he forced out the next words. "And you know what? It is." There. He'd said it. Finally.

"Liar."

Scores of women would barter their personal trainers to hear those words, but he'd had the horrible luck of falling for one who apparently didn't believe them. "Why are you doing this? Are you trying to get a confession out of me? Is that what you want?"

"That would be a good starting point."

He cursed under his breath. "Okay, you want your confession? Here it is—I love you."

Her swollen eyes stretched open and she slapped him across the face with her dirty glove.

Rourke fell back but recovered and grabbed her wrist as she prepared for a second strike. "Stop it!"

"Go to hell! I know all about you, Mr. Rourke Flannigan owner of Reese Construction." She twisted in his grasp and tried to get away, but he grabbed her other wrist, preventing her escape. "When were you going to tell me you owned the company that killed Clay? That you'd come here to broker a deal so I wouldn't sue you?"

"Kate—"

"Tell me!"

"I had no idea it was you when I made the decision to visit the man's widow." Right now, he wished he'd never come back. "And then I saw the file and heard he was from Montpelier and I asked myself how many demolition contractors were from a town the size of a grapefruit. I was going to tell you as soon as I got here." His voice faltered as he pushed past the memory of seeing her again. "Once I saw you, I couldn't tell you. Not right then. But I was going to, just as soon as—"

"As soon as I gave you my lawyer's entire game plan. What a fool I was, asking for your advice on Clay's case. You must have had a good laugh at that one. Advising me how not to sue you."

"I didn't find anything humorous about it." This was past disastrous and getting worse. "I did give you my honest opinion on the case."

"Honest? You don't know the meaning of the word."

"I planned to tell you the truth, just as soon as we figured things out between us."

"Really? Don't you mean as soon as you got me into bed?" she hissed, trying to break free of his gràsp.

Rourke gripped her wrists tighter until she cried out. "Stop fighting, damn you."

"I can't believe I was such an idiot."

"Kate, listen to me—"

"You killed Clay. He's dead and it's your fault." The accusation clung to the thick, night air. "Now you're trying to cheat us out of what little solace we can gain from his tragic loss."

"That's not true."

"Of course it is. You're a businessman. It's about the bottom line, isn't it? What's one lowly demolition contractor when you own eight other companies?" She sneered at him. "Mr. Dupree prides himself on his investigative abilities, especially when big business is involved, and you're big business."

"Let's go inside and discuss this. Calmly."

"Fine. Let me go."

He eyed her. "You won't run?"

"No."

As soon as Rourke released his grip, Kate tried to bolt toward the house. He grabbed her around the waist and dragged her to the ground, smothering her with his weight. "You're being ridiculous."

"Get off of me, you jerk!"

"Funny, you weren't complaining earlier."

"Go to hell."

"Kate—"

"I'm going to sue you."

Her lips were soft and full under the half moon. "I know." He lowered his head an inch closer.

"And I'm going to take millions of dollars from you."

"No doubt." He'd give her anything for one more chance.

"According to your financials, you've got lots of it." Her eyes glittered with anger and something he refused to think of as hatred. "We were a real family, something you might not understand. We liked our Sunday afternoon barbecues and playing Frisbee in the backyard, and driving to Mel's for a Tastee Freeze. We didn't need glitz and newspaper reporters and ten-thousand-dollar gowns to tell us we were happy." Her voice rose until it pinched his brain. "You stole it from us, you and your company that demanded work get done faster than humanly possible, and Clay did it because he wanted us to have a better life." Her voice cracked and she turned away, sobbing until her shoulders shook.

"I'm sorry." The truth sliced him—she'd loved Clay. She might have given him her body these past few days, but it was out of need and loneliness. Clay Maden was her real love and Rourke had taken him from her. "I'm sorry," he said again, stumbling to his feet.

"Go away. Please. Just go away."

Whatever shred of hope he'd harbored for a future together died with her words. She'd never forgive him. "Good-bye, Kate." His gaze lingered on the gloss of hair touching her neck. A few hours ago he'd buried his face in its silkiness, kissed it, whispered words of love into it. Now it was all over.

Rourke turned and headed for the back steps. He'd scoop Abbie up and head back to Chicago as soon as possible. He was so busy trying to figure out a way to deflect his niece's impending anger, he didn't notice the figure standing just inside the screen door. "Julia?"

"You killed my father."

Chapter 18

"Well, are you really going to leave Mrs. Maden behind?"—Maxine Simmons

Journal Entry—May 4, 2004

I dreamed of you again last night. We were sitting on our deck and you'd grilled steaks for us. I'd made a coconut cream pie.

It was so relaxing, it felt like a meditation. Then I woke up.

Since I found that picture of you in People *last year, I've been imagining us together. Before I saw that magazine photo, when I thought of us together you were always still eighteen. After the photo, I realized the truth in glossy print—you're a powerful man who takes what he wants, though most people, especially women, probably never even make you ask. I hate writing that but I know it's true. Why wouldn't it be?*

Are you still with the blonde from the picture? Was she your girlfriend then? Your friend? Maybe not even that?

I wish you could see the model dollhouse I built. It is so perfect and has everything we wanted for our own home, down to the ceiling-to-floor stone fireplace in the master bedroom and the turret washed in lavender. You would love it.

I think.

I wonder sometimes if I could see you again, say you were standing in the next room and all I had to do was open the door and step over that threshold, knowing once I did nothing would be the same, would I do it?

I promised myself and God that you'd be relegated to a once–a-year memory in a red velvet journal. And I've been so good, but that picture has tormented me. I almost did an Internet search the other day, just to see what might come up. Thank God Julia came in the room before I typed your name.

Where are you?

Why can't I stop loving you?

***

"Mr. Flannigan, I've booked our flight for Saturday at 12:50."

Rourke glanced up from the page he'd been reading, or rather, the paragraph. Eight sentences in ten minutes.

"Mr. Flannigan?"

"That's the first available?"

"I'm sorry, sir, there's nothing else."

Was that sympathy peeking at him from behind those cat-eye glasses? That was the last thing he wanted. "Fine. We'll have to make do."

"Yes, sir."

Today was only Thursday. He'd been in hiding since the grand blowout Tuesday night. He hadn't ventured near her house or her shop. Hell, he hadn't even been to Sophie's for a cup of coffee. But in two and a half days, he'd emerge and never have to worry about running into Kate again, except maybe in a courtroom.

His stomach knotted at the thought. She'd been decibel-deafening clear that she had no desire or intention of establishing any sort of relationship with him, other than as a means to make him pay for her *husband's* death, the husband she'd loved with such intensity. She hadn't added that last bit, but it had been sitting between her words like a soggy piece of bad intention.

"Mr. Flannigan?" Maxine cleared her throat and asked, "Would you like me to see to Abbie's lunch?"

Rourke glanced at his watch. "Lunch. Right. Seeing as she hasn't spoken to me in two days, I doubt she'll want to have lunch with me. Besides, she might try to put something in my hamburger." He pulled out his wallet and asked, "Do you know where she is?"

"Julia Maden's."

"Ah, of course." Apparently Abbie was outside the circle of exclusion they'd placed him in. He could care less.

"Abbie and Julia really are quite fond of one another."

Rourke turned back to his computer. "Hmm."

"They've been inseparable these last few days."

"Hmm."

"I imagine they've found common ground in the loss of their parents."

He scrolled through the reports on the screen and jotted down a few notes.

"That can be very important. Especially now." She cleared her throat and continued, "Critical, actually."

Rourke tossed his pen on the desk and swung around. "Is that Maxine Simmons, doctor of psychology speaking, or Maxine Simmons, mother of ten?"

A brilliant red stained her cheeks but she didn't turn away. "I know I'm neither, Mr. Flannigan, but those girls need one another right now."

"I'm sorry about Julia's father and I'm sorry for the company's part in it, no matter how accidental. I'm even sorry that my screwed-up sister couldn't pull out enough maternal instinct to parent her own daughter and got herself killed. But sorry doesn't matter, because we're leaving Saturday."

"Yes, sir."

"All three of us, Maxine."

She clasped her hands in her lap and murmured, "I'll let Abbie know, Mr. Flannigan."

"You do that." So, his little niece had enlisted Maxine to buy her extra time here. Not very likely.

"Pardon my asking, sir, I know it's not my business," Maxine squeezed her hands so tight he thought she'd burst a blood vessel. "Well, are you really going to leave Mrs. Maden behind?"

She must have seen the answer on his face because she jumped from the chair, snatched her purse, and raced out the door mumbling something about lunch.

***

Georgeanne Redmond followed the second hand on the clock above the bookcase. The instant it hit twelve, she lifted her glass and sipped. The smoothness of the vodka warmed her blood. One more sip, small enough to drag out eight minutes. Such a long time. In her day, she'd have gulped ten times that amount and wanted more.

The wanting never stopped, though she could pretend for Kate, and the minister, and the town. There were times when she teetered on the brink of crashing headlong into her former life in all of its alcohol-imbued glory. But she wouldn't. She couldn't.

She took another sip, longer this time, and licked the vodka from her lips. Rourke Flannigan would finally get his comeuppance at the hands of Katie, and she, Georgeanne Elizabeth Redmond, would be in the front row of the courtroom, cheering her daughter on. People tried to hide behind money and power, but right found a way around them every time and Katie had right on her side.

Did that man really think he could waltz into town and treat them like they were trailer trash? Toss a pittance their way and never question the why? Ha! He'd soon see how resilient her daughter was, how she could strip him of his good will and take what belonged to her. What belonged to all of them.

Finally, Georgeanne would be vindicated. She lifted her glass and drained the last two tablespoons of vodka. It had only been six minutes. *Breathe.* She inhaled through her nose and blew out a long breath through her mouth. She'd kept her secret fourteen years. A lifetime. But it had all been worth it. She closed her eyes and remembered the moment her life changed.

The sticky July night clung to her as she drove the Plymouth into the inky darkness of Indian Road. Damn, why couldn't the city install a street lamp or two? Last week, Shep Greely nearly ran over a slew of geese. The week before that, Harriett Carlson hit a skunk that stunk all the way to the grocery store.

She clutched the steering wheel and squinted into the night. Katie would be in an uproar if she got home and found Georgeanne gone. Then the lectures would start. Since when did children think they could give their two cents to their elders, especially a mother? No matter, there should be enough time for a few quick ones before Katie got home. That girl barely made midnight curfew these days, ever since she hooked up with that Flannigan boy. Hmph. Something about him didn't sit well. Too damn good-looking for one. Those silver-gray eyes and that big white smile, just ready to break a girl's heart. Well, it wasn't going to be Katie's. He couldn't head to college fast enough.

And if he thought for one minute—

Something lunged in front of the car and Georgeanne hit it head on with a thump. She slammed her foot on the

*brake so hard the car spun around, then swerved to a stop.
"Jesus, Mary, and Joseph." What on earth had she hit?
Too big for a dog. Too small for a deer. She eased the door
open and made her way to the front of the car. The
Plymouth's headlights illuminated the lump on the ground.
Georgeanne inched closer. Squinted. Screamed.*

The lump moved. Groaned. "Please…"

*Georgeanne knelt and peered at the body's face. It was
Rourke Flannigan's mother. The woman's legs were
twisted at odd angles, her arms limp at her sides, her
forehead smeared with blood. "I'm sorry. I swear I never
saw you."*

*Barbara Flannigan moved her lips and a whisper of
sound fell out.*

"What?" Georgeanne leaned closer.

*The woman opened her mouth again and said,
"I…jumped…in front of…you."*

*"Why?" Was she hallucinating? One drink wouldn't
make Georgeanne hear voices. They didn't start until half a
fifth was gone. When the woman didn't answer,
Georgeanne touched her hand. "We have to get help." She
scanned the blood—so much of it. "You need a doctor."*

*"No." A surge of strength filled that word. Barbara
Flannigan's eyes fluttered open. "Leave me." And then,
"Please."*

*The woman was in shock. She had to be. "You hold on,
okay?" Georgeanne scanned the black road. No one came
down this way, which was why she'd decided to take this
route to The East End Grille.*

*"Georgeanne, please. I can't go on without him."
Pause. "Tell Rourke the truth."*

Crazy talk. Shock stripped people of logic and made them act in bizarre ways. Once she had an IV and some pain meds, she'd see things differently. "It'll be all right."

"No." *She shook her head.* "Tell Rourke."

"Tell Rourke what?"

And then Barbara Flannigan whispered a truth that startled Georgeanne as much as it filled her with compassion.

The second accident happened after she left Rourke's mother. She just wanted to get home, back to the quiet of before—without blood, without a twisted body in the middle of Indian Road, without a dying woman's secret resting heavy on her soul. Georgeanne pressed the gas pedal hard. She missed the curve, jumped the embankment, and crashed into the guardrail, ramming her leg against the steering column. Pain tore through her as she threw the Plymouth in reverse and crept home. She hid the car in the garage, dragged her body inside, downed a pain pill, and fell on the bed with Barbara Flannigan's bloody face imprinted on her brain.

She would honor a dying woman's last wish. God and the law might not see it as right, but in Georgeanne Redmond's paltry life, she'd always shunned right for easy.

This time would be different.

***

"Georgeanne? You in there?"

Georgeanne jerked awake and shoved the glass beneath the stash of newspapers. Len Slewinski. He'd said he wanted to talk to her the other day when she ran into him at the grocery store and she'd gone and told him to come around when he had a minute. The man made her uncomfortable with those beady eyes and a conscience that would turn in a jaywalker. She reached for the peppermints she kept on the end table and popped three in her mouth. Just in case.

"Georgeanne?"

"Come on in, Len." What on earth could he want? Hopefully, not to reminisce about Clay again. The poor boy was dead and going on and on about him wouldn't bring him back, even though Georgeanne suspected it eased Len's conscience since he was the one who left Clay alone at the work site.

"Howdy, Georgeanne. Day treating you well?" He tugged off his ball cap and tried to smooth tufts of gray hair.

"It's another day. Can't complain and it won't do much good if I do anyway, will it?"

"Guess not. Mind if I sit?"

"Certainly." Why was he looking at her that way? Could he smell the vodka?

"I was hoping we weren't going to have to have this conversation, but it looks like it'll be necessary."

Damn, Sally Rinsel told him she'd bought Georgeanne a fifth. "There's a perfectly logical explanation, Len."

He cocked a brow and scratched the back of his head. "Sad enough, that's true. Just wish it didn't have to come from me."

Oh, damn his self-righteous soul. "Len, just say it."

He shook his head. "It's about Clay."

A whoosh of relief fired through her. Listening about her son-in-law for the twenty-fifth time she could tolerate—not enjoy, but tolerate. Anything was better than getting nabbed for drinking.

Len spread his weathered hands across his work pants and sucked in a breath. "That boy was mighty important to me."

I know, like a son. "Like the son you never had."

"True. And Katie, well, she's a beauty and just as sweet, too."

"I agree." Two hours and fifty minutes before the next drink. If Len wasn't such a lily white, she'd pull out the vodka and share a drink with him.

"He was the most righteous person I ever knew. I'd lay out the first one who tried to tarnish his good reputation."

Oh, Len, go see a priest if you want to unload your guilt. Georgeanne sipped in a breath and wished for that drink. Even a teaspoon would do. She couldn't tell Len to take his guilt and go to hell, because he was an important part in the case against Rourke Flannigan.

"You know Clay was all about honesty."

Georgeanne sat back in her rocker and pictured everything.

"…and he'd want the truth told…"

Who would have thought a gray-haired scarecrow in denim and flannel would bring down the mighty Rourke Flannigan?

"…which is why I'm here right now…"

See who ended up in disgrace and ruin.

"…sorry to say this, Georgeanne…"

The Flannigans of Chicago would have their comeuppance and she'd be in the front row to watch.

"Clay wasn't wearing a safety harness."

And then she'd laugh in their faces, especially… "What did you say?"

He'd gone all sweaty and pale. He pinched his fingers together and bowed his head. "Forgive me, Lord Jesus, Clay wasn't wearing a harness when he fell. I put it on him before I called the police."

Georgeanne heard nothing after that, not Len Slewinski's scrambled apologies, not his unsteady gait moving past her, not the soft click of the front door. Her brain shut off everything but the truth. *Clay hadn't been wearing a safety harness. Len would not lie about this in a court of law. Once again, the Flannigans would come out on top. Once again, the Redmonds would look like trailer trash.*

"Damn it." Georgeanne yanked the vodka from under the stash of newspapers, unscrewed the cap, and swallowed straight from the bottle. No measuring, no timetables, no pauses. Nothing but the burn filling her body, cleansing her mind, easing her into a calm.

Now she could think. She took another swig, wiped her mouth with the back of her hand, and blew out a long breath. She'd sold her soul fourteen years ago so Katie would be safe, so life could go on as it was supposed to. In Montpelier. With Clay Maden.

Chapter 19

"My father's eyes were brown."—*Julia Maden*

"I hate that man. *Hate* him."

"I know he's kind of a pain, but once you get used to him, he's not so bad."

Julia flung herself on the bed and stared at the ceiling. "He killed my father."

Abbie plopped down beside her. "It's not like he actually pulled a gun on him or anything."

"Might as well have."

"Maybe it really was an accident, you know?"

Julia slid her a mean look. "Now you're just trying to protect him, but there won't be any protecting that man once the lawyer gets through with him."

"I'm not trying to protect him. I hardly know the man but he's not a murderer."

"Right."

"My mother died in a plane crash but I didn't sue the airlines."

"Maybe you should have."

"You can't sue the whole world when accidents happen. She shouldn't have been flying over the ocean in a little plane with a tropical storm brewing. But she did anyway, just like she did everything else she wasn't supposed to do. Just like your dad shouldn't have been there all by himself, but he was."

"He was trying to hurry because that asshole wanted his apartments renovated in forty days."

"Still," Abbie shrugged, "it's not Rourke's fault." Pause. "Does your mom really think it is?"

"Who knows? We're not allowed to say his name. I tried to talk to her about it, but she says she's going to let the lawyer handle it now, that it's totally out of our hands."

Abbie stretched out next to Julia and stared at the blue ceiling. "When you come to visit next summer, we'll swim in the pool every day. It's the exact color as your ceiling."

"Are you crazy? You think my mom's going to let me come within two states of your uncle? No way."

"I'm just saying, maybe."

"Right. I don't know about you sometimes, Abbie. Even if she did agree, which she never would, think about it; my mom sues your uncle for a gazillion dollars and then he just says, 'Don't worry, your daughter can come and visit Abbie, stay in my house, eat my food, swim in my giant blue pool.'"

"My uncle never loses," Abbie said quietly.

"Well, he's going to this time."

"Did you ever notice the way they look at each other?"

"What are you talking about?"

"I don't know." Abbie scratched her head and squinted at the ceiling. "It kinda seemed like they liked each other a little bit. Maybe. Didn't you think?"

"No." Julia twisted her mouth into a snarl.

"I'm just saying, maybe."

"No way. Besides, my father just died. My mother loved him more than anyone else on this earth, except for me maybe."

"Okay. Sorry." Minutes passed with no sound between them but Mr. Rexter's lawnmower next door. "Julia?"

"Yeah?"

"Are you really not allowed to leave the house?"

"You heard her when I called to ask if Maxine could take me to lunch. She almost flipped. I'm under house arrest until your uncle leaves town. You shouldn't even be here."

"If she comes home, I'll sneak out the window."

"You're crazy."

"So, what are we going to do? I'm bored."

"I don't know. Watch *Pretty in Pink?*"

"Again? No thanks."

"I've never been under house arrest before so I don't know."

Abbie sighed. "I've been plenty of times."

Julia leaned up on an elbow and asked, "So, what'd you do?"

A tiny smile slipped over Abbie's face. "Pay them back. I'll show you if you want."

"Like what?"

"Ever snoop around in your parents' dressers? Look in their underwear drawer? In the back of the closet?" Julia shook her head. "It's called payback. You find out all kinds of things. Want to do it?"

"My mom doesn't have any big, dark secrets."

"How do you know?" Abbie sat up and challenged her.

"I know."

"Okay. It was just an idea."

Julia scanned the room and glanced at the clock on the nightstand. "She's not going to be home for another two hours. I guess we could do a mini search, but we're not going to find anything."

"Well, then let's at least look through her clothes, maybe try on shoes and stuff?"

Julia hesitated. "I don't think she'd like that."

"Do you like being under house arrest for something you didn't do?"

The words hadn't even formulated a question before Julia jumped off the bed and raced down the hall to her parents' bedroom. She yanked open the top drawer of her mother's dresser. "I'll start here. You take the closet."

Fifteen minutes later they'd unearthed a red negligee, a black lace bra, and a bottle of Chardonnay 1991. "Your mom's boring," Abbie announced as she yanked out a shoe box. "I guess she doesn't have any secrets."

"Told you."

Abbie lifted the top off a shoe box and pulled out a pair of black sandals with tiny rhinestones on the buckle. "These are cool." She threw off her flip-flop and shoved a foot into the black sandal. "Very cool."

"You should see the other black ones she has with tiny pink beads sewn on the straps. She wore them in a wedding one time." Julia crouched on the floor and peeked inside the closet. "Let me see if I can find them." She yanked out several boxes, stacking one on top of the other until she had twelve boxes.

"Does your mom have some obsession with shoes?" Abbie asked, buckling the other strap on her sandal.

"I guess. I never realized she had so many." Julia lifted the top box off the pile and the other boxes crashed to the ground, upending shoes and tissue in a big thump.

"Timber!"

Julia groaned. "Damn. We have to make sure everything gets put back the way it was. I don't want her to know we were snooping."

"Snooping for her bottle of wine? Or the red negligee that's not even see-through? If these are the biggest secrets she has, I'd say she should have been a nun."

Julia giggled. "Actually, I think she might have thought about it at one time."

Abbie rolled her eyes. "We'd probably have more luck finding secrets in a nun's closet."

Julia reached for the black sandals with the pink beads and shoved them on her feet. Both girls wobbled around the room laughing and pretending they were airline stewardesses. "Let's try on another pair," Julia said, flinging off her sandals. "There used to be these really cool suede boots…" She sorted through the boxes in search of the boots. When the last box produced no results, she crawled back toward the closet and peered inside. "I thought I had all of them." She squinted into the filtered darkness and spotted a box. "Here we go." She tossed the cover off the over-sized shoe box and gasped.

"What is it?" Abbie inched closer and peeked inside the box. "Ooh. A red diary."

Julia snatched the box to her chest. "Not so fast. First, we get this stuff cleaned up, just in case she comes home early. Then, we peek inside."

"Oh, all right." Abbie shoved boxes together in neat stacks and lined them up in the closet while Julia straightened her mother's drawer and tucked the negligee and bra in the back. When she picked up the bottle of wine to bury it in the back of the closet, Abbie stopped her. "We could sneak a few tastes and nobody would know."

Julia shrugged. "Sure. But just a little. I don't want her to find out."

"Get two cups. Hurry."

Julia tucked the book under her arm and raced to the bathroom, where she grabbed two paper cups. When she returned to her mother's bedroom, Abbie was lying on her back on the floor, making crisscrosses in the air with her rhinestone-sandaled feet.

"Here." Julia handed her the cups. "You pour. I'll start reading."

"Okay." Abbie shimmied onto her belly and grabbed the wine. She unscrewed the top and poured an inch into each cup. "Here's to secrets," she said, holding up her cup.

"Secrets," Julia echoed.

"Okay, I'm dying. Read."

Julia laid the red velvet book on the carpet and opened it to page one. Her mother's neat handwriting jumped out at her and for just a second, guilt squeezed her belly. She pushed past it and read, *"This book is dedicated to the love of my life."*

They giggled and sipped their wine. "Ooh, sounds sexy," Abbie said. "You sure you want to read this? Maybe you should let me take a look at it first." She inched her fingers toward the book but Julia slid it out of reach.

"This is my mother, my secret. You find your own."

Abbie made a face and said, "It's probably some sex book about your parents."

"Or their love story."

"Hmm. Probably how they met, how they fell in love, blah, blah, blah."

"If you don't want me to read it, just say so and I'll look at it later."

Abbie wrinkled her nose and muttered, "No way. I want to hear every little detail."

Julia grinned. "Thought so." She leaned over and began again. *"May fourth, nineteen ninety-seven. It has been six hundred and thirty-three days since I last saw you. I destroyed all the pictures of us—everything—first out of anger, then despair, and finally, fear. I didn't want to remember the thick silkiness of your hair beneath my fingers, or the tiny chip in your bottom front tooth...or the fierceness in your voice when you promised to love me forever."*

Julia stopped reading. "This doesn't make any sense."

"Sure it does. Your mother bought the book when they were separated for some reason. Very romantic. We're going to get some juicy stuff out of here, I can tell. Keep reading."

"I didn't want to remember there ever was an us, but your voice, your touch, your eyes, the color of a summer storm, have consumed me for almost two years."

"Wait," Julia blinked hard, "this isn't right."

"What? Keep reading."

"But—"

"Read the rest."

"No!" Julia slammed the book shut and threw it across the room.

"Hey, why'd you do that? Julia?" Abbie scooted over to her. "What's wrong?"

Julia refused to look at her. "My father's eyes were brown."

"Yeah, so?"

"Have you ever heard of a brown storm?"

"Oh. Shit."

The next words fell out of Julia's mouth in a cold, emotionless jumble. "I guess she had a secret after all."

Chapter 20

"Do you know anyone with eyes that color, Rourke?"— *Julia Maden*

Rourke hung up the phone and tossed his pen on the desk. "Done. Miles will draw up the papers. You ready, Maxine?"

She nodded and pulled out a pad and pen. "Mr. Flannigan, you're certain this is what you want to do?"

"When have you ever known me to second-guess myself?"

She turned the color of a pickled beet. "Actually never, sir." She let out a discreet cough and lifted her bony shoulders in what might have been called a shrug. "But Mrs. Maden—"

"Wants her money. And she shall have it." *Damn, Kate. She really thought it was about the money.* "Every last cent of it. How many pennies are in four-million dollars, Maxine? No, don't pull out a calculator. Just guess."

"Why, I don't think I can." She fidgeted in her chair and gave him a helpless, confused look.

"Exactly. It's a damn lot of money, excuse my language." He'd been a fool to think Kate would see through his guise to his heart. "When we get back to Chicago, Miles can review the letter and take care of the details."

Maxine pulled out a tissue and wiped her forehead. "You aren't going to inform her of your decision?"

"I see no point involving her any further."

"But, sir, I think she would want to know."

It would change nothing between them. He'd been hoping for her heart and she'd been holding out for money. "I don't want to see her again."

"But, Mr. Flannigan—"

"I'm going to draft this letter and then we're through here. I've been thinking of driving to Syracuse this afternoon to take a look at the construction site. Abbie would be bored to tears staring at concrete and beams, so she'll stay here with you. I'll be back early Saturday morning to take us to the airport." He had to put distance between himself and Kate before he did something foolish like try to see her again.

"Yes, sir."

Rourke rubbed the back of his neck, trying to ease the gnawing ache centered at the base of his head. He knew it was tension and he knew the cause. He'd just decided on the first sentence of his letter when the front door burst open, and Abbie and Julia flew in like twin tornadoes.

"Well, no one can accuse you girls of not knowing how to make an entrance." Rourke's smile slipped when he saw Julia's face. "Julia? What's wrong?" *Do not let it be Kate.*

"Where is she?" Julia advanced on him in a gust of hostility. "Is she here?"

"Who?"

"My mother."

"No." He glanced at the red book plastered against her chest. "Isn't she at work?"

She stepped toward him and shook her head. "Angie said she left an hour ago. Don't lie to protect her, Rourke."

What was going on? "Why would I do that?"

Her gray eyes burned liquid silver. "Everybody seems to be lying lately." She inched closer. "What's one more lie?"

He shot a glance toward Maxine, pleading for help, but her thin face had paled under her makeup. "Look, I'm sorry I didn't tell your mom about my association with the company right away. I wanted to give her time to adjust to…" *Hell, adjust to what? Seeing him again? His touch?* "I didn't want to rush things."

"I'm sure." Her eyes turned to tiny slits.

"Your father's death was an accident, Julia. As difficult as it is to hear, demolition is a dangerous profession. Sometimes people die."

Her lower lip quivered but she shot out the next words. "Actually, that's why I'm here. To talk about my *father*."

The way she said the word made him uneasy. Had she somehow figured out he and Clay couldn't stand each other? "What's going on?"

That tiny mouth opened again. "I came to talk about my father."

He'd argued politics with senators and come out on top. He'd negotiated city blocks of condominiums and received abatements many said would never be granted. He'd even received a governor's blessing and the promise of a sizeable amount of acreage in Alexandria, if he'd only agree to marry the man's daughter. Julia's words held some sort of accusation, but damn if he could identify it.

"Julia." It was Maxine, thank God, saying something to fill the silence. "Please calm down and let us figure this out."

Julia swung around and confronted her. "There's nothing to figure out." She lifted the red book and slammed it against the desk, knocking a stack of papers to the floor. "I'm not stupid. This is my mother's handwriting. And my father—" she crumpled into a heap in a nearby chair "— isn't even my father."

Rourke's lungs closed with the swift horror of an allergic reaction. He gasped and choked, sipping in drafts of air, all the while focusing on the words he thought he heard.

"Mr. Flannigan!" Maxine whacked the middle of his back with surprising strength. "Are you all right?" She pounded on him harder and faster until he reached around and grabbed a wrist.

"Enough," he rasped. "Are you trying to kill me?"

"No, sir. I...are you all right, sir?"

Actually he thought he was going to be sick, right here in the middle of his desk. Rourke ignored her and groped for his voice. "Julia, what did you just say?" She lifted her face to look at him and before she opened her mouth, he saw the truth in the pain and betrayal of those silver eyes, eyes that were familiar in their abject grief. Had he not stared in the mirror for days after learning of Kate's marriage and seen those same eyes? That same pain?

"He's not my father."

Why couldn't she cry? Start bawling all over the place? Big tears? At least that would provide an outlet for some of her grief. He knew the cost of holding back and keeping it all bottled up.

"He's not my father," she said again, louder, her gaze flashing to the red book squeezed against her chest. "You knew my father, though, didn't you?"

Rourke forced his voice to remain even. "I knew him."

"What color were his eyes?"

His senses heightened. "Why would you ask that?"

"Please. What color were his eyes?"

Rourke shrugged. "The same color as the work clothes he wore every day. Brown."

"Unmistakably brown," she repeated. "But this book says my father's eyes were the color of a summer storm. Do you know anyone with eyes that color?"

There were no gasps, no cries of outrage or denial. Maxine stood beside him, her eyes glued to the edge of the desk. Good old Maxine knew how to conduct herself, even in the face of a shocker like this one. Abbie didn't squeal or rant either, not a peep. In fact, she looked merely sad and confused.

"No, I'm afraid I don't." What a lie. *Look at me*, he wanted to say. *Can't you see for yourself?* He'd guessed the truth the first time he'd spotted her, but Kate had sworn he was not Julia's father. He'd believed her because the Kate he remembered was decent and honest, not a traitorous liar.

"But you must remember someone," Julia insisted, her lips quivering again around the edges. So hopeful. So desperate.

Now the tears will come. "Sorry, I don't. It was a long time ago."

She moved one step closer, determined to have answers. "Look at me, Rourke. See the way my eyes turn colors— just like a storm. A summer storm with lightning," her voice trailed off. He knew the second she recognized the truth. Her mouth screwed up and she blew out a tiny breath of sound, so soft he had to lean close to hear the words. "Just like yours."

"Julia."

"You." It was a simple statement. "You," she repeated again.

Damn you, Kate. How could you do this to me?

"You didn't know, did you?"

"Not until two seconds ago."

"You and my mother…"

167

"I'm sorry." What the hell else could he say? *Your mother thought I wasn't coming back so she married your father?*

"My father's dead." She pronounced each syllable with perfect clarity and stunning conviction.

"Yes." What could he say? He didn't even know what a father was.

"I don't need a father."

Rourke rubbed his jaw and buried his other fist under the desk to keep from yanking her by the shoulders until she cried. *Cry, damn you.*

But Julia stood tall and resolute as though she were reciting a documentary about someone else's life. "Abbie said she never had one and she's fine."

"Oh, yes, Abbie's fine." He let the sarcasm spin through his words as he glanced at his niece. The child was about as fine as an arachnophobiac in a tarantula nest. He gestured to the red book. "Is that for me?"

She thrust it at him. "My mother betrayed us all. Me, you, my father." She inched back, one step at a time. "I'll never forgive her for it." Then she turned and ran out the door, making an indistinguishable noise that sounded an awful lot like a sob.

"I'm so sorry, Rourke." Abbie did nothing to hide her tears. "It's all my fault. I was just trying to cheer her up and give her something to take her mind off of me leaving, so I suggested we go on a hunt and see what we could find."

Of course his niece would be behind something like this. Julia had lived thirteen years without questioning her genes, and it had taken Abbie less than three weeks to wreak havoc. "That's a dangerous game."

"Man, how was I to know you were going to be Julia's father? That's really twisted, but I was wondering about it, especially when I watched the two of you together."

"What's that supposed to mean?"

"When Janice showed up here, I could tell it bothered Mrs. Maden by the way she watched her, and then when the two of you were near each other—" she shrugged and jammed her hands in her back pockets "—it was like this electrical force kept pulling you apart and pushing you back together at the same time. Very weird."

"I think you've been watching too much TV."

"I am sorry, Rourke. You might be a jerk sometimes, but you didn't deserve to find out you had a kid this way. Julia didn't deserve this, either."

"No, she didn't."

"Now what? If you get partial custody, she can come visit and stay with us."

Custody. Damn, he had a thirteen-year-old daughter. Somehow he thought if he ever had a child, he'd start from the infant stage and work his way up instead of springing right into the talking-back stage.

"Well?"

Rourke reached for the red book, which was made of velvet and looked like something a young Kate would choose to spill her heart in.

"Rourke? Say something."

He fingered the cover. How many times had she turned to this book? Had Clay known? Once Rourke opened it, nothing would ever be the same. "I think I'd like to be alone."

Maxine jumped out of her chair and said, "Of course, Mr. Flannigan. I'll take Abbie back to the Manor." She grabbed her purse and scooted around the desk. "Come along, Abbie." When she reached the door, she turned. "What would you like me to do about Saturday's flight schedule, sir?"

Good old Maxine. She wanted to ask if they were still heading back to Chicago on Saturday but her properness just wouldn't let her. "I don't know, Maxine. Right now, I just don't know." He waited until the door clicked behind them and then turned to the red velvet journal and opened it to page one.

Chapter 21

"You might have fiction in those pages, but you've got a lot of truth in there, too."—Rourke Flannigan

Journal Entry—May 4, 2005

They say you only have one true love in your lifetime. Do you think that's true?

This past year has been the worst for missing you, maybe because of Clay's mother. Death is a real wake-up call. Whatever the reason, I'm antsy and agitated more than I've ever been. I even drove to the airport one night and sat for two hours watching the planes land and take off, wondering which ones were heading to Chicago.

God, how I miss you—even after all these years.

***

He would be here soon. To laugh in her face? To pity her ridiculousness? To stare at her as though she were an anomaly crumbling before his eyes? If only Julia could have been protected.

Kate huddled in the darkness of the living room and pressed her face into the softness of the cushions. She'd thought she was being so noble by limiting her memories to a single book and a single day each year, but one second of Julia's accusations made Kate realize the selfishness of her actions. True nobility would have weathered the pain in silence. True nobility would not have married someone with the assumption that love would come later. But she wasn't noble or selfless. She was weak and desperate, and her daughter, who wasn't speaking to her, had called *him* and demanded he confront Kate. That same beautiful child had packed a bag and announced she was staying with Angie for a few days.

When the doorbell rang at 8:35, Kate eased off the couch and switched on the table lamp. She'd spent fourteen years dreaming of Rourke Flannigan's face and now she dreaded the sight of him. She opened the door and there he was, handsome, powerful, and as impenetrable as granite. How had he reacted when he first learned he had a thirteen-year-old daughter? Had he lost even a hint of the control he wore like an arrogant shroud? Stuttered? Or better yet, been rendered speechless? Probably not. Those things didn't happen to Rourke Flannigan.

She turned away and moved toward the couch. "You may as well sit down," she mumbled, fixing her gaze on the edge of the coffee table. Kate sensed him behind her, moving closer, but thankfully he chose the flame-stitch chair instead of the couch. Even then he was too close. "Just say it." Thankfully, the tranquilizer she'd dug out of her drawer earlier had wiped out the first layer of conscious behavior.

"What could I possibly say?"

His voice sounded almost gentle. If she closed her eyes and wiped out the words, she might mistake the sound for a preview to a romantic interlude.

When she didn't answer, he continued in the same persuasive huskiness. "I could ask if you were writing a piece of fiction and that's what I read in your journal. That would be reasonable." He paused and she noticed the tiniest twitch on the left side of his jaw. "God knows there are enough ill-fated loves stories out there—Romeo and Juliet, Gatsby and Daisy, Bonnie and Clyde. People are always clamoring for just one more." He paused again and the gap between his words made her light-headed. "But if that's not the case, then one would have to assume the journal is based on reality. Correct?"

Kate lifted a shoulder and half turned her face into the cushion.

"The question then becomes, which life is the real one? There's the life in the red journal, and then there's the one you lived the other 364 days for the past fourteen years."

She squeezed her eyes shut and rubbed her temples, wishing the pill weren't making everything so fuzzy. "Don't yell."

"I'm not yelling. Yet."

"Just say what you've come to say and be done with it."

"Let's get one thing straight, Kate. You're not calling the shots anymore."

She inched her eyes open and glared at him. "I was *never* calling the shots. I was merely reacting to them."

"Poorly, I might add."

"Go to hell."

"Less than forty-eight hours ago, you demeaned me with your self-righteousness. Yet, while you were berating me, you kept a secret that made my error in judgment look like a white lie."

"I was protecting my daughter."

"*My* daughter, too, Kate, not just yours."

She bit her lip and waited for the explosion. When he spoke again, his voice slipped two notches to a persuasive rumble. "You don't really know much about my business, do you?"

She shook her head.

"I'm a renovator, apartments and warehouses mostly, big-ticket items. I gut the places, fix them up, maximize my profit, and sell them off. Once in a while, I encounter a company that tries to cheat me or attempts to change the terms they've agreed upon. Do you know what I do then?"

"No." There was an important message here but she couldn't sift through the drug haze clogging her brain to find it.

"When someone tries to cheat me, that's personal."

The soothing quality of his voice chipped at her defenses with such silky persistence she wasn't sure if he was angry or merely looking for a way to tell her he understood why she'd done what she had. Maybe he was going to forgive her. Maybe he wanted them to have another chance.

"…and then I buy up a few of their other properties, not necessarily ones I even want, and certainly not ones in the original contract, and you know what I do, Kate?"

"Hmm?" Her eyes drifted shut. He really did have the most calming voice.

"I gut them and I continue to do this until I've bought up the controlling share of the owner's business. At that point, I move in my own people and take over."

She squinted at him. "Take over?"

"Exactly."

"You mean you destroy them? Deliberately?"

"No, I deliberately protect what's mine. You do understand that, don't you?"

"I guess. It seems rather harsh."

"Maybe, but it's a lesson that's never repeated."

"Only a fool would cross you again." It was obvious there were dark pockets of Rourke Flannigan's psyche that were foreign to her.

"Exactly. Now if I go to such lengths to protect my company from liars and cheats, imagine what I'd do to protect my own flesh and blood?"

His words sliced through her drug-addled brain. "What do you want?"

"Answers, Kate. Goddamn answers."

She rubbed her temples and tried to clear her head. She had to think. "I was never supposed to see you again. The book was just a fantasy."

"That's sick."

She shrugged. "I got bored. Everyone doesn't jet set all over the world like you. I had a husband and a baby and I needed an escape." *Make him believe it's all a lie.*

The left side of his jaw twitched. "You're lying."

"Why? Because it's not the answer you want to hear?"

"No, because you kept it hidden in a shoe box in the back of your closet."

"So? Clay wouldn't have understood."

His lip curled. "I doubt many men would, unless they were part of the fantasy."

"Angie thought it would make a good story."

"You told her about it?" He looked at her as though she'd just admitted to stripping in church.

"Of course I did." That was such a lie. "She thought it would make a great story."

"You wrote in that journal once a year for fourteen years about how much you *loved* me because you were working on a *story*? Do you think I'm an idiot?"

"I wrote it last year, all of it. I just made it seem like it was a once-a-year entry." *Lie, lie, lie.* "Angie thought it would be more effective that way, you know, touch the readers' hearts."

"Not really."

"You can ask her." She'd have to call Angie as soon as Rourke left. There'd be a mountain of questions but she'd rather confess to Angie than risk Rourke finding out the truth.

"I plan to speak with her."

"Fine."

"You might have fiction in those pages, but you've got a lot of truth in there, too."

"Some truth," she admitted.

"Right." His silver eyes sparked with anger and something close to pain. Kate watched with growing uncertainty as a fine white line creased the edges of his full lips. "You should have told me."

The memory of discovering she was pregnant and had no idea where Rourke was welled inside and exploded. "You deserted me!"

"I did not desert you."

Those horrible weeks resurfaced, forcing her to relive the pain once again. "After the first week, I was sure you'd come back or at least call. Angie said you were gone for good, but I didn't believe her. When the third week passed, I started to get nervous. Then I missed my period."

"Damn." He raked a hand through his hair and blew out a deep breath.

"Your aunt saw the problem the second she landed here, holding her nose so our little town wouldn't contaminate her. She wanted you out."

"She said I needed distance to sort things through."

"Distance from the scandal is what she meant. It wouldn't look good for an Ivy League boy to date a girl whose mother ran over his mother—even if the woman were walking down the middle of the road in the black of night."

He eyed her with distaste. "Even if the girlfriend's mother flees the scene and hides in her bedroom until she almost bleeds to death and is forced to go to the hospital?"

"She was scared. She said people would accuse her unjustly."

"You mean of drinking and driving?"

"Yes."

"We both know our mothers had faults. I blamed myself for the accident." His expression darkened. "If I hadn't been with you that night, she wouldn't have been out on the street."

"That makes no sense."

"I knew my mother's witching hour came every night around ten o'clock. Why do you think I always stopped home for a half hour when we were out?"

"You said she was lonely and you had to settle her in for the night."

Pain laced his next words. "I had to settle her in with her drugs and twenty minutes at her bedside. She couldn't drift off if I wasn't there. It was like that every night since my dad died."

"I didn't know."

He lifted a large shoulder and shrugged. "I tortured myself for weeks." He met her gaze, held it. "But the really sick truth was that I wouldn't have changed a thing."

Her heart tumbled back to the night on the lake…to him wrapped around her, over her, inside her…

"What kind of son admits something like that?"

"I'm so sorry."

He sighed and ran a hand through his hair. "You didn't trust me very much, did you?"

"I didn't have the luxury of time to trust you."

His voice dipped. "I wish I had known."

"What were you going to do, drop out and play dad? Your aunt never would have stood for it."

"I would have married you."

His words stung her heart. "Do not say that."

"I'm sorry you gave up on us so quickly."

If only he knew the truth. "It wasn't just about us; there were other people to consider, especially Julia. I was not going to bring up an illegitimate child."

"So Clay came barreling to the rescue in his pickup. If I'd returned before you married him, would you have married me?"

"You didn't return, so what's the point?"

"Humor me."

Lie. But she couldn't. She opened her mouth and let this one speck of truth fall out. "Yes." The tension on his face eased a fraction. Why did it matter now? Why did any of this matter now? "Face it, Rourke, you're a bachelor leading a bachelor's life. You don't have room in your life for a child. Before Clay's death, you didn't even know Julia existed."

"You're right, but now I've seen her, now I know she has my eyes, and my smile. Do you really think I can just walk away from that?"

"You have to."

"If you think that, then you've seriously underestimated me. I may have missed the first thirteen years of my daughter's life, but I won't miss the next sixty."

Kate's heart skipped two beats. "You're moving to Montpelier?" she whispered.

"No. Julia's moving to Chicago."

Chapter 22

"Speaking of marriage, do you love her?"—Julia Maden

Rourke tucked the button-down shirt inside his jeans and fastened his belt. He glanced at his watch and grabbed a jacket. He had a date in fifteen minutes and he hadn't been this nervous since the first time he asked Kate out. Julia had called and invited him to Sophie's Diner for hot fudge sundaes. Not that he'd be able to eat anything, but food wasn't the reason for the meeting.

He locked the door to his room and headed down the wide staircase to the parking lot and his rented Mercedes. He'd read Kate's journal three times already and would read it at least twice more before bed, and still he couldn't uncover the truth. What if it really had been just the fantasy of a lonely housewife? Then again, what if it had been the truth? A sick ache gripped his stomach and he unrolled the window to suck in several deep breaths.

When he reached Sophie's, he parked the car and glanced through the large stenciled window of the diner. Julia sat in a booth, long hair pulled in a high ponytail that accentuated her cheekbones and reminded him of the way Kate used to wear her hair. He gulped another breath and opened the door. She spotted him as soon as he walked in. Her small lips turned up in a half smile and he forced his own lips to stretch until they hurt. "Hello there." He hesitated a half second wondering if he should kiss her cheek or hug her. He decided against both and slid into the booth opposite hers. "I like your shirt."

She scrunched her nose. "You don't think it makes me look like a candy cane?"

"No. And if it did, I like candy canes."

"I wasn't going to get it but Mom said—" she faltered and cleared her voice "—she said it would look good on me."

"She's right." Was this the beginning of the most awkward night of his life? Maybe he should have invited Abbie and Maxine. At least Abbie would have kept the conversation going with her never-ending comments. "What do you want to eat?"

Julia shrugged. "I'm not really very hungry."

So, she was nervous, too. "Well, I remember Sophie used to have the best hot fudge sundaes around and I think the last time I had one was here."

Her gray eyes filled with doubt. "When you lived here?"

He nodded. "Light years ago."

"Okay, I'll have one if you do."

Rourke ordered their sundaes and turned to his daughter. *Calm, stay calm.* "Thank you for inviting me. I'm sure you have a lot of questions."

"Yeah."

"Shoot."

"Did you used to live on Oliver Street?"

He blinked. "I did. How did you know?"

"*She* used to make me ride my bike down there with her all the time. I hated it because there were too many hills. I complained enough so she finally stopped."

"*She* is your mother." Kate said the journal was all a lie. Maybe *that* was the lie.

"And you're my father, right? Only I had a father but he's dead and now you're here."

"Sort of." Rourke had no idea where this was going.

"It's like a bad soap opera. A woman sleeps with one man but marries a different one. Then that man dies and the first one returns and the daughter finds out about them. So she goes to her real father and tells him. And then what?" She bit her lower lip and he swore the tears were going to pour out any second, but a few blinks later she said, "If she didn't love my father, she shouldn't have married him."

"I think she loved him in her own way." Now he was defending Kate's feelings for Clay Maden.

"Why didn't you come back?"

The sad longing in her voice pinged Rourke's heart. "It was complicated back then, or at least I thought it was." How could he make this child understand something he still didn't? "My mother had just been in an accident, and my aunt, whom I didn't even really know, flew in and took me back to Chicago to live with her while my mother recovered." Did she know about Georgeanne? If he were going to have a shot at making her understand, he had to tell her the truth. "Your grandmother was driving the car that hit my mother." The shock on Julia's face told him she hadn't known. "She didn't stop."

"You mean like a hit and run?"

He nodded. Now Kate would really hate him but he would not lie to his daughter. "I was really messed up and angry. Then my aunt started dangling Princeton in front of me and saying things that made me believe what your mother and I shared was just an infatuation and would pass." He let out a sigh, wondering if the pain of recall would ever dull. "It took two months to realize she was wrong, but it was too late. Your mother was already married."

"Because she was pregnant with me," Julia said quietly.

"Yes." She had his same quirky habit of moving her jaw from side to side when she was thinking.

"A few years ago, I figured out my birthday and their wedding day were off; that's how I knew she was pregnant when she got married."

"Your mother loves you very much."

"She should have told me."

"Maybe she was protecting your dad."

"Then she should have told you and if she couldn't find you, she should have waited longer than two months to marry somebody else."

He didn't disagree.

The waitress plopped their sundaes in front of them and Julie nibbled a hunk of chocolate fudge before asking, "Do you think, I mean is it even possible that someday, *maybe*, you could love my mother again?"

Bam, straight to the heart. He dug around for a spoonful of ice cream, getting just the right mix of fudge and ice cream before he answered. "Anything's possible."

Chapter 23

"If my daughter were traveling hundreds of miles with a stranger tomorrow, I wouldn't be able to think either."— Angie Sorrento

"How could this happen?"

The high pitch in her mother's voice, the glitter in her eyes, the red around her neck, all reminded Kate of Georgeanne's drinking days, but that was ridiculous. She'd promised on Julia's life that she would never take another drink.

"Kate? Answer me. How could this happen?"

There was no way around it but to tell the truth. She could hedge, though. "Mom, you know I loved Clay, right? No matter what happened before or anything else, you know I loved him." *Not a heart-stopping, once-in-a-lifetime love, but still, love.*

"Of course you loved him. What a ridiculous statement." She rubbed her neck and made it even redder. "What I want to know is how that damn man ever found out about our Julia."

Because of my selfish, inexcusable stupidity. There was no other way around it. "Julia found my journal." There.

The glitter in Georgeanne's eyes sparked. "You kept a journal? You wrote about you and Rourke Flannigan? That he was Julia's *father*?"

She made it all sound so sordid.

"Answer me."

"I only wrote in it once a year." As though that made everything right.

"Once a year," Georgeanne mocked. "Such restraint." She massaged her leg, dug her fingers into the cotton material. "For how long?"

Kate had expected anger and disbelief, but the bitterness outweighed both. "Mom—"

"How long did you write about him?"

"Fourteen years."

Georgeanne let out a strangled cry. "Do you have any idea what you've done?"

"I'm sorry. I know Clay deserved better—"

"Clay?" her mother snapped. "I'm not talking about Clay though God knows that man did not deserve this. I'm talking about what you've done to me." She pounded a fist against her chest. "I sacrificed everything to protect you and Julia and you threw it all away, and for what? Some silly words in a journal."

***

Kate hadn't slept in two days. Julia was leaving for Chicago in the morning. It was unfair, and frightening, and yet Rourke had made it clear he'd fight for the right to be in his daughter's life. The hardest part was Julia's eagerness to go with him.

Angie glanced up from her computer and said, "Why don't you head home? You've been sitting there for twenty minutes and haven't taken a single brush stroke."

Kate forced the brush along the railing of a mock colonial porch. "I'm just thinking about how I want it to look."

"Kate. Go home."

"I need to stay busy." She bit her lower lip and concentrated on a spindle.

"If my daughter were traveling hundreds of miles with a stranger tomorrow, I wouldn't be able to think either."

"That stranger is her father."

"Sperm donor's more like it. That man doesn't have a parental bone in his body. It's all a power play and you know it. He's pissed you kept it from him and he's pissed about the lawsuit."

Kate rubbed her left temple. "I wish I'd never pursued the case."

"He would have come anyway. Damage control and all that."

"I just want him to leave."

"He will, don't worry. Leaving is Rourke Flannigan's specialty."

***

"Everything is set, Mr. Flannigan. I've made Julia's plane reservation and contacted the house to prepare a room for her."

"Thank you, Maxine."

She cleared her throat. "The girls have asked me to take them to see a *chick flick* this afternoon if you have nothing else for me?"

Rourke glanced up from his report. *Did she even know what a chick flick was?* If not, she'd find out soon enough. "That's fine. Make sure Julia's mother knows we'll be leaving at 7:30 tomorrow morning." He'd resorted to addressing Kate as "Julia's mother." How sad was that?

"Yes, sir." She hesitated. "I've sent her a copy of Julia's itinerary with the appropriate phone numbers and street address."

"Good thinking."

"Yes, sir."

He thought she was about to add something else, but she nodded twice, grabbed her purse, and left. There was something different about Maxine. Her gait? Her hair?

Then it hit him. The tweed was gone! In its place, she'd worn a light gray sweater and black slacks, a first for Maxine since he'd hired her three years ago. Rourke was contemplating Maxine's new look when the bell above the door jangled and Angie Sorrento stormed in. He tried to ignore the instant pain that jolted his right temple and said, "Well, if it isn't my favorite nemesis."

She stalked to his desk and thrust both hands in her pockets—probably so she wouldn't take a swing at him. "You really are an asshole, aren't you?"

He leaned back in his chair and smiled, just to annoy the hell out of her. "Is that a rhetorical question or would you like an answer?"

"How can you do this to her?"

"Do what? To whom?"

Her dark eyes sliced him. "Doesn't it bother you, even a little, that you're tearing mother and daughter apart?"

"Cut the theatrics, Angie. She played me and you know it."

"Just how did she do that, Mr. Brilliant? By getting pregnant?"

"By keeping it from me."

"You're right. I guess she should have started calling all the Flannigans in Chicago and surrounding suburbs and maybe told them she was looking for the father of her baby?"

The woman reminded him of a terrier with fleas. "How about she didn't run to the altar with the first guy who came along?" He did not want to have this discussion with this woman.

"You don't know anything about it."

"And you do?"

"I was there, buddy." She jabbed her small chest. "You weren't, were you? No, you were too busy having a blast at your big, fancy college."

He wasn't even going to qualify that with an answer. He had been at Princeton but the thought of Kate or rather trying to forget Kate had consumed him.

"And I'll just bet you had fun with that journal, didn't you?"

"If you were a man, I'd deck you."

"If it were legal, I'd shoot you."

That he believed. "What do you know about the journal?" The one he'd become obsessed with and carried in his briefcase, even if none of it were true.

Angie shrugged and narrowed her gaze on him. Someone did her wrong long ago, probably a man, and she'd lost her softness, if she ever had it. "I knew there was one. I was with her when she bought it."

"And you read it?"

She squared her shoulders and challenged him. "Why do you ask?"

He'd be damned if he'd let her see how much the book meant to him. "Kate said none of it's true. She said it was just a fantasy."

"And I'm Abe Lincoln."

"She said she was bored and lonely, so she started creating 'what if' scenarios."

"Yeah, right."

He kept his voice casual. "Are you saying that's not true?"

Angie pulled both hands through the tangle of black mop she called hair and sighed. "Okay, I'm not going to lie. I never read the book, but I was with her when she bought it. Velvet. Blood red. She said she bought it so she could jot down events in Julia's life, but I saw the way she looked at it and I knew she was going to write something much more private in it."

"So you think it's true?" Hope thumped in his chest.

"I'm only going to tell you this so you ease up on her. Kate's fragile right now. She lost her husband and now she's worried she'll lose her daughter. If that weren't enough, you just danced back into her life. We both know you live in different worlds but there's a part of her that's always believed you belonged together." She spit out a laugh. "Isn't that absurd?"

"Not really."

"Come on, you've got your Barbie-on-a-stick girlfriends and your cars and your paparazzi. Where would a homegrown girl from Montpelier, New York, fit in? Please don't hurt her anymore than you already have. Let Julia visit but don't tell everyone she's your daughter. Not yet. The reporters would barrage Kate and she can't handle that."

"I don't want to hurt Kate." *She still cared about him. Maybe loved him?*

"Then prove it. Let her go to Chicago with Julia. You can make it look like she's keeping an eye on Julia and Abbie while you work. You'll think of something. You're very good with the spin."

Kate in his home? He started to panic. She'd see the heart-shaped tub, the pond, the fireplace in the bedroom, the lavender turret—everything they'd talked about building together. She'd realize he'd never gotten over her and once she saw inside his heart, she could hurt him again. Angie could say the journal was true but how did he know Kate hadn't set him up by sending her here to tell him just that? He didn't know anything anymore. But he intended to find out. "Okay," he found himself saying, "tell her she can go. I'll have Maxine take care of the details. We'll pick her and Julia up at 7:00 tomorrow morning."

"Thank you."

She seemed almost civil as she said it and Rourke wondered again if he'd just been set up. This could all be a grand plan, with Kate behind it. And if it were, Heaven help them all.

***

This had to stop. Now. Georgeanne glanced at the clock. She'd had her last drink two hours and fifty-five minutes ago, right after lunch. Or was it one hour and fifty-five minutes ago? She rubbed her leg and tried to remember. The glass with the blue mark stared back at her with the half-finished bottle of vodka peeking from the magazine rack.

She was slipping, hour by hour, drifting back toward her earlier life. Who could blame her? To learn the person responsible for your son-in-law's death was now honing in on your granddaughter? It was just a matter of time before they had Julia wishing she lived in Chicago. Who knew what would happen then? She could decide Montpelier wasn't where she wanted to be. She could choose a new life. A new family, one which didn't include Katie or Georgeanne. *How could this have happened?* Georgeanne hefted the bottle from the floor and splashed another drink in her glass, eyeballing the vodka toward the blue line. She might be a quarter-inch off, but right now, she needed that quarter-inch.

By the time she finished her drink—four minutes ahead of schedule—she had a plan. Life had battered her around, pitching her between choice and circumstance. She'd loved and lost, grown bitter and desperate, turned to drink, and eventually, found snippets of contentment with her daughter and her family. Now even that small pleasure was threatened.

The time to stand up and protect what was hers had come. She wouldn't lie meekly as Rourke Flannigan and his entourage trampled what little happiness she had left in life. She'd stop him. And she'd make him pay. Maybe not in a court of law, but he and his company would pay...and if it took dredging up old secrets to get the job done, so be it.

***

Kate sat in the back seat of the Mercedes with Julia and Abbie while Rourke drove with Maxine next to him, checking off her to-do list. Kate still couldn't believe he'd agreed to let her travel to Chicago with Julia but she wasn't about to question his decision. Other than grab her suitcases and extend a curt nod, he'd barely acknowledged her in the forty-five minutes she'd been in his company.

The airplane ride wasn't much better. Rourke and Maxine sat in first class, which left Abbie, Julia, and Kate in coach and served as one more reminder of the difference in social and economic status separating them.

"You are so going to love Chicago," Abbie said. She hadn't stopped talking since they'd boarded the plane. "Wait until you see Rourke's house." She spread her fingers and said, "The carpeting's so thick you can sleep on it. Surround Sound. Twelve flat screens. Pool. Sub-Zero fridge." She scrunched her nose and gushed, "I am so glad you two are going to be there. I hate being by myself."

Julia squeezed her hand. "You won't be by yourself anymore."

"Yeah, I'm going to love these next two weeks. And Rourke hasn't been such a pain lately, either." She darted a quick glance at Kate and added, "Overall."

It was awkward having Abbie and Julia know about Kate and Rourke's past, but at least he'd chosen to keep his parentage from the public eye. He probably figured the truth would unearth itself soon enough.

"Mrs. Maden, have you ever been to Chicago?"

"No, I haven't."

"She hasn't been anywhere but Niagara Falls," Julia said, her tone just shy of rude. She still wouldn't discuss Rourke or what they'd talked about the other night.

"Well, Rourke does have a pretty cool house," Abbie went on, apparently unaware of the cold war Julia was staging against her mother. "You have got to see that tub. It is so bizarre. A heart tub." She giggled. "It's like the kind in one of those honeymoon places."

"I'm more interested in the pool," Julia said.

"It's Olympic size with a diving board and a hot tub."

I'll build you a pool, Rourke had told Kate years ago, *and we'll swim naked under the stars...*

Kate pushed the memories aside and closed her eyes. She'd wondered about Chicago for so long and now she'd finally get an opportunity to see it. When the plane landed, O'Hare Airport met her like a noisy, stifling monster, filled with too many people and too much activity. Rourke herded them along with a sweep of his large hand and one-word commands. He hadn't spoken directly to Kate since they got off the plane but she could tell he was aware of her by the way his gaze sliced past her in a valiant attempt *not* to notice her.

Why did she care? Why had her heart done a tiny back flip when Abbie mentioned the heart-shaped tub? Rourke might have had it built for whatever lover he had at the time, certainly not for a teenage romance gone bad. So why did that notion bother her? It wasn't as though they could ever share anything closer than a casual acquaintance. People who lied to one another didn't make good partners and she would do well to remember that.

Chapter 24

"What happens if you spread caviar on fish sticks?"—
Rourke Flannigan

"The papers are ready for Mrs. Maden to sign." Miles Gregory sighed and added, "You can say good-bye to four million dollars."

Rourke glanced up from his paperwork. "I take it you don't think this is a wise decision."

Miles adjusted his perfect bow tie. "You know my feelings, but it's your company, and your choice."

"I pay you a hell of a lot of money for your advice."

"All right then. You don't owe that woman a penny."

"I couldn't even have a decent meal on what she's going to receive from social security and worker's comp."

Miles glanced at him over the top of his glasses. "Rourke. This woman is not a Dom Perignon/caviar connoisseur. She'll do fine."

Rourke fiddled with his pen, flipping it end over end between his fingers. "I want to do right by her and the child."

"You owe them nothing. Do you want to read the insurance commission report again? Or OSHA's findings? It was an accident."

"Maybe I pushed them too hard."

Miles pressed his fingertips against his right temple. "Are you trying to throw your money away? Or looking to make a charitable donation somewhere? If it's the latter, I'll be happy to provide you with a list of needy causes."

"It's not that."

"What then? It isn't like you to turn to mush in the heat of battle. Usually, you're aiming your sword at the jugular."

Damn. Miles was not going to let this go.

"You're giving them full asking price. What happened to the art of negotiation? I almost hate to take my paycheck this week." Rourke shot him a look that made Miles smile. "I said almost."

"It's a touchy thing, I guess."

"Oh. Please don't tell me you've fallen for the woman. That's it, isn't it? You're interested in the widow." He fiddled with his bow tie again. "What you're doing is admirable, but I must advise you that more than one man has lost his shirt and his fortune at the hands of a woman."

You have no idea.

"I imagine she's enamored with your attention. Who wouldn't be? You are one of the city's most eligible bachelors."

"Miles, you don't know what you're talking about."

"That's what you said in the Wentzler deal."

"How was I to know the old man was paying off the chief engineer to get to the planning commission?"

"You couldn't know. That's why you pay me." Miles paced the room, hands clasped behind his back in typical closing argument form. "Kate Maden is a country girl. I doubt she knows what a Rolex is, let alone owns one."

"When did you turn into such a pretentious ass?"

"I'm being realistic. You don't live in the same universe. She's fish sticks. You're caviar."

"What happens if you spread caviar on fish sticks?"

"Simple. Spontaneous combustion."

Rourke nodded. "But it would be one hell of a ride, wouldn't it?"

A smile slipped over Miles's face. "Yes, I imagine it would."

Rourke closed his briefcase and stood. "One more thing. I'll need a trust set up for Julia Maden."

"You *are* joking, aren't you? What else do you want to do for those people? Give them your name?"

"Now there's a thought." The man would lose the crease in his pants when Rourke told him Julia was his daughter. Soon.

***

Rourke knocked on his aunt's door and poked his head inside. "Sorry I'm late."

She glanced up from her paperwork and pierced him with one of her "How dare you" looks. "You don't appear sorry. Not in the least," she said in a tone meant to intimidate.

Diana's tactics might work on the rest of the staff and a good half of the company's business associates, but they didn't work on him. Beneath his aunt's starched and fearsome demeanor lay a woman with a heart, even if she preferred to keep it in a freezer.

"Well, come in and sit." She gestured toward the chair opposite her massive cherry desk. "Need I remind you I detest lateness?"

Rourke slid into the chair and crossed a leg over his knee. "I'm sorry. It couldn't be helped."

Her lips flattened and she studied him with keen eyes that had a way of unearthing exactly what people didn't want uncovered. "Why were you detained?"

"Extenuating circumstances."

"Indeed?" She arched a brow and waited.

"Yes." He played with the tassel on his loafer, debating how to break the news about Julia to a woman who took issue with cheap pens and incorrect punctuation. There really was no good way to prepare for a shocker. Sometimes it was best to just thrust it out there. Rourke took a breath and said, "I have some rather startling news for you."

She grew still. "How startling?"

Here goes. "You're an aunt. Again. I'm a father." *There.* Now it was out.

She flinched as though the news had physically assaulted her, but the movement was so quick and faint, if he hadn't been studying her, he'd have missed it. When she spoke, her voice contained a matter-of-factness about it that perplexed him. "I see. Is that why you're late?"

"That's all you have to say?"

"No." She toyed with her pen. "I never pictured you with a baby."

"She's not a baby. Julia's thirteen."

Diana's expression remained blank. "Thirteen? Who's the mother?"

"Kate Maden."

"Ah."

"I never knew."

"That's the first good piece of news I've heard since you entered the room. Had you known, you might have felt honor-bound to marry the girl, and then what? Good-bye Princeton, good-bye opportunity." She jabbed the tip of the pen into a notepad. "Good-bye life."

"I don't see it that way," he said quietly.

"What other way is there to see it?" she asked, her voice sharp and determined. "Raging hormones don't make for compatible partners. It would have been a disaster." When he didn't respond, she pressed, "One-sided love is even worse. She married someone else. Don't forget that."

His heart closed up but the pain still seeped through. "Not likely."

***

"Rourke, why are they in Chicago?" Janice perched on the arm of his recliner and crossed her legs. They were long and sexy and supple. And he wasn't interested.

"Julia wanted to visit Abbie. Her mother wouldn't let her come alone."

"But why do they have to stay at *your* house?"

Had he really never noticed her petulance? Of course he had, but he'd let other attributes make up for it. But a double-D cup and dancer's legs only carried a man so far.

"I suppose I can't stay over, not that I've been doing much of that lately, anyway." She leaned toward him and her cleavage spilled out of her top an inch from his face. "You can always stay here."

Was she cooing? He turned away and shifted in the recliner. Kate would never stoop to cooing. "I don't think so."

She slid her hand along his thigh, red nails glistening against his dark slacks. He thought of Kate's hands, small, efficient, her nails natural and blunt-cut. Rourke closed his eyes and imagined Kate's hands gliding near his crotch, cupping him, stroking...

"That's my boy."

He jerked his eyes open and grabbed Janice's hand. "Stop. I'm not in the mood."

A wide smile slithered over her red lips. "That's not what it looks like to me."

Disgusted with her antics and his own roaming thoughts of Kate, he pushed out of the recliner and stood. "I've got to go."

"What about dinner?"

She stood and smoothed her short skirt over tanned, Pilates-toned legs and lifted the hem just enough to give him a peek of black lace. Half the men in Chicago would give a month's salary for a romp with Janice. He just wasn't one of them anymore. Maybe he never had been.

"Rourke? I already made reservations at Mon Ami's. We are going to go, aren't we?"

He checked his watch, a guise to buy time for his next excuse. "I'm sorry. I can't tonight. I promised Abbie and Julia I'd take them to Red Robin for burgers."

Janice tossed back her luxurious mane and said, "You're turning into a real Mr. Dad."

"I'm just trying to show a little consideration to my niece and her friend."

"Right. You don't even like kids."

"They're growing on me." Odd but true.

Her eyes glittered. "I suppose *she's* going."

He feigned ignorance. "Who?"

"The mother."

"Kate?" Janice knew her name but she liked to play this game.

"Right. Kate." She mouthed the name like a vinegar mouthwash.

He shrugged and pulled out his keys. "I don't know if she's going or not. I didn't invite her."

"She'll be there." She slithered her tight body against his. "And I'll be here." She licked his lower lip, sucked on it, softly, slowly, with extreme intent. Then she stepped back and ran her hands over her breasts and thighs. "I'll be here. Waiting for you." Her hands drifted to her crotch. "In case you want dessert."

Of course he wanted dessert. A sugar-filled, adrenaline-rush confection named Kate.

When Rourke swung by the house to pick up the girls, he casually mentioned Kate's name but Julia told him her mother had gone for a walk. Again. Since they'd arrived yesterday afternoon, he'd only seen Kate once. He'd watched her from the bedroom window as she stood on the stone path leading to the garden, surrounded by bursts of red and pink and lavender, her expression filled with misery and pain. *Twenty walks a day wouldn't erase the garden they'd once designed together.*

He'd wanted to get out of the house and Maxine joined them for burgers dressed in a button-down shirt and tailored jeans. She almost called him Rourke before she caught herself and reverted to Mr. Flannigan. No tweeds. First names. Maxine was loosening up. When she offered to take Abbie and Julia to see a movie after dinner, they giggled and begged with such gusto, Rourke could have sworn they'd just set him up. But for what?

He drove home alone after Abbie rejected his third attempt to get an invitation to the movies, telling him it was a chick flick. Right now, seeing a chick flick was more desirable than heading home where he might have to face Kate. Why had he ever agreed to let her come? He'd need three bourbons before he tackled that question. For now, he'd settle on exhausting his body by swimming laps. Then he'd have his bourbon and contemplate his love-hate obsession with Kate.

Chapter 25

"Kate. What are we doing?"—Rourke Flannigan

She sensed someone watching as she gripped the edge of the pool to catch her breath. It had taken ten laps to relax, another five to feel the exhilarating pull of muscle against water, and three more to forget whose pool she was swimming in. Kate dipped her head back in the water, smoothed her hair, and turned around. Rourke stood at the opposite end, his broad chest bare, his lower half covered in dark trunks. From his tense stance it was obvious he hadn't expected her.

"I was just getting out," she said, making her way to the pool steps.

"No need to leave on my account. This pool's big enough for both of us."

Who are we kidding, Rourke? This continent isn't big enough for both of us. "That's okay. I was done."

Before she could move, Rourke tossed his towel on the ground and dove in, his powerful body slicing the water as he swam toward her. When he was within arm's reach, he sprang from the water and slicked his dark hair from his face. The glittering silver of his gaze scared her. Or was it the way that look churned her insides that scared her?

"Stay," he said.

"I'm tired." She started to back away. "I should go."

"Kate. What are we doing?"

She opened her mouth to throw out a flip response but the tone in his voice spoke of confusion and desperation, two feelings she knew well. "I don't know."

"I should despise you for keeping Julia from me, and yet, I find myself thinking about you constantly. That afternoon at the Manor, I thought it was the start of something new between us and then it all blew to hell."

Careful. You're risking your heart here. "Fate has a way of doing that."

"Don't be coy." He brushed a strand of hair from her cheek and settled his fingers on the base of her neck.

Could he feel her pulse pounding like a frightened bird? "I don't know what to say."

"The truth?" He leaned toward her, lifted her chin so she could meet his gaze. "Was that journal really just a fantasy? Was there even a paragraph, a few sentences maybe that were true?"

"Does it matter?"

"Very much."

She leaned her face against his hand and whispered, "It was true."

"All of it?"

She pressed a kiss in the palm of his hand. "Every word."

"Thank God." he breathed, crushing her to him.

They clung to one another, their bodies hot and wet and filled with passion. "I never stopped loving you," she whispered against his chest, "not for one second of all those years."

He loosened his grip and looked down at her. "I swear to God, Kate, when I came to Montpelier, I meant to tell you right away about my company. But then I saw you," his voice grew rough, "and I was eighteen again."

"I know."

"Give me another chance to do it right this time?"

She clasped her arms around his neck and rose up on tiptoe. "Yes," she murmured, brushing her lips against his. "Oh, yes," she breathed, exhilarated by his closeness. He lifted her in the water and swung her around twice, laughing. "Rourke, stop! You're making me dizzy."

"Stop? Did you say stop?" He hoisted her in his arms and hugged her against his chest. "Sweetheart, in five minutes you'll be begging me *not* to stop."

She kissed a spot above his left nipple. "I have a feeling you're right."

He carried her to the edge of the pool and eased her along his body, slowing as she rubbed against his erection. "Come to me, Kate." Water glistened from his lips as he spoke. "Give yourself to me."

She'd always been his and years and a marriage hadn't changed that. Kate unfastened the top of her two-piece and eased the fabric over her breasts.

"Perfect," Rourke whispered, cupping her breasts. "You were always perfect."

She stepped out of her bottoms, not caring that she no longer possessed the suppleness of an eighteen-year-old. Rourke still wanted her, stretch marks, wrinkles, and all. She dipped two fingers beneath his trunks and pulled them down. His penis jutted out, full and ready. She offered him a shy smile, dove underwater, and took him in her mouth. He held her head between his hands and jerked against her with quick, spasmodic strokes. When she came up for air, his eyes were slits, his breathing harsh, his chest heaving.

"Sit here," she said, tapping the side of the pool. "I've been dreaming of this for years."

He lifted himself onto the edge of the pool and groaned when she slid between his legs and took him in her mouth once more. She worked her tongue and mouth along his hardness, stroking, sucking, teasing. "Kate," he moaned. His hips jerked with fierce determination. "You have to stop now. Stop, before it's too late."

She worked her tongue along his shaft and murmured, "What was that about five minutes and begging?"

Rourke let out a growl and slid into the water, grabbing her hips and entering her in one swift motion. Kate cried out and rode him, desperate to get closer, to become a part of him. "Deeper," she pleaded, wrapping her legs high around his waist. She clung to him as he pumped into her, his eyes clamped shut, the cords of his neck bulging, his mouth a flat line, until with one final stroke, he spilled himself deep inside her.

He was still pulsing when he reached between them and touched her with slow, delicious intent. "I've never been able to forget you," he whispered against her neck. "Never been able to forget this." He circled his thumb against her swollen flesh, faster and faster, until she couldn't stand the torment any longer. She cried out his name as jolts of pleasure tore through her in one brilliant climax.

"This is only the beginning," he murmured, pulling her against him. "We have fourteen years to make up for."

His words were still on Kate's mind when the girls arrived home an hour later and raided the kitchen for lemonade and chocolate chip cookies. Rourke remained in his study, as agreed upon so as not to create suspicion, but turned up in the kitchen twice, saying he needed a chocolate fix to go with his beer. She dared not look at him for fear the girls would know what they'd been doing—in the pool, in his bed, in the shower.

Would the wanting never go away? This Rourke was much more than the tender lover he'd been at eighteen. This one possessed skill and determination blended with a persuasive ardor she could not and did not want to deny. An hour later, she drifted to sleep dreaming of Rourke. His smile. His laugh. His fingers…The feather-light touch on the back of her neck woke her. Once, twice, three times. She slapped at her neck and jerked around. "Rourke! What are you doing here?"

He tucked a chunk of hair behind her ear. "Last I checked, this was my house."

"Shhh. You're too loud."

He chuckled and whispered, "Bossy woman. Give her an orgasm and she turns bossy."

"Quiet, the girls might hear."

He pulled her to him and dipped his tongue inside her mouth. "And you don't want them to know how you were writhing and moaning beneath me a few hours ago."

"No, I don't."

He trailed a finger along her collarbone and traced the outline of her breast. "Then I don't suppose you want them to hear about what you were doing to me in the pool either."

How did he make her forget caution whenever he touched her? "Definitely not," she whispered, running her hands over his chest, down the muscles of his belly and lower still, to the hard erection jutting beneath his shorts.

"Ahhh, baby." He jerked against her hand. "This is going to be a long night."

She stroked his hardness and whispered, "Very long. Very hard. And very, very quiet."

Chapter 26

"I understand you and Rourke knew one another years ago."—Janice Prentiss

July 23, 1995
Huntington Lake—after midnight
"Danielle, Alexandra, Laura, Olivia, Gabrielle, Maria." She paused and gazed up at him. "Do you like any of those?"

Rourke smoothed a tangle of hair from her face and murmured, "All of them."

"I am not going to have six babies."

His laugh settled over her like soft caramel. "Six is my lucky number."

"Well, seven is mine but I'm not having seven children."

"Alex," he said. "And Ben, and Max. Maybe Lucas."

"No Rourke Junior?"

"No thanks. That name's tough enough without adding a junior on the end of it."

"Hmm. You've got a point." Kate laid her head on his bare chest and breathed in his scent. He smelled of pine and their recent lovemaking.

"As soon as we finish college, we can get married. We'll get engaged the Christmas before."

Just hearing him talk about their future made Kate half-dizzy. She wanted to marry him more than she wanted her next breath. A whisper of panic brushed over her. "Tell me this isn't all a dream that's going to disappear in the morning."

Rourke rolled Kate onto her back and burned his silver gaze into her. "This isn't a dream. It's reality, Kate Redmond, our reality. We will be married. No one can stop us."

"Yes," she murmured, opening her mouth to meet his. "No one can stop us."

***

Georgeanne pulled out the scrap of paper from her shirt pocket and dialed the number. "You promised to take care of things."

"I'm working on it."

"That's not good enough."

"There've been a few complications."

"Excuses. You have three days. Either I see results or I start talking."

***

"Thank you for keeping this our little secret." Janice Prentiss flashed Kate a brilliant smile. "I am truly beside myself." She sashayed into Rourke's house like a runway model, dressed in a black slack suit with a low-cut jacket revealing ample cleavage and a striped scarf tied at the neck.

Kate felt like a frump from the Goodwill store next to the woman. Her stomach had flip-flopped between jumpy and full-blown nausea the second she'd agreed to see Janice for what the woman insisted was an urgent situation. Kate should have told Rourke about the phone call before he left for the office this morning but she hadn't wanted anything to tarnish last night.

"Why don't we go into the sunroom? It's much more private there."

Kate had never even been in the sunroom but obviously this woman had. *What's the urgent situation?* she wanted to ask. *Tell me now.*

"Would you like something to drink? Bette makes a wonderful chai tea."

She spoke as though she were the hostess and Kate the guest. "No, thank you. I just finished breakfast, but help yourself to whatever you like."

Janice smiled as if to say *I always do.* She tapped the intercom button with a lacquered nail and said, "Bette, this is Janice. I'd like a chai and a few of those delicious shortbreads you keep on hand. We're in the sunroom. Thank you." She released the button and sank into an overstuffed leather chair. "Please sit."

Kate thought of refusing but the act would appear petty and ridiculous. She perched on the edge of the chair opposite Janice, feeling like an actor in a play whose lines had been deleted.

"I understand you and Rourke knew one another years ago." Janice's hazel eyes zoomed in on Kate.

"Yes, we did." *I will not let my voice wobble.*

"Did you date?"

"For a time."

Her eyes narrowed the tiniest fraction. "How sweet. I always say young love is like cotton candy—gooey and much too sticky, especially unrequited love."

Kate bit her lower lip.

Janice lifted a slender, perfect brow. "Was that what you two shared? An unrequited young love?"

How could she possibly tell this woman the love she and Rourke shared had migrated and imbedded itself into their adult lives and finally, thankfully, burst forth in full bloom last night? She couldn't tell her so she merely said,

"His mother got sick and he moved away." *Close enough to the truth.*

"Ahhh. Even worse. Love torn apart." She trailed her red nails along the arm of the leather chair and let out an exaggerated sigh. "It's the stuff of movies, isn't it?"

"Sometimes, I believe it is."

"Does Rourke know he has a child?"

Kate's lungs clamped shut and she gasped for air.

"Is that why he's suddenly auditioning for Father of the Year?"

Kate swallowed twice and forced out the words. "He knows."

"I thought so." Her full lips curled. "He won't marry you."

"I didn't ask him to." *He will marry me. No one will stop us this time.*

"You seem like a nice person, but we both know you don't belong in his world. You belong with the other Kates of the world, teaching school and baking cakes. Rourke loves the glitz and glamour of this life." Her eyes sparkled. "He's magnificent to watch."

But he was still Rourke. Her Rourke.

Janice examined her diamond bracelet and said casually, "I haven't told anyone about my discovery. It would take someone looking for it, or a person who knew Rourke very well to mesh the eyes, the hair color and texture. They even have the same bites, have you noticed that?"

Of course she had. "What do you want?"

"You should take your daughter and go home, Kate."

"I don't think what I do is any of your concern."

Janice sighed. "I know what you're trying to do here. You think you can convince him to marry you and eventually adopt Julia so no one has to know he's her real father."

"That's not true." *Was it?*

"Of course it is. Who wouldn't want Rourke as a husband? I'm sorry to disappoint you, but that is not going to happen."

What had Rourke ever seen in this woman, aside from the obvious? Maybe the obvious had been all he'd wanted. "I really have nothing more to say."

"Of course you don't, but then I didn't expect you would." She settled back in the leather chair and fingered a lock of hair. "There is one more thing to consider before you set up house here."

Kate dragged her gaze to the woman, forcing politeness into her words. "What would that be?"

"I'm pregnant."

***

"Maxine, what's the name of the florist I use? Madelino's? Gabelino's?"

"Gabrellino's, sir. Would you like me to place an order for you?"

"No, I'll take care of it." Rourke flipped through the Rolodex to the *G*s.

"Very well, sir." Maxine paused halfway to the door. "Would you like the number for Tiffany's as well?"

He looked up and grinned. "Some things should be done in person, don't you think?"

A hint of a smile slipped across her lips. "I do indeed, sir."

"I thought so, too. I was thinking a platinum setting with an emerald cut. Two carats?"

"One can never go wrong with that, sir."

He nodded and flipped through the Rolodex. "My thoughts exactly."

Rourke left the office shortly before lunch and stopped at Tiffany's. This purchase would be a lot different from the one he would have made at twenty-two. Tonight he'd give Kate the ring and ask her to marry him. They loved each other. They had a child together. They could work out the details later.

***

Rourke found Kate in the sitting room upstairs, perched on a window seat overlooking the garden. The perfect setting for a proposal. He tiptoed over and planted a kiss along the back of her neck. "Miss me today?"

She stiffened. "Hello."

Her voice sounded clogged and worn. "What's wrong?" He moved so he could face her. "Why are you crying?" She eyed him through puffy lids and swiped her nose with a tissue but remained silent. "Kate, talk to me."

"I'm leaving in the morning."

He couldn't have heard her right. "What?"

"I'm leaving. Julia can stay another week."

"You're not making any sense. What's going on? Did something happen?"

She didn't answer right away. Instead, she lifted a shoulder and shifted her gaze out the window as though the answer lay in the patches of colorful garden below. He'd been gone less than eight hours; what could possibly have happened?

Finally, she spoke. "We talked about making this room the nursery, do you remember?"

Maybe she wanted to talk about babies. Fine. "I remember every room we designed. That's why I built this house."

"I went through each one today and I see so many things we talked about. You must have memorized them all."

Okay, so maybe she didn't want to talk about babies yet. Maybe she wanted to talk about their dreams and the way they were at eighteen. That, he could handle. He tucked a chunk of hair behind her ear and said in a gentle tone, "I remember the tiniest detail of things that are important to me. Like you. We can talk about all the plans we made but I don't want to resort to old memories anymore. I want to make new ones with you." He reached in his pocket and pulled out the case from Tiffany's. "This is for you," he said gently. Her hands trembled as she fingered the case and eased it open. "I've never stopped loving you, Kate. Marry me."

Her face collapsed and tears spilled down her cheeks to her chin in a fine, steady stream. He swiped at them with his thumb and said softly, "We can be together. Finally." Rourke stroked her hair, loving the feel of it against his skin. "Every morning, you'll wake up in my bed and every night, we'll fall asleep in each other's arms. We'll travel together. I want to show you Greece and Italy. Julia will love—"

"I can't marry you."

"Well, not right now, but maybe after six months we could start planning." He wanted her as his wife tomorrow, but he'd force himself to wait.

"No." She clamped the case shut and shoved it in his hand.

What was she doing? She loved him. "Talk to me, tell me what's going on so we can get through this."

"It's too late. We came so close and now," she sniffed and turned to stare out the window, "it's gone."

"Look at me."

"I can't. I already have too many memories of you I can't erase. I don't want to remember anything else about you. Can't you at least appreciate that?"

A slow bead of panic spiraled through him, filling every pore in his body. "You're not making sense. We have a second chance and now you're going to just throw it away?"

"The chance is already gone."

"It's here." He grabbed her chin and forced her to look at him. "Right here, with you and me. Tell me you know that."

She shook her head and let out a tiny whimper. "Please, let me go."

He couldn't breathe. "What about last night? Didn't that mean anything to you?"

"It meant everything to me. It's what will get me through these next years."

"Stop talking like that." He heard the desperation in his own voice. She could not turn him away, *not again*. "What about the journal? You told me you meant every word."

"I did."

"Make me understand, Kate. Why are you doing this?"

The pain in her beautiful blue eyes gouged his heart. "Janice is pregnant."

***

"What?"

Of course he didn't know yet, but it didn't matter.

"Answer me."

Why did he always look so handsome and sincere just before he broke her heart? "Janice came to see me this morning. She told me then."

"That's bullshit."

"Not if it's true."

"Janice would choose leprosy over motherhood."

"So there's no way she can be pregnant?"

His eyes narrowed to liquid silver. "I'm saying there's a higher probability of a cloistered nun being pregnant than Janice."

She threw him a cold look and said, "Not if you're anywhere in the vicinity."

He yanked her to her feet, his large frame towering over her. "Damn you, Kate, do not ruin this."

"I'm not the one being accused of fathering a child."

"I did not father her child." His grip burned into her skin as he leaned closer. "There is no child," he bit out, and then in a softer voice, "there can't be."

"Is that a fact or merely wishful thinking?"

His expression hardened. "Janice doesn't even consider children human beings. Besides, she loves her body too much to mutilate it with a child."

"I think you might need a little more effective birth control than that." She fought the image of Rourke and Janice, their beautiful naked bodies wrapped around one other.

He threw her a disgusted look. "She was on the pill and I always used protection."

"Always?"

"Always."

He sounded so certain that she wanted to believe him but women had been tricking men with pregnancy for centuries. "So maybe she poked a hole in your condom and forgot to take her pill."

He ignored the comment and insisted, "I did not get her pregnant."

Kate looked away so he wouldn't see the pain on her face. "What are you going to do?"

"Force the truth out of her."

"How? You'll need a pregnancy test and then it could be wrong or too early or—"

"Kate." She flinched when he touched her shoulder. "I'll handle it. I have a man who checks things out for me. He'll get answers and she'll never even know it."

"You mean a private investigator?"

"Right. He's very discreet. This guy can get a person to spill their life story and never realize they've done it."

His words made her uneasy. "You sound like you've used him quite a bit. How many other women did the PI scare away?"

Rourke traced a finger along the back of her neck, massaging in slow circles. "A few. He's like a second line of defense."

"Kind of like an antibiotic ointment."

"More like SPF50. I was not going to put myself in a position to make any woman a permanent fixture in my life."

The words stung but she forced a casual tone in her voice. "Then I guess I should consider myself lucky I didn't run after you when I found out about Julia."

His hand stilled. "I'm not talking about you. I'm talking about Janice and all the other Janices in this world."

"Of course you are."

He swore under his breath. "I knew she was looking for a ring the night I met her."

"But that didn't stop you from seeing her."

He did have the good grace to blush. "I never pretended I was going to marry any of them. They all knew it and yet they all thought they could change me."

"You used them."

His jaw twitched. "They didn't have a hard time drinking four-hundred-dollar bottles of wine or flying first class to Switzerland."

"Oh, so, you used each other," she corrected.

"That's right, so what?"

"I'm not used to people being so blunt about their ulterior motives. Usually, they sugar-coat it a little bit."

"When you're tossing hundred-dollar bills at somebody, you can give it to them any way you want. And you know what?" His body tensed as he closed in on her. "They'll take it every time."

Who was this stranger with the cold eyes and jaded heart? "Is that why you bought me this gigantic ring? Because you thought you could treat me any way you wanted and I'd just take it as long as the carat was large enough?"

"Stop being ridiculous."

"I'm being serious." She pointed at the velvet case in his hand. "Something like that should buy you quite a bit."

"I wasn't talking about you, Kate."

Wasn't he? She couldn't tell anymore. "You play games with people, Rourke. You say one thing but your actions indicate something altogether different. Maybe your other women closed their eyes to your manipulations, but I can't."

"What the hell does that mean?"

Could he really not see? "I can't live this life, wondering if," she paused and corrected herself, *"when* you'll hire someone to check me out. Just in case." His face paled and she spotted the truth beneath his tan. "You hired someone to spy on me, didn't you?"

When he didn't answer, she jabbed his chest with her finger. "Tell me the truth, damn you."

"Okay. I checked your financials." He turned away and stared out the window. "It was all public information—the loans, the liens, the second mortgage."

Kate slipped into a chair and glared at his back. She hated him right now, hated how he'd peeked into her life with the casual disinterest of a passerby. "Did you have a good laugh? Did you think it comical that I drove a ten-year-old car and ate burgers while you had chauffeurs and room service?"

"I found no humor in any of it."

"Really?" Now she really hated him and his demeaning tone. "You pitied us then, is that it?"

He shook his head. "No."

"Then why did you do it?"

He didn't respond right away, and when he did, his words were barely intelligible. "I couldn't seem to help myself."

"You make it sound like an illness. Where are the reports? I want to see them." She wanted to know every detail of those reports and the information they'd dug out of their lives.

"I destroyed them years ago."

"Years ago? How long has this been going on?"

He turned to face her, his expression unreadable. "Too long."

"You knew about Julia and my business."

He nodded. "And Clay's financial troubles."

"Of course. Do you know what color my sheets are, too?" He tensed but said nothing, which only further infuriated her. "Do you have any idea how grotesquely bizarre this is? It's like someone watching through a peephole while you shower."

"I never meant to hurt you or make you uncomfortable, and I certainly wouldn't demean you in any way."

"That's exactly what you did."

He moved toward her and knelt down on one knee. "I'll make it up to you. I promise." He clasped her left hand and slid the ringer on her finger. "Marry me and let me make it up to you."

She stared at the diamond glittering on her finger like a beacon of hope. This had been her dream since the first time she kissed him. And now he was offering it to her in vibrant carats.

"Can you promise me there won't be any more Janices lurking in the shadows? That one won't come to the door next month or next year and present me with a child and tell me it's yours? What happens when I'm older and heavier and the young things flit over you like butterflies? Will you still want me then?"

"I will always want you," he said with uncompromising fierceness.

"I think you believe that now and I appreciate your words. I really do. But Janice made me realize something today. We're too different, Rourke—our lives, our backgrounds, everything. I don't belong here."

"You said you loved me. How can you just walk away from that?"

"I'd rather walk away now than have you toss me away later."

"Stop talking nonsense."

She eased the ring from her finger and laid it on the table next to her. "Julia can see you during breaks and when it doesn't interfere with her schoolwork. I'd like her home the end of next week so we can get ready for school."

"Kate, let's talk this out. What can I say to change your mind?"

"Don't say anymore. Just let me go."

His jaw twitched. "I can't do that."

"You have to." She stood and faced him. "After all, you're going to be a father."

"I told you she's manipulating me."

"I guess I should thank her then for making me realize what life would be like with you." His expression darkened as he clenched his teeth and stared at her. "Good-bye, Rourke." She turned and walked away from the dream and the man she'd loved forever.

Chapter 27

"How long are you going to feed me this line before you tell me the truth?"—Angie Sorrento

"…and then he had the nerve to try and tell me to stay." Kate whacked at a finishing nail, missed, and hit her thumb. "Damn!" She threw down the hammer and grabbed her injured thumb.

Angie glanced up from her computer. "Ten minutes ago you spilled paint all over your pants. Now you hammered your thumb. Maybe you should just go home and take a little rest."

"I'm fine."

"Sure you are."

Kate studied the red spreading over her thumbnail. "Really, I'm okay."

Angie sighed. "If you say so."

Kate heard the clicking of the computer keys and knew Angie had turned back to her work. If only it were that easy. "Okay, so I'm not fine."

The clicking stopped. "It's been six days since you came back and all you'll tell me is Julia learned how to water ski and is thrilled to be going to a Cubs game?"

Kate shrugged and dragged her gaze toward Angie. "Julia's impressionable. How many thirteen-year-olds get a chance to meet a professional baseball player?" Actually, it was the whole team, but Kate was not going to go there. So what if Rourke Flannigan knew everyone?

"You're right." Angie shrugged. "I'm sure you're just moping around here because you miss Julia."

"Right." *You know that's not the only reason.*

Angie picked up her pen and rolled it between her fingers in the exact same way Rourke had. "She'll be home in eight days and then you'll be fine." Her voice slid an octave. "Then *everything* will be fine, won't it?"

"Yes. Of course."

"Good."

He broke my heart again and it's a miracle it's still beating.

"Kate?"

Why couldn't he have stayed away?

"Kate!"

She jumped and forced Rourke Flannigan from her brain. "What?"

"I just want to know one thing?" All traces of the earlier compassionate tone disappeared and in their place was Angie's usual no-nonsense voice. "How long are you going to feed me this line before you tell me the truth?"

"His ex-girlfriend's pregnant." There.

"Oh." Angie eased from her chair and moved toward Kate. "I'm sorry," she whispered, wrapping her arms around Kate's shoulders. "What a bastard."

Kate swiped at a tear. She needed Angie's barrage of ill-intentioned curses to remind herself Rourke Flannigan was no good for her. "He said it wasn't true," she sniffed, "that it was all a set-up and he was going to get to the bottom of it, but what's the use?"

"Could it have been a set-up?"

"Maybe, but either way there's always going to be another woman gunning for him."

"Hmm. I don't like the guy but you can't fault him for the women out there trying to hook up with him or his money."

"He had no business associating with that kind of woman."

"Honey, three-quarters of the male population have no business but given half a chance, they'd all grab onto a silicone Barbie."

"Men are pigs."

"Most are."

It felt good to slash Rourke's name. Kate opened her mouth and spilled out more dirt. "Do you know he hired a detective to spy on the woman? Said that's what he does so he can stay *uninvolved?*"

"You can't really blame the guy, considering all the traps women are setting for somebody like him."

"But do you know what the sickest thing was? He spied on me, too."

Angie pulled back and looked into Kate's eyes. "Spied on you? When?"

"Here. He said he knew all about my loans and Clay's business problems." She dragged a hand over her face and forced herself to continue. "He even admitted he's been doing it for years."

"Years?"

"I know, it's bizarre."

"Yeah. Bizarre." Angie toyed with a coil of dark hair, twisting it around her finger, tighter and tighter. "But why would he spy on you for years? I always thought the guy walked out of Montpelier and never looked back. It doesn't make sense."

"I know. He said he couldn't stop, which made no sense at all." Kate closed her eyes and willed everything about Rourke Flannigan to disappear.

"Oh my God."

"What?" Kate blinked her eyes open and stared at Angie. "What's the matter?"

"Don't you see? If he told you he *couldn't* stop spying on you for all these years, it could only mean one thing."

"What? The man's a control freak who won't let anything go, even when he doesn't want it anymore?"

Angie opened her mouth and the words inched past her lips. "All these years, I never would have guessed."

"Guessed what?"

"He loved you, Kate. From the very beginning, he really loved you and he's never stopped."

***

Rourke was in a foul mood tonight, just as he'd been the last several nights. He hid it when he was with Julia, or at least he tried to, but other than that, he was miserable and bent on making everyone else miserable, too. Janice had evaporated and reappeared in New York on a photo shoot—a hand and foot lotion ad, very busy she'd said, no time to talk until she returned tonight. She was giving him a line and he'd been half-tempted to fly to New York and confront her, but common sense and a fear he wouldn't be able to control his anger won out. So he waited. She'd be here soon enough and then he'd drag the answers out of those lying red lips.

Maxine had taken Abbie and Julia out for pizza and a movie. She'd developed a strong maternal tendency these past several weeks, ever since her trip to Montpelier. Rourke refused to think of anyone associated with that town, except for Julia, of course. He sipped his bourbon and considered the evening ahead. Janice would pounce on him shortly, overflowing with chatter and buzz like newly uncorked champagne. She'd bring him a tie or cuff links or some other nonsensical gift he didn't need or want. All he wanted was the truth so he could go about reconstructing the rubble that had become his life six days ago. At least he still had Julia.

The front door opened and the *clickety-clack* of heels on tile broke through the quietness. "There you are."

"Hello, Janice." He lifted his bourbon and sipped.

Perfume suffocated his breath as she stepped closer. Had he really thought her antics tantalizing or had she merely been another distraction from his real problem—trying to forget Kate? She inched toward his mouth but Rourke turned his head seconds before she kissed him.

Janice sighed and perched on the arm of the couch. "Okay, you're angry."

Had she purposely crossed her legs just now so her skirt rode up her thigh, inches from the garter belts she loved to wear? "Why would I be angry?" He hadn't mentioned Kate or what she'd told him. In fact, he hadn't mentioned anything to Janice other than ordering her back to Chicago immediately. An order she'd avoided.

"I can read body language, Rourke." She ran a hand down his arm and inched closer. "I've always been very good at that...bodies, I mean." She eased her fingers along his chest to his belly and settled on his thigh. "I think you're tense," she said, working slow circles over the muscles of his leg. "And I know just how to relieve that ache."

He shoved her hand away. "I'm not in the mood for your games, Janice." He stood and moved to the fireplace, several feet from her groping hands.

"Rourke."

"Start talking."

She sniffed, twice. She was a much better actress than he'd given her credit for. The tears appeared on command, along with the sniffling. And somehow she conducted the theatrics without smearing her makeup. Now that was truly an art.

"Oh, Rourke, I don't know where to begin. Hormones. I can't seem to control them these days." She offered him a teary smile. "I'd hoped to tell you under different circumstances. I was thinking a table at Gianoni's and a bottle of Cristal but..." she lifted her slender shoulders and a fresh wave of tears fell.

Despite his anger, a tiny thread of panic gripped him. She *was* just acting, wasn't she? That's why she'd thrown the hormone thing in, wasn't it?

Janice turned to him and murmured in a voice heavy with anguish. "I know you never wanted a child. I know you think them bothersome and demanding. I know." She buried her face in her hands. "I am so sorry."

Rourke sucked in the last whiff of oxygen from the room and forced his legs to move toward her. "Janice." He reached out and awkwardly touched her shoulder.

She clutched his other hand and gazed up at him. "Do you want me to get rid of it? Is that what you want me to do?"

He pictured someone else in that seat and knew *she'd* never consider that an option. "No, of course not." He raked a hand through his hair and rubbed the knot at the back of his neck. "It's just that, well, it's a damn shock."

"I know."

"How the hell did this happen?" He still wasn't convinced anything had happened but there was a minute fracture in his previous degree of certainty, and that disturbed him.

She giggled. Janice never giggled. "I'd say it happened in the usual way."

"That's not what I meant." *No, please no.* "You were on the pill. I used a condom."

She settled back against the couch and crossed one long leg over the other. "There is such a thing as human error. We're both human." Her lips curved into a full smile, reminding him of sex and lots of it. "Apparently we both erred."

He was going to be sick. "How do you know for sure?" He'd read that super-skinny types like Janice didn't always get their periods on time. Maybe that was it. She was just late. *Dear God, please let that be it.*

She swung her leg again, long and silky and tanned, strapped in a three-inch red stiletto. "Women just know, silly. And I'm late."

"How late?" He was sure he'd read underweight women could miss three or even four periods. Sometimes as much as a year. Where had he read that?

She slid him a shy smile. "A month. This will be a spring baby."

The three bourbons he'd downed earlier burned a hole in his gut. He swallowed hard and pictured Janice's concave middle protruding against those tight jersey dresses she loved to prance around in. The visual slipped through his mind, sharp, precise, and nauseating.

"Rourke? Are you okay?" She was beside him, stroking his back. "You look gray and you're sweating. Here. Sit down." She let out a soft laugh and settled herself next to him on the couch. "I don't blame your reaction." The stroking continued, along his shoulders, neck, down his arm. "But I guess we'll both get used to the idea and just think what a beautiful baby it will be."

"Did you take any of those home pregnancy tests?" There had to be a mistake. Somewhere.

"Of course I did. The little line showed up. That means it's positive. "

He opened his mouth and gulped in air. *Positive.*

"Do you want to know the sex of the baby?"

"I don't know." He stared out the window at the sliver of moon floating over the blackness of night and wondered what *she* was doing right now.

"I absolutely think we need to find out as soon as possible. Then we can plan the room. We'll need a decorator."

Did she believe me when I told her I wanted to marry her? Or did she think it was all a sham because of this? How can a man have every material possession in the world and lose the one thing he wants most? Again?

"Rourke? Did you not hear a thing I said?"

"What? I was listening."

She snuggled closer and rested her head on his shoulder. "You smell so good. Good enough to devour. Let's go to bed."

"I'm not tired." *How could he touch her after Kate? How could he ever touch another woman after Kate?*

"Good. Neither am I." She wrapped her arms around his neck and kissed him on the mouth. When he didn't respond, she pulled away with a pout. "I see you'll need a little time to adjust to the idea of being a father. So where does this leave us?"

The tone in her voice put him on immediate alert. "What do you mean?"

She bounced off the couch and paced the room. "Just that. Where does this leave us? Are you going to be an involved father or just one who pays child support and maybe sees his son or daughter every other weekend and on the occasional holiday?"

"Of course I want to be involved." He wasn't about to let another of his offspring roam the planet without knowing who his or her real father was.

"And what about us?" She wheeled around and squared off like a gunfighter, hands on hips, chin thrust forward.

There is no us. There's never been an us. "I haven't thought about it." What a lie.

"I'm not raising this child alone. If you aren't interested in the whole package, I'm sure I can find someone who is."

He flew off the couch and planted himself next to her. "I won't have another man raising my child." *Not again.*

She lifted a graceful shoulder and shrugged. "It's your choice, but if you wait too long, it won't be."

Chapter 28

"I mean, here's my mother, but when I'm reading that stuff, she's not really my mother then."—Julia Maden

July 23, 1995
Huntington Lake—midnight
Slivers of moon cast soft halos on their naked skin as they clung to one another, breathing in the night scent of grass, and sweat, and virgin sex. "I love you," Kate whispered against Rourke's chest. He made her feel strong, and safe.

"I love you, too."

"I'll never stop loving you." It was a truth she wanted him to know.

His hand stroked her back, pulled her closer. "My heart is yours. Forever."

***

He dreamed of Kate at night, her long dark hair skimming his chest as she knelt over him, her lips moist and warm against his. The sheerness of her white negligee exposed the curves and dips of her beautiful body, a body that smelled of hyacinth and passion. He needed to touch that body, stroke the silky skin, lift her onto his hardness. "Come to me," he whispered. "Let me make you mine." He closed his eyes and reached for her, anxious to feel her softness drape him. His hands grasped air where her hips should have been. His eyes flew open to nothingness. Kate had vanished. The dream returned three nights in a row, and each time she disappeared just as he was about to touch her.

"Damn it," Rourke growled, jolting awake from another anguished dream. He threw back the covers and padded to his study where he poured a shot of bourbon and downed it in one swallow. He hadn't slept much since Janice's sucker-punch announcement and when he finally dozed off in the early morning hours, damn it all if he didn't dream about Kate and her disappearing act. He'd tried to call her at least twenty times in the last three days—twenty-two to be exact—but she wouldn't take his phone calls. He bet Angie, the Wicked Witch of the West, loved that.

How had he messed things up so badly? He was a responsible, articulate, educated man who managed his life and his business with precision. But put a woman in the mix, and it went to hell. He cursed and made his way to the kitchen where he fished around in the pantry for something to eat. Since Abbie had come to live with him, he had his choice of high-fat, high-calorie goodies. He pulled out a bag of potato chips and dove in. Hadn't he seen a container of French onion dip in the fridge? Maybe having a kid around wasn't so bad after all. He yanked open the fridge and stuck his head inside, peering around a carton of chocolate milk and a container of yogurt.

"Rourke?"

He jerked back and hit his head on the refrigerator shelf. "Damn!"

"Are you okay?"

Julia stood in the doorway wearing shorts and a Chicago Bulls T-shirt. Rourke rubbed the side of his head and said, "Yeah, I'm fine. What are you doing up at this hour?"

She shrugged. "I couldn't sleep."

"Hungry?"

She worked up a small smile. "I'll take a few chips and there's dip on the second shelf. Want some?"

"Actually, that's what I was hunting for when you snuck up on me."

Julia pulled out the dip and lifted the lid. "Abbie and I ate some earlier but I think there's still enough for you."

He eyed the half-eaten dip. "I haven't eaten this stuff in ten years."

She dug out a handful of chips and plunged one in French onion dip. "You've been missing out."

Rourke jabbed his chip in the dip, scooped out a hunk, and plunked it in his mouth. "You've got that right." They sat in silence, chomping on chips and dip. He began to relax and enjoy the companionable quietness of sharing a late night snack with his daughter. *His daughter.* He choked on a chip, which sent Julia into panic mode.

"Rourke?" She whacked his back. "Rourke? Are you okay?" *Whack, whack, whack.*

He raised his hand, coughing and sputtering. "Stop! Are you trying to kill me?"

"Oh. Sorry."

"Maybe I shouldn't eat these things after all." He peeked in the bag and grabbed another handful. "Oh, what the hell."

"Rourke?"

He scooped a gob of French onion dip on his chip. "What?"

Julia hesitated, then opened her mouth and blurted out, "Are you going to marry her?"

Had Kate told her? "I—"

Julia's silver eyes turned accusing. "You can't marry her. I won't let you."

She didn't have to worry about stopping him. Her mother had thrown a two-carat diamond at him and walked out. Why couldn't he have fallen in love with a woman who possessed a more agreeable disposition? "I don't know what's going to happen. Maybe in time we can figure out a way to make it work. Maybe you'll get used to the idea. What do you think?"

She scowled. "Not in ten thousand centuries."

"Do you hate me that much?"

"I don't hate you." She swiped both hands across her cheeks. "I hate *her*."

"You hate your own mother?"

She stared at him like he'd just asked her to spit out silver dollars. "No, of course not."

"Then who are you talking about?"

Her gaze narrowed on him and she crossed her arms over her almost flat chest. "Who are *you* talking about?"

"Your mother."

"My mother? *My mother?*" Her shoulders relaxed and she uncrossed her arms. "Really?"

"Who were you talking about?"

Her small nostrils flared. *"Janice."*

"Janice?" Where did she get a crazy idea like that?

"I heard her talking to Greta. She told her the grout in the bathroom needed scrubbing and once she moved in, things would be different."

He didn't think he'd heard her right. "Once who moved in?"

"Janice." Her dark brows pushed together. "Abbie and I call her Janice the Anus."

No wonder Julia was upset. "Do you always call people names?"

"Only when it's the truth."

He couldn't fault her for that. "I am not going to marry, Janice." *Even if she is pregnant with my child.*

"Promise?" Her eyes shone bright and half-hopeful.

He clasped her hand and squeezed. "Promise."

She sighed. "Abbie will be relieved. We were all worried but Maxine said not to but I said—"

"Maxine? Abbie? What were you all doing? Taking bets on my love life?"

A dull pink smeared her cheeks. "More like betting against it."

"Gee, thanks. What's Maxine got to do with it?" For a woman who still refused to call him by his first name, she certainly had gotten involved in his personal affairs.

"Maxine said it wasn't going to happen. 'Not in the next two lifetimes' is how she put it. I wasn't sure and Abbie said she thought Janice would do something to blackmail you into it, like get pregnant."

The oxygen swooshed from his lungs. Had Janice said something? Worse yet, had Kate?

"I told her that was crazy because Janice loved her body too much to turn it into Play-Doh for nine months."

He took a small breath. And then another. Julia didn't know. Yet.

She giggled. "Can you imagine her trying to walk around on those spikes she wears with a pot belly hanging out?"

He smiled and shook his head. "No, I'm having a hard time with that visual." But he could picture Kate pregnant, all soft and round and glowing. The image grew so vivid it felt real.

Julia's giggle morphed into a full-blown laugh. "And those tight dresses, that would be a real picture for *People*." Her face turned serious and he thought she'd make a hell of a prosecutor one day. "Were you really talking about my mother?"

"I…" He picked up a chip and studied it.

"Rourke?"

He could give her a damn convincing lie but she deserved the truth. "Yes. I was talking about your mother."

"You love her, don't you?"

"I do."

Her lower lip trembled and her eyes glistened with fresh tears. "I knew it."

"Look, Julia, I know you loved your father," he stopped, "I mean, Clay. No, that's not right either." Damn, he'd turned into a babbling idiot. "The man who raised you loved you like a father. I'm like the quarterback who comes in during the fourth quarter when the team's up forty to nothing." She stared at him and he knew the analogy was lost on her. He tried again. "I never had a chance to be your real father, but that doesn't mean I wouldn't have wanted to be."

"I loved my father."

"He was a good man. I can't replace him, and I don't want to. I don't know what's going to happen between your mother and me, but that doesn't change the way I feel about you or the fact that I want you in my life."

"She won't talk about you."

"I didn't think she would."

"She won't tell me what's wrong either. If she doesn't tell me, how can I try to make it right?"

"That's not your job."

She looked away. "Sometimes I wonder if I even know her."

He touched her chin and coaxed her to look at him. "You mean since you found her journal?"

She nodded. "Everything just kind of exploded in my head. I mean, here's my mother, but when I'm reading that stuff, she's not really my mother then. She's some other

person who's in love with somebody who's not my father."
She blinked hard. "Well, not the father I thought was my
father."

"It's a lot for me to understand, too."

"All these years she's kept it bottled up inside. If my
dad hadn't died, maybe I'd never have known about you or
any of that stuff," her voice drifted off, "almost like she had
another life, separate from the one she had with us."

What could he say? She was right.

"This is so screwed-up."

Right again.

His daughter heaved a big sigh and pinned him with
eyes so like his own. "So, since you two obviously love
each other, you're going to have to figure out a way to get
her to marry you."

Chapter 29

"Life passes by those who refuse to get on the train."—
Rourke Flannigan

"Let me see if I understand this correctly. You want me to draw up a trust for the daughter of the man who was killed in the Syracuse accident, *and* you are willing one half of your estate to her?"

Rourke clasped his hands behind his head and nodded at Miles. "Correct."

"Need I advise you this is absolutely ludicrous and considering my capacity as your legal counsel, I cannot, in good faith or otherwise, permit you to do so without making you fully aware of the consequences of such actions?"

Rourke hid a smile. Miles could get so huffy when someone veered outside his interpretation of legal parameters. "You don't need to remind me. I'm of sound mind and possess all of my faculties as I ask you to draw up this agreement."

"You're already paying the woman an exorbitant amount of money."

"I'm talking about the child here."

Miles cleared his throat. "I had no idea you held such an affinity for children. Had I known, I'd have asked you to sponsor a scholarship or two for the underprivileged."

Rourke ignored Miles's sarcasm. "Next year, tell Dexter to put it in the budget."

"Why are you doing this?" Miles worked his temples with the tips of his fingers. "This makes absolutely no sense."

"I'm sure you find it confusing."

"Confusing?" Miles closed his eyes and continued to massage his temples. "I find it insane."

"What if I told you the child in question was my daughter."

Miles's eyes shot open. "What?"

"If Julia Maden were my daughter, then it would make perfect sense to have these provisions for her, wouldn't it?" For the first time in all the years Rourke had known Miles Gregory, the man with the golden tongue and thousand-dollar words, was speechless. "A man does right by his child, doesn't he, Miles, even if he never learns of the child's existence until years later? Years after another man has been raising that child as his own? And if the discovery comes as a result of a horrible, unfortunate accident in which the real father is indirectly responsible for the death of the surrogate father, imagine the guilt and need for recompense that would generate?" Rourke kept his gaze fixed on Miles, who remained speechless. "Yes, well, that would make an interesting case, wouldn't it?"

"Are you saying," Miles reached for a handkerchief and blotted his forehead, "are you saying the child is yours?"

Rourke nodded. "So it would appear."

"But," he stared at Rourke as though he couldn't assimilate his words. "How could that be possible?"

Rourke lifted a brow.

"No, that's not what I meant to say." He dabbed his forehead with increased effort. "But how *can* that be?"

Rourke had toyed with the poor man long enough. Miles was a man of contracts and litigation and codicils. Emotion was like an algebraic equation written in a foreign language. "Kate and I knew one another when we were teenagers." Now for the blast. "Her mother was driving the car that hit my mother."

"Good God."

"Exactly. Diana flew to Montpelier, scooped me up, and dumped me at Princeton before I realized what was happening. At the time, I hardly knew my aunt, but she was so efficient and so damned authoritative, I never thought to question her."

"That's Diana," Miles said. "I'm sure she abhorred the publicity."

"That's the thing; there wasn't any."

"Ah. She must have called in quite a few favors to keep that quiet. I was working here at the time and never heard a word. I never knew she had a nephew until you showed up for work."

"That was a long time ago. The old bird's softened a bit, wouldn't you say?"

Miles lifted a brow. "I'm afraid I must abstain from answering on the grounds that I may incriminate myself."

"Okay, okay, I got it. But she's on the verge of softening."

"Any century now."

Rourke saw the soft side of his aunt, not often and not for long stretches, but it was there, no matter how much she tried to hide it.

"So you broke off with Mrs. Maden and never knew she was pregnant?"

"More or less." No sense telling him she'd found his replacement mere weeks later.

"And you never knew?"

Rourke shook his head. "Not until recently, no." He thought of the journal tucked safely in his briefcase next to the file on Kate. How ironically appropriate.

"Good Lord, this is a shock."

"Now do you understand?"

"Yes, now it all makes sense. But *half*, Rourke? Do you know how much money that is?" Rourke didn't bother to answer. "Of course, you do, that's not what I meant. But isn't there another relative, perhaps a distant cousin?"

"This is my daughter we're talking about, Miles."

"What does Diana have to say about this?"

"She doesn't know."

Miles cleared his throat. Twice. "I wouldn't want to be you when she finds out."

"I'll handle Diana."

Miles converted to lawyer mode. "How do you know she's really your child? Hearsay? The woman told you?"

"I know." Even if Kate hadn't admitted it in the journal, Julia had his eyes, and his chin, and his fingers...the more he looked, the more he found himself in his daughter.

Miles let out a resigned sigh. "What about the woman?"

"What about her?"

"Are you going to inform her of the trust?"

"Eventually."

"Is there nothing I can do to dissuade you?"

"No."

Miles sat up straighter and began making notes. "I'll have the papers drawn up. Will there be anything else?"

"One more thing. Set up a trust for the other half of my estate."

Miles paused and stated in a tight voice, "I'll need the recipient's name."

"Relax. This one's more flexible. I'll know in the next eight months or so." He thought of Janice and her claims. And then he thought of Julia and her vehement statement that Janice would *never* have a child. "I'll know by then if I need this trust or not."

Ten minutes later, Miles left Rourke's office with notes and a promise to have papers ready in twenty-four hours. The man would have to learn that everything wasn't about legalities and the bottom line. Sometimes there were far more important things, like people.

He rang Maxine and she entered carrying a pad of paper and a pen. "Yes, sir?"

"Miles just left," he said, waiting to see if she'd offer any comment. He'd seen the two of them talking at the coffee station and from the look on Miles's face, there was more brewing than coffee.

"Yes, sir, he did just leave." She kept her tone even but he swore her cheeks turned a few shades brighter.

"Did he have anything to say?"

"No, sir."

"Take a seat, Maxine." She'd been in Montpelier, she'd met Kate, she'd spent time with Julia. "Miles isn't very happy with me right now."

"I wasn't aware of that, Mr. Flannigan."

"That's why I'm telling you. You see, I asked him to set up a trust for Julia, and he doesn't think I should do that." She looked down at her pad and said nothing. "I told him Julia's my daughter and I'm going to do right by her. She'll visit me during breaks and in the summer, and I'll be heading to Montpelier whenever I can get away to attend school events and whatnot."

Maxine nodded. "I'm sure she'd like that, sir."

He toyed with his pen. "I think so, but I'm not sure about her mother." There it was, his real purpose for calling Maxine in. He slid a glance her way. "What do you think?"

She busied herself with her pad and pen though he'd not asked her to write anything. "I'm sure I don't know."

"But what do you think, Maxine? That's all I'm asking. Just your thoughts."

"Well, sir, it could create a bit of a stir, I imagine."

"How so?" Maxine knew more than she was letting on.

She fiddled with her glasses and avoided his gaze. "Julia's mother might not be so welcoming."

"Has she said anything to you?"

"No, sir, not directly."

"Have you spoken with her recently?" He felt like a prosecutor trying to force out a confession.

"Not directly, no sir."

Maxine was a damn good protector. "I could use your help here, Maxine."

She dragged her gaze to his and said in a quiet voice filled with conviction, "She loves you, sir. She's always loved you. But you've gotten yourself into a bit of a predicament here and perhaps you should sort it out before you go involving Mrs. Maden."

She was talking about Janice. "You know?"

Maxine nodded her curly head. "There's only one thing that changes a man's mind about a woman he doesn't particularly care for."

"You're a smart woman, Maxine."

"Thank you, sir."

"So, do you see a way out of this or should I just load a gun and shoot myself?"

"I'm not sure that's necessary, Mr. Flannigan."

"What do you mean?"

"There are some women who would say anything to achieve their goal."

He spread his hands on the desk and leaned closer. "You mean lie?"

"I prefer to think of it as fabrication."

Rourke rubbed his jaw and considered her words. "We're on the same page here. I've been trying to trip her up, which is why I've been spending so much time with her, but so far, nothing. I have a private investigator checking into things. I'll know in a few weeks."

"That's very wise, sir."

He was already past Janice and thinking of Kate again. "Why won't she return my calls?"

"Perhaps she's afraid of getting hurt again."

Afraid, it always boiled down to that. Anger seeped through his veins and into his words. "She's afraid of life; that's her problem."

Maxine paled. "Some people have a difficult time, sir."

It didn't take an Einstein to see she was referring to herself. He wondered what she'd do if he told her he knew she had a thing for Miles and he'd lay money Miles had a thing for her, too. "Life passes by those who refuse to get on the train."

"Yes, sir."

He flipped open a notebook and scanned the lines. "I've called her seven times a day for the past eleven days and she refused my calls. I've e-mailed her twenty times with no response, and sent seven letters. Do you think she doesn't want to talk to me?"

"It would appear so, sir, but in time, I'm certain she'll come around, especially if things don't work out with Ms. Prentiss."

"Things are not going to work out with Janice because even if on the two-tenths of a percent chance she *is* pregnant, I'm not marrying her. Men support children all the time and don't marry the mothers."

"Very true, sir."

He sighed. "I suppose you know she refused my ring."

"Mrs. Maden, sir? Yes, I had heard."

***

September 25, 2009

The days roll into one another, week stumbles over week, and suddenly I realize it is almost October.

We were almost perfect, you and I. And now, all that remains is the torment of what could have been. I can't talk to you, think of you, be with you, and yet you have invaded every pore of my body and I can't get rid of you.

I hope it's the same for you. I hope you bleed when you think of me. If you think of me. I don't blame her for loving you or for carrying your child. I don't even blame you for your part in that. I blame you for giving me hope, for touching me again and making me think we had a chance, after all this time, after all the waiting.

And then, just like that, it's gone.

Chapter 30

"If you care anything about her, if you ever cared, leave her alone."—Angie Sorrento

To file:
Client: Rourke Flannigan
Subject: Kate E. Redmond
Date: September 26, 2009
Ms. Redmond left her house at 8:45 a.m. and drove to Dream Houses by Kate where she remained for 1.25 hours after which time she drove home. No sign of Ms. Redmond again until Tuesday, September 25, when she left her house at 11:35 a.m., picked up her mail and drove to work. Party remained for 3.5 hours and left. Returned home. No stops. Wednesday, September 26th—not sighted. End of report.

Rourke shoved the report into his briefcase and picked up the phone. *Something was wrong.* "Dream Houses by Kate, may I help you?"

"Angie, it's Rourke. Don't hang up."

There was a long pause and then, "What do you want?"

"Is she all right?"

"What do you think?"

"You've got to help me."

"So you can tear her apart again? No thanks. I'm a better friend than that."

"I need to see her."

"Go to hell."

"I just want to talk to her."

"Right. She hasn't eaten in three days, she hasn't slept in four, and she looks worse than she did after she buried Clay. You're not getting near her again."

"Angie, please."

"Stay away, Rourke Flannigan. I wish you'd never come back into her life. If you care anything about her, if you ever cared, leave her alone."

***

"Hello, Abbie." Janice swung in on a cloud of perfume that snuffed out half the oxygen in the room. "Where's your uncle?"

Abbie thought about ignoring her but Janice would tell Rourke because that's just how she was and then he'd give her the lecture on respecting other people. Yada, yada. It was so not worth it. Abbie pointed a finger at Rourke's study and said, "He's on the phone."

"Oh." Janice glanced toward the closed door. "I'll just sneak in and tell him I'm here."

Abbie would bet a hundred bucks Rourke wanted to see her about as much as a vegetarian wanted a strip steak. So, let her find out for herself. "Sure. Whatever."

Janice laid her jacket and purse on the chair and said, "I think we're going out for Japanese later. Care to join us?"

Right. "No thanks. I've got a lot of reading to do."

Janice floated over and glanced at the title of Abbie's book. "*Of Mice and Men*," she murmured. "I remember reading that. Excellent. But why did poor Lenny have to die?"

Abbie slammed the book shut. "Thanks for ruining the story."

"Oh." Janice threw her a swift smile. "Sorry."

That smile wasn't even a tenth apologetic. The witch ruined the story just to show Abbie who had the power.

Janice flounced her hair over her shoulder and headed down the hall with a casual, "If you change your mind, you're welcome to come with us."

Abbie swore under her breath and glared at Janice's skinny legs. In the last few weeks, Janice had been slinking around more than usual, acting like she belonged here. It was pure sickening. There had to be a reason and Abbie was determined to figure it out. She waited until Janice disappeared down the hall and then jumped off the chair and grabbed Janice's purse. Truth and lies hid in the lining of a purse. Maybe she'd find a bit of both inside this Coach. She unlatched the satchel and dug a hand inside. Lip gloss, lip plumper, lip liner. What a piece of work. She unzipped the side compartment and pulled out a square, flat box with writing on it. "Shit," she mumbled, staring at the label. "Shit, shit, *shit*." She threw the purse on the chair, mindless of the lip accessories scattering to the carpet, and ran toward the study.

***

Rourke had never experienced a migraine in his life but the spot above his right eyebrow pierced his brain with enough pain to make him wince.

"I don't think I like this sudden self-righteous persona who's taken over your body." Janice threw him a seductive smile and fingered her cleavage. "Where's the old Rourke Flannigan, the one who didn't let time *or* circumstance alter his libido?" Her voice dipped in throaty coquetry. "I want that man back. Bad."

The pounding in his head slammed him again. "I'm really busy right now, Janice." He shuffled a few papers on his desk and slid the red journal into his top drawer. That's what he'd been busy with, reading it over and over until every word rested in his memory.

"You're just cranky." She slid out of the chair and slithered around to his side of the desk. "I know what you need." She cupped his crotch and started stroking.

"Stop!" Rourke yanked her hand away and flew out of the chair. "What the hell are you doing? Abbie's in the next room."

"That's never stopped you before."

He shrugged and moved to the window. The sky sprawled the horizon in crisp, vibrant hues, a perfect imposter to Kate's eyes.

"I know why you're doing this."

He could feel her behind him but he didn't turn. "Enlighten me."

There was the slightest whimper in her words as she said, "You'll just try to deny it, but I'm no fool."

She was right. His behavior had nothing to do with Abbie and everything to do with—

"It's because I'm pregnant, isn't it?"

He swung around. "What?"

"I know." She clutched her concaved belly and bit her lower lip. "Some men are like that. Once a woman is pregnant or has a child, he won't touch her. It's the Madonna complex."

"Janice—"

"No. Don't pretend."

Her red-tipped fingers massaged her belly and Rourke had an absurd picture of Janice trying to change a diaper with three-inch nails. In a designer dress. And designer pumps.

"I love you, Rourke." She clutched his arm and peered into his face. "We could be a family. We could be happy. You, me, our baby."

A swirl of nausea clenched his gut. The sweat started next, prickling over his forehead, his neck, his back, followed by the pounding over his right eyebrow, so intense he had to squeeze his eyes shut.

"Rourke? What's the matter? You look like you're going to pass out."

He shook his head and ran past her to the bathroom where he proceeded to puke up his turkey Reuben and half his stomach. So much for carving out a family with Janice. Did she really think her possible pregnancy—he wasn't buying it until Graves submitted his report—would make him want to marry her?

"Rourke, are you all right?" Her throaty voice slipped under the door and clung to him.

"I'm fine. I think it's the flu."

"Oh. Well, maybe I should leave." Her voice dimmed and he pictured her tiptoeing from the door. "You know, because of my condition and all. I wouldn't want to get sick." Humor seeped through her next words. "I've been sick enough already."

Rourke splashed water on his face and rinsed out his mouth. "Sure. Good idea."

"Okay, then I'll call you later."

He gripped the sink and sucked in a breath. "Fine." *Go, just go.*

"Can I have Greta pick up anything? Or call something in? Chicken soup? Ginger ale?"

"No. Thanks."

He leaned against the wall and waited for her to leave. Soon, he'd have to deal with this situation, but not today. He closed his eyes and willed his head and stomach to settle down.

"Where's my uncle?" Abbie's words banged on his temples and slid to his gut.

Janice's irritation followed. "Why? What's wrong?"

"I'm not going to let you trap him."

Rourke's eyes flew open. Trap whom?

"What are you talking about?"

"This."

"Where'd you get that? Give it to me."

"Not until I tell my uncle. Rourke? Where are you?"

"Give that to me, you little brat."

"No!"

Rourke pushed away from the wall and flung open the bathroom door. "Abbie? What's wrong?"

His niece waved a small box in the air. "Ask her!"

Janice tried unsuccessfully to snatch the box. After three swipes that landed her nothing but air, she changed tactics. "She had no business going through my purse. That's invasion of privacy, which is a punishable offense."

It was? Rourke squinted at the flat box. "What is that?"

Janice rushed toward him, clearly no longer concerned about catching the flu, and said, "It's not mine."

"Don't listen to her. See for yourself." Abbie thrust the box at him and cast a triumphant smile in Janice's direction.

"Ovulation Time," he read aloud. "'Predicting the best two days to become pregnant.'" He flipped the box over and started reading the directions. "What the hell?"

"I told you, it's not mine." Janice inched closer and smothered him with explanations. "It belongs to Claudia. She's been trying to get pregnant forever, and I told her she should start tracking her ovulation cycles and well, you know she's not good with technical things unless they're all spelled out. So, I bought it for her."

He held the unopened box up and said, "You bought an ovulation kit for a friend."

Her dark head bobbed up and down like a Chicago Bulls bobblehead. "Yes."

"That's bullshit," Abbie spat out.

"Abbie, that's enough."

"She's lying, Rourke. Can't you see she's going to try and get pregnant?"

"I *am* pregnant."

"What?" Abbie's face turned gray.

"I said I am pregnant, little Miss Know-it-all. So, why would I need an ovulation kit?"

"You're lying."

Rourke settled his arm around his niece and said, "Abbie, it's okay. I didn't want to say anything so soon but Janice *is* pregnant and starting now, I'm going to be very involved with this child." Janice's face split open in a blaze of triumph. "Janice, I'll need the name of your doctor and a list of your appointments so I can schedule accordingly."

"Oh. Well, there's no need for you to go right away."

"I want to." He smiled at her as she wet her glossy lips and shifted from one stiletto to the other. "And I'll need a copy of the pregnancy report." He scratched his head and added, "Oh, and the ultrasound schedule. I want to know the second they find the baby's heartbeat."

"Okay. I'll let you know."

"Good."

"Rourke, she's lying," Abbie persisted. "That woman is about as pregnant as Maxine."

The phone rang, cutting off Janice's retort. "Let the answering machine kick in," Rourke said. "We're going to get a few things straight right now." Like how he was not going to marry Janice.

August Graves's voice filled the line, blurring Rourke's thoughts. "Rourke, this is Graves. I got the information you wanted. Negative. Repeat, negative. I'm faxing you the complete report now. Call if you have any questions. And about the other, call me."

Janice advanced on him and demanded, "Who was that?"

The pounding in his head stopped. And his stomach wasn't threatening to heave again. Amazing what a few well-placed words could do for a person.

"Rourke? Aren't you going to tell me?"

He smiled. "He's a detective."

"A detective?" A hint of anxiety swirled through her voice. "Why in heaven's name would you hire a detective?"

He walked toward the fax machine, which had started printing, and said in a casual voice, "Sometimes that's the only way to find out the truth."

"Then I feel sorry for you if you have the need to spy on your friends."

He shrugged and lifted a single sheet of paper from the machine. "Sometimes your friends aren't really your friends."

She inched closer. "What is it? What's the detective investigating?"

Rourke finished scanning the page and handed it to her. "You. You're not pregnant."

Chapter 31

"I guess this whole thing takes some getting used to, doesn't it?"—Kate Redmond Maden

Kate set the bowl of spaghetti on the table and sat down. "One meatball or two?"

"One."

"One scoop of pasta or two?"

"One."

Kate paused midway between retrieving a meatball. "What's wrong? This is spaghetti and meatballs we're talking about here. Homemade. Your favorite."

Julia shrugged. "I'm just not that hungry."

Julia was always hungry. Her pediatrician called it part of the growth-hormonal phase. If she wasn't eating, something was wrong.

"I see Abbie called last night," Kate said, making a big deal out of twirling her spaghetti in a perfect pattern around her fork.

"Uh-huh."

"What did she want?"

"Just to talk."

"You still want to go to Chicago next weekend for your father's birthday?"

Julia's head shot up. "Of course I do. Why are you asking? Don't you want me to go?"

Kate hesitated a half second. "If that's what you want, then yes, I want you to go."

"I do but I hate to leave you alone."

"I'll be fine." It would just take a little time getting used to sharing Julia with Rourke. She'd thought of the detective he'd mentioned the last time she saw him and Angie's comment about it. *He loved you, Kate. From the very beginning, he really loved you and he's never stopped.* It wasn't true. It couldn't be true. And then there was Janice. What would Julia say when she discovered she was going to have a sister or brother? "I guess this whole thing takes some getting used to, doesn't it?"

Julia shrugged. "I guess."

"I know it's going to be hard to go there. I felt the same way. But if at any time you don't want to go, you don't have to." She had to let her daughter know that Rourke Flannigan did not own the world.

"I know."

Kate speared a chunk of lettuce and onion. "Good. And if you ever go and feel uncomfortable, all you have to do is call me."

"Mom. Stop."

"What? I'm only trying to make you feel comfortable about going."

"Is it me you're trying to make feel comfortable, or yourself?" Those eyes buried her with their silver stare. "Rourke and I talked about it. He's not trying to replace Dad. He just wants to get to know me. What's so wrong with that?"

He's going to break your heart. "Nothing."

"He's actually pretty cool." She smiled. "It's funny to watch him try to deal with two teenage girls. He is so absolutely clueless."

Kate jumped on that. "My point exactly. He's incapable of spotting a problem."

Julia rolled her eyes. "I cannot believe you just said that."

"It's true. He can run a multimillion-dollar business and flit from Hong Kong to London but what does he know about PMS?"

"With Janice around, I'd say a lot."

Which brought to mind another subject. "And what if he gets married and decides to have another child. How will you handle that?"

"He's not getting married."

"You sound pretty sure about that."

Julia snatched a piece of bread and tore a hunk from the middle. "I am sure." She took a deep breath and said, "I wasn't going to say anything because I know how upset you get when we talk about Rourke."

"I do not get upset."

Her daughter eyed her with the wisdom of an eighty-year-old and said, "Yes, you do."

"Okay, maybe the mention of his name makes me a little tense." Again, the look. "Okay, a lot."

"Janice told him she was pregnant."

Oh God, that's why Julia was so upset. "Oh," was all she could manage.

"Yeah, but turns out it was all a big lie and Rourke caught her in it."

Janice wasn't pregnant? Hearing about Rourke and the woman he'd been sleeping with from her daughter was against every self-help book she'd ever read, but she couldn't resist. "How did he find out?"

Julia started shooting details like an investigative reporter. "Abbie found an ovulation kit in Janice's purse. Okay, I know she shouldn't have been snooping, but we all know Janice is just trying to get Rourke any way she can.

So, Abbie confronts her with this kit and Janice makes up some big story about how it's for a friend, and then the phone rings and it's this detective Rourke hired."

The same detective he hired to track me?

"And guess what? This detective got some medical records that said Janice is *not* pregnant." Her eyes sparkled as she regaled Kate with the details. "The kit was to *get* pregnant."

Kate hated herself for asking but she couldn't help it. "So what happened?"

"He booted her skinny backside out."

"Oh."

Julia nodded and took a bite of meatball. "Oh, yeah. Abbie said it was better than reality TV. You know, I think I will have another meatball and more pasta."

Janice wasn't pregnant. Kate struggled to process the ramifications of it all.

"Mom, the meatball and pasta?"

"Oh. Sorry." Kate scooped out more pasta and another meatball onto Julia's plate. Janice wasn't pregnant…

"Mmmm." Julia dug into the pasta, twirling a gigantic forkful on her plate. "Boy, I wish I'd been there to see the fireworks. Abbie said Janice oozed sweetness all over the place but Rourke wouldn't have any of it. Told her to leave and he never wanted to hear from her again."

"I'm sure Janice didn't like that," Kate said, prickling with satisfaction.

"I'm sure she didn't. Abbie told me something else, too."

"What?" This secret camaraderie was addictive.

"She said she made a discovery of her own. It was right under her nose and even Abbie didn't notice it until it smacked her on the head."

Kate leaned in close and demanded, "What secret?"

Julia sat back, munching on a crust of bread, and said in a casual voice, "Rourke still loves you."

***

Kate's life changed in the produce section of the grocery store. She'd been sorting through heads of broccoli when Len Slewinski sauntered over carrying a ten-pound bag of Yukon Golds.

"Howdy, Kate. How's the prettiest girl this side of the Mississippi doing?"

"Hi, Len. I'm fine." Truth was, she wasn't fine. Might never be fine again. "How did Loretta get you to go to the grocery store?"

He lifted the bag of potatoes and shrugged. "She said if I wanted home fries with my sausage and biscuits, I had to bring home the taters." He pushed back his ball cap and scratched his head. "You figure I should get two bags?"

"Uh, no. I think ten pounds should hold you."

"Hope so. She don't make 'em but three times a year. Says it gets grease on the walls and such."

Kate smiled. "If you get hungry for them, you let me know. I've got a big bottle of degreaser to take care of the walls."

Len nodded and cleared his throat. "You're real special, Kate. Clay called you his princess."

Guilt seeped through her. She did not want to talk about Clay right now. "Thank you."

He cleared his throat again and swiped a hand across his eyes. "I'm real sorry about what I did. I know it was wrong but I didn't want them disrespecting Clay. He didn't deserve it."

"Excuse me?" She hadn't discussed the accident with Len since the day it happened. Had he told her something then? Something he'd been sorry about?

Len shifted from one booted foot to the other. "Didn't Georgeanne tell you?"

"Tell me what?"

He looked away, kicked the linoleum floor, and said in a quiet voice, "Clay wasn't wearing a harness when he fell."

"But that's crazy. That's the first thing the safety inspectors would check for. He had to have one on. Unless…"

"Unless someone put it on after."

****

Just three sips. Eight minutes. Georgeanne sloshed a little more vodka in her glass, recapped the bottle, and stuffed it in the magazine rack. Kate had called sixteen minutes ago, demanding to speak with her in person. Georgeanne tossed back the last drops of vodka, wiped her mouth, and hid the glass in the seat cushion of the rocker. Her daughter arrived in less than eight minutes. A bad sign since she lived across town and normal travel time was twelve.

The kitchen screen door banged open and seconds later Kate stood in front of Georganne, hurt and disbelief smeared across her face. "Why didn't you tell me Len came to see you?"

Of course. Len Slewinski had a conscience that kept him awake at night until he checked and double-checked every possible misdeed, even when it wasn't a misdeed. Damn the man. "I was going to tell you, but you've been busy with Julia and her trips."

"You should have told me right away. Do you know what this means?"

Kate looked like she was about to throw up. "Of course I know."

"We have no case against them."

"Says who? That big fancy lawyer from New York?" Bottom line, Clay died on Flannigan property. That made the Flannigans responsible, didn't it?

"I don't need Mr. Dupree to tell me our chances are seriously reduced." Kate dragged her hands over her face and shook her head. "How could you keep this from me?"

Georgeanne felt for the glass nudged against her right hip. A drink would slow things down and help her gain perspective. What would Kate say if she unearthed the bottle from the magazine rack and poured a short one? "Now settle down." She ran her tongue along the roof of her mouth, hunting for traces of vodka. "I don't appreciate being talked to that way."

Kate threw her hands in the air and paced back and forth. "Well, I don't appreciate being lied to."

"I didn't lie to you."

She swung around. "What do you call it? Withholding the truth? Permitting misinformation? Take a pick, Mom. They're all wrong."

Georgeanne started to stand but remembered the glass hidden in the rocker cushion and sank back down. "I was only trying to protect you."

"At what cost? Do you think I'd want a penny of their money if it wasn't due me?"

"Clay's life didn't earn you that due?"

"Not if he wasn't wearing his safety harness." Kate sank onto the chair next to her mother and rubbed her temples. "He had a chance to do right and if he didn't, for whatever reason, he was wrong."

"So the Flannigans just get off free?"

"They've got nothing to do with this anymore."

"No." *Damn them, no.* "They have Julia now, don't they? They've waltzed into this town and snatched her up. Where's the justice in that?"

Kate shrugged but said nothing.

"It's not right." Bursts of anger exploded in Georgeanne's gut. Someone had to tell the truth. About everything. If she died, so did the truth of what really happened that night fourteen years ago, how lives were manipulated, sacrificed. Even destroyed.

"I'll make this right, Katie. I swear I'll get our girl back."

"It's too late, Mom. Maybe it's always been too late."

***

The envelope from RF Renovations, Ltd., arrived in the afternoon mail. Was this Rourke's new tactic to win her back? She'd avoided his phone calls since returning to Montpelier, and then five days ago, they'd stopped. Kate placed the letter on the coffee table and sank onto the couch. She couldn't sit here without remembering Rourke's long body spread out in elegant comfort as though he belonged here. The man continued to fill every cranny of her life with his voice, his touch, his smile. And that was a very big problem.

It didn't matter if Janice had lied about her pregnancy. There would always be other Janices. Rourke only wanted Kate now because he couldn't have her, and of course, because of Julia. He'd told her he didn't like to lose, probably the truest words he'd ever spoken. A man like Rourke wasn't about love or commitment. He was about winning.

Damn you, Rourke Flannigan for coming back into my life.

Kate snatched the letter and tore it open. See if she'd give in to his new tactics. See if she'd budge one micron. She snapped the letter open, ignoring the check that glided to the floor.

Mrs. Maden:

Please accept our condolences regarding the loss of your husband. While no amount of financial recompense can begin to assuage your loss, RF Renovations, Ltd., offers the enclosed check to you with deepest sympathy. Acceptance of this check will negate all rights to bring future suit against the aforementioned company or its owner, Mr. Rourke Connor Flannigan.

With deepest sympathy,

Miles M. Gregory, Legal Counsel for RF Renovations, Ltd.

She glanced at the check lying face down on the carpet. Was this another of Rourke's ploys? Pay a fraction of what Mr. Dupree asked to avoid the chance of a lawsuit? Kate scooped up the check and flipped it over. She squinted, counting the zeroes three times. Four million dollars. Two million more than Mr. Dupree said they'd settle for.

Why, Rourke? Why did you do this? Her gaze slipped to the signature on the check. *Rourke C. Flannigan,* stared back at her, a bold reminder that she really didn't know him at all.

Chapter 32

"Can you imagine loving someone so much you can't think of anything else, even while you're telling yourself it would never work?"—Abbie Flannigan

"Maxine, we've got to do something." Abbie buried a French fry in a mound of ketchup. Mervin's Burgers was not Sophie's Diner but then Chicago was not Montpelier. "Those two are worse than Andie and Blane."

Maxine blinked. "Who?"

"Andie and Blane," Abbie repeated with great patience. "You know, the Romeo and Juliet from *Pretty in Pink*."

"No, I don't know."

"We'll add it to your must see list. Anyway, Rourke and Mrs. Maden are made for each other. We just have to help them realize that."

"Mr. Flannigan would not like us discussing his private affairs."

"We're all they've got, Maxine. Me, you, and Julia." Why couldn't she see that? The woman might hide behind her perfect grammar and stick-straight posture, but underneath it all, she was about as tough as mashed potatoes and getting softer every day. Abbie grabbed three more fries and plunked them in ketchup. "Oh, for heaven's sake, can't you just call him Rourke for once?"

Maxine cleared her throat and dabbed her mouth with a paper napkin. She looked almost pretty in her baby-blue sweater and pearls. Maybe it was the loose curls brushing her neck or the way her dark eyes softened when she spoke.

Something had changed these last few weeks but darned if Abbie could tell what. "Maxine?"

"Mr. Flannigan—Rourke—is a very private man despite his enormous social presence. He trusts me, Abbie, a gift he doesn't grant many. I will not betray him."

Abbie should have figured Maxine would go all self-righteous on her. She hadn't even heard what Abbie wanted her to do yet. Adults were so afraid to take a chance, even when they knew a gamble could change someone's life. Maxine had probably never gambled in her fifty-some years on this earth, not even at something as lame as bingo.

"What were you going to ask me to do?"

Abbie shrugged and studied the ketchup smears on her plate. "Don't worry about it. Julia and I will take care of it."

"Oh." And then, "I don't think I quite like the sound of that."

"Not your problem. Forget about it." Abbie sipped her milkshake and swiped a hand across her mouth. "This place is good, but it's not Sophie's."

"I admit, Sophie's had a certain appeal. I did love their malts."

"Right." Here was her chance. "The whole town had a certain appeal, didn't it?"

"Yes, it did."

"The people, too. They were special."

"Indeed." Her voice drifted to an indistinguishable sigh.

Keep pushing. "Kind of a nostalgic place, what with Sophie's and the Manor."

"Hmm."

She looked dreamy. *Dreamy? Maxine?* Abbie pushed a bit more. "Kind of a fairy tale feel about it."

"Exactly."

"Makes a person believe in happy ever after."

261

"Hmm."

Bingo. "Which is why Rourke and Mrs. Maden belong together."

Maxine's mouth shot open but Abbie spoke first. "I want you to invite Mrs. Maden to Rourke's birthday party."

"She'd never come."

"If it looks like it's from Rourke she might."

Maxine shook her head and murmured, "She'd never accept an invitation from him."

"Darn it, Maxine, we have to think of something. I am tired of watching documentaries with him every night or listening to him talk about bonds and futures. I've even started reading *Money* so I can get him in a conversation. He's killing me here. You have to save us both."

"What would I do? I have no way of controlling what Mr. Flannigan does."

Maxine had more power than she knew. "Let me ask you this—does he love her?"

"You mean Mr. Flannigan and Mrs. Maden?"

"Stop stalling, you know who I mean."

"Yes," she said, "I believe he does."

"And she loves him?"

Maxine nodded.

"Can you imagine loving someone so much you can't think of anything else, even while you're telling yourself it would never work? So, you make up excuses and give reasons to fill your days?"

"Hmm." Maxine's eyes were closed, the paper napkin held to her mouth in a crumpled ball.

"Weeks go by, and then months and years."

"Hmm." She bowed her head and sniffed.

Abbie leaned over the wooden table and whispered, "And before you know it, you're all alone. Forever. With nothing but a pile of stale memories."

Another sniff. Maxine swiped at her cheeks with the paper napkin and straightened her glasses. Abbie pretended not to notice the tears rimming her eyes.

"We're the only ones who can help them. Me, you, and Julia. Will you do it, Maxine? Will you find a way to bring them together?"

Maxine yanked off her cat-eye glasses and swiped a hand across both eyes. "Yes. I'll do it for them and for all the unrequited loves roaming this earth."

Something in the way she said it made Abbie wonder if Maxine might be talking about herself.

***

Rourke sipped his bourbon and stared out over the expansive lawn that *Chicago Life* called "stunning and glamorous." He'd never planted a single bulb or trimmed a tree branch. All he'd done was point at pictures he liked and write a check. What did that say about him? Beauty could be bought? He was a visionary who didn't waste time on day-to-day decisions?

Tomorrow was his thirty-third birthday. Abbie had insisted on a party. *Damn,* the kid could be persistent. She wanted balloons and streamers and all that other nonsense. He'd spotted her list under a magazine. That alone spelled disaster, but coupled with the fact that Julia was arriving shortly to help, made the probability of a successful outcome less than 1 percent. What the hell. Maxine had provided a birthday list and Miles Gregory's name was first on the list.

He reached for the red velvet journal that had cursed him since the day he first opened it. If Pandora's Box proved tragic, this journal was equally fatal. He leafed through the handwritten sections until he located the first blank page. Then he pulled out a pen and began to write.

***

Angie grabbed the phone on the second ring. Kate would be on her way back from the airport and if this month's drop-off were like last month's, Angie would have to scoop her off the floor. *Damn Rourke Flannigan to hell.* "Dream Houses by Kate, may I help you?"

"May I speak with Kate Maden, please?"

The woman's voice was cool, concise, and unfamiliar. "She's not here. Is there a message?"

"This is Maxine Simmons. Rourke Flannigan's secretary." Pause. "It's imperative I reach Mrs. Maden as soon as possible."

Right. So you can act as minion to that beast? Not likely. "I don't know when she'll be back."

"Has she taken Julia to the airport yet?"

"Possibly." *Damn if I'll tell you.*

"Ms. Sorrento—Angie, this is extremely important."

"To whom?" *Rourke Flannigan, who else?*

His secretary remained unperturbed. "To all parties concerned."

"I don't know about all *parties*, and I could care less other than where Kate and Julia are concerned."

"Understandably, which is why I'm trying to reach Mrs. Maden."

Was that sincerity beneath the woman's aloofness? It certainly sounded like it. Nevertheless, Angie was not about to hand over vital information that would get to Rourke Flannigan, the ultimate manipulator. "I'm not telling you anything until I know what this is about."

There was a long pause followed by a stifled sigh. "I'd like to fax something for Mrs. Maden. Once she's read it, maybe she'll change her mind about Mr. Flannigan. Maybe you will, too."

"Doubtful."

"Please see that she gets this as soon as possible."

"Fine." Angie relayed the fax number and hung up. *Witch.* Within minutes, the first paper inched through the fax machine. Angie snatched it up and began to read.

***

Kate stepped out of the car and made her way toward the shop. Her heart ached as it did every time she said good-bye to Julia, and it would continue to ache until her daughter returned home four days from now. She opened the shop door, devising ways not to think about Julia, when Angie swooped on her in a rush of agitation. "Thank God. I thought you'd never get here."

"What's wrong?"

Angie thrust a handful of papers at her. "There's something you need to see."

"Not the Gillents' bathroom sample again. I know it's the wrong color but Precisely Plum is a tenth of a shade away from Perfectly Plum. If Mrs. Gillent wants that, she'll have to wait two more weeks for the special order."

"This is not about Mrs. Gillent's bathroom."

"Good."

"It's about Rourke."

"Rourke?" Kate's gaze fell to the papers in Angie's hand. "What about him?"

Angie held out the papers and said in a soft voice, "I think you should read this."

There were eight of them. Locations. Times. Dates. Brands of coffee. Shoe choices. Kate read each account carefully, trying to recall the occasion. The detective was good, she'd give him that because she'd never noticed *anyone* watching her and he'd been doing it for eight years.

The last two pages of the fax looked as though they'd been copied from a book. They were handwritten and the penmanship was unmistakably Rourke's.

I miss you. It's been twenty-seven days since you left. Twenty-seven days of wandering through life like a sleepwalker, knowing nothing but the truth I should have admitted years ago. There will never be another woman like you, and the greater, more painful yet peaceful truth—I'll never stop loving you.

I've spent eight years telling myself the reason I employed August Graves to investigate your comings and goings was to make sure you lived the life you deserved for marrying someone else. A life of wanting. That might have been the reason in the beginning, but after the first report, I only cared about you and re-creating you in my mind so I could subconsciously place myself in the master bed on Laurel Street, next to you. I visualized myself lying beside you on the blanket at Huntington Lake, sharing coffee in the morning, taking walks together. It was the life I wanted. With you. Instead, I let wealth and power seduce me with their desires that, in the end, turned up shallow and empty.

You think there are other women, yet all I see is you. All I've ever seen is you. I've always loved you. I'll never stop loving you.

Chapter 33

"It's taken three vodkas to dial this number. Don't let Katie think it was in vain."—Georgeanne Redmond

The phone call came at 3:05 p.m. Maxine didn't bother to knock, just poked her head in and mouthed, "Georgeanne Redmond is holding on line two."

Rourke wouldn't have been more surprised if she'd told him the pope was on the line. What could the woman want with him? He considered ignoring the call, but of course he couldn't because it might have to do with Kate. Georgeanne Redmond was responsible for igniting the spark that burst into a wildfire and destroyed life as he knew it fourteen years ago, life as he thought it would be. He pressed line two and said, "Rourke Flannigan."

"Hello, Rourke."

She sounded like Kate, but more mellow, with echoes of pain pulsing in the beats of her voice. "Georgeanne."

She attempted a laugh. It failed. "You must be wondering why I'm calling."

"You could say that."

Pause. "Just let me get this out now, before I lose my nerve." Another laugh. "It's taken three vodkas to dial this number. Don't let Katie think it was in vain. I have two things to tell you. First, Clay wasn't wearing a harness the day of the accident. It was put on after."

"After he fell? By whom?" *Did she realize what she was saying?*

"Doesn't matter. The person who did it was only trying to protect Clay's memory so he wouldn't look like a reckless fool. Nobody was trying to get money from you and Katie didn't know about it until a few days ago." Pause. "She told me about the check, too. She's sending it back."

Rourke couldn't get past the fact that Clay hadn't worn a safety harness. "Why in the hell didn't he have a harness on?"

Georgeanne didn't answer right away and when she did, sadness coated her words. "Probably in a hurry, trying to get his hours in so he could buy Katie something else he thought would make her happy. He never stopped trying and he never stopped competing with you."

"Me? Kate married him. He won the prize."

"But he never won her heart. That's all I'm going to say about that other than if you ever cared about my daughter, you'll take your money back and leave this alone. Now, the second thing I have to say is about the night of the accident...the one with your mother."

"I'm really not interested." He had enough to think about without adding Georgeanne's mess on top of it.

"Please."

He sighed. "Dredging up that night serves no purpose. It's done."

"Just listen. Please. Three minutes, that's all I ask."

Rourke rubbed the back of his neck and glanced at his watch. "I'll give you two."

"I swear on my granddaughter's life I was not drunk that night. One drink, that's all I had before I got in the car. When I turned on Indian Road, it was pitch-black. Your mother jumped out at me. At first I thought it was a big dog or a deer. I got out to see..."

"I know the rest," he said, because whether he did or didn't was not the point. Stopping pain and memories, that was the point.

"But you *don't* know, Rourke," she rasped. "You don't know at all. There was so much blood, I thought your mother was dead. Then she moved and murmured something. I had to kneel down to hear her." Her voice faded, then grew stronger. "She told me to leave her. She said she couldn't go on, said she didn't want to."

He couldn't have heard her right. "What are you saying?"

"She begged me to leave her there." Her sobs stretched through the line and grabbed him. "I swear on my granddaughter's life, I'm telling you the truth. I did it for your mother—for the pain on her face and the misery in her words."

He knew his mother was depressed, but suicidal? "Why didn't you come forward that night and tell the police? You could have cleared yourself right there. Instead you got charged with a hit-and-run."

"I couldn't."

"Couldn't? Or wouldn't?"

"Couldn't. I was so shaken up all I wanted to do was get home. I was driving too fast and smashed into a guardrail. That's when I messed up my leg. I waited several hours but the pain was horrible and I finally called 9-1-1. When I woke up from surgery, it was already too late." And then she proceeded to tell him why.

***

Len Slewinski stared at the phone number, written in his chicken scratch on the back of a gas receipt. He'd memorized the dang number, which wasn't saying much since he'd been gawking at it for near an hour straight.

There was no way around it. He had to make things right and take the consequence, even if it meant jail time.

How could a good intention end up in a pile of manure? He'd only been trying to rescue Clay's good name so the boy would be remembered with pride and Katie wouldn't be subjected to snide comments about the reckless foolishness that made her a widow. But then that danged lawyer started snooping around and next thing Len knew, they were talking trial, which meant he'd have to testify. He'd eaten a pack of antacids a day since he heard that news.

But the crap hit the fan when he ran into Katie in the produce section of the grocery store and it came back to smack him square in the head. He'd almost dropped the Yukon Golds when he realized she didn't know about the harness. When she told him Rourke Flannigan owned the company Clay was working for when he died, well, that almost gave Len a coronary. Things had to end now, one way or the other. He picked up the phone and dialed the number. There was nothing left to do but own up to what he'd done. Mr. Self-Important would decide the rest.

"Mr. Flannigan's office."

Len closed his eyes and made the sign of the cross. "I need to speak with him."

"May I ask who's calling?"

He wiped his forehead with his handkerchief and said, "Name's Len Slewinski. Tell him it's urgent." Len said three Hail Marys and started on his fourth when Rourke Flannigan came on the line.

"This is Rourke Flannigan."

"Mr. Flannigan, don't know if you remember me or not, but—"

"I remember you, Mr. Slewinski. You called me a big city boy with a fancy car and shiny shoes."

Len mopped his forehead again. "Yeah, well, I might have been a bit hasty with my words."

"What do you want?"

There was steel in the man's voice. Probably the same kind that was in prison bars—the place Len was going once he told this man what really happened to Clay. Len gulped in a breath, maybe his last one as a free man, and said, "It's about Clay. He wasn't wearing a harness when he fell." Pause. *Jesus, Mary, and Joseph, give me strength.* "I put it on him afterward." Rourke Flannigan didn't answer. Was the man going to torment Len by making him repeat himself? Dang it all, he was. The SOB was a real jerk. Len opened his mouth to suffer through his confession again when the man spoke.

"You realize you've committed a crime."

"'Course I do." He didn't have to be all snooty about it. Len might be going to jail but he'd walk there with his head held high—even if he was in handcuffs and leg chains. "I meant no harm. I never thought there'd be a trial or the like. I just wanted to protect Clay and Katie."

"I see."

Crap, the man was going to draw this out and make Len suffer. "Just so you know, I plan on turning myself in as soon we finish here. Got my bag all packed. I know the sheriff. I'll have him contact you once I'm fingerprinted and such."

"Mr. Slewinski—"

"Clay was a good man. When the town finds out what really happened, they'll call him a fool and Katie and Julia will have to live with that."

"Aren't you worried about what they'll think of you?"

"Not particularly."

"I'm going to hang up the phone now, Mr. Slewinski, and forget we ever had this conversation."

"I don't understand."

"I'm not going to press charges."

"You're not? Why?"

"Because the truth will harm more people than it will help. And because I might have done the same thing in your situation."

"Oh. Well, thank you, then." The phone *clicked* and Rourke Flannigan was gone. Len clutched the receiver in his left hand and made the sign of the cross with his right. Maybe he'd been wrong about Rourke Flannigan after all.

***

Rourke hung up with Len Slewinski and wondered if any other Montpelier residents would call today to expose secrets. He doubted any would top Georgeanne Redmond's. Who would have thought she'd be the one to unearth the lies and shed truth on his life? What would the world think if they knew Rourke Flannigan was not really who they thought he was? Maybe he would tell them all—starting with Diana. Minutes later, he knocked on her door and waited the customary three seconds for her response.

"Come in."

She'd think it was Margot, her secretary, since no one contacted Diana without an appointment, not even to discuss making an appointment. Rourke opened the door and stepped inside. Diana glanced up, nodded, and continued stirring her tea. At 3:15 p.m. every day, she drank spiced black tea to boost her immunities and keep her mind alert. At 4:00, it would be green tea, at 6:00, oolang. Diana would need all of her mental capacity for what he was about to divulge.

"What's wrong? Did Chemstrol refuse our latest offer?"

He sank into the chair opposite her and picked up a paperweight. "Madame Butterfly," he said, studying the fine yellow script on the paperweight. "Didn't she kill herself?"

"She did."

"Hmm." He looked up and met Diana's gaze. "This isn't about business."

"I see." She set down her spoon. "Is this about the child?"

He heard her tone, her words. Her meaning. "No. It's about Georgeanne Redmond." The woman's name sent an allergic reaction through Diana. Her eyes narrowed and shrunk into their sockets. Her face turned ashen, then darker still. Her fingers shook, then stretched flat on the desktop, gripping the smooth wood. "So, you remember her?"

"How could I forget the woman who ran over your mother?"

"Interesting. That's not how she remembers it."

"Of course not. Do you expect a woman like that to tell the truth? Why, she's probably never told a single truth in her entire life. She should have gone to jail."

Ah, Diana was morphing back to her old self. "She said it was an attempted suicide."

"Suicide?" Diana spat out the word.

"Why is that so hard to believe? My mother never got over my father's death. She lived on pills. Surely, you knew that."

Diana looked away. "She needed a little boost over a rough time."

"That rough time never ended. She got hooked and depressed and nobody could help her because she didn't want to be helped. Let's be honest here, she could have been rehabilitated after the accident, left the house, driven a car. She didn't want to. She didn't want anything but those damn pills and they finally did her in."

Diana threw back her slender shoulders and held her head high. "That's not true. What happened to your mother was a result of one woman's selfish behavior."

"I agree."

"That woman is behind your mother's destruction."

"True."

"Yet she's walking free."

He stared at Diana. "Yes, she is."

"What are you looking at? Is it because I speak so boldly about the woman?"

"No, that's not it at all." *She really had no idea.*

Diana sipped her tea and studied him. "I've always believed in getting to the point. I would prefer you not speak with the woman again."

"I see no reason to, do you?"

"No, I don't. She'll only cause you more grief."

"More than she's already caused?"

"Absolutely." She nodded her silver head. "You've no use for her anyway."

"I think you're right."

"Good. I'm glad we're in agreement." She eased back in her chair and her voice softened. "I do enjoy our conversations, Rourke."

"So do I," he said, then added, "Mother." The word cracked the expression on her face, splitting the smugness she wore so casually into a thousand pieces. She tried to recover, but fear rimmed her next words.

"I've never heard a more ridiculous statement in my life."

"Really? You don't think the truth ate at the woman I thought was my mother? That maybe before she died she wanted me to know?"

Diana shook her head and stumbled to her feet. "This is crazy talk and I am not having this conversation."

Rourke stood and made his way around the desk until he towered over her. "We're going to have this conversation and you're going to tell me the truth. If not, I'll expose you and then see what your precious stockholders think of the great Diana Flannigan." She met his demand with silence, but she had to be panicked.

The standoff continued until finally she stepped back and paced the room. "I was studying at Cambridge. He was working on his doctorate in economics. I got pregnant. Your grandfather wouldn't hear of an illegitimate child so he devised a plan."

"Was marriage such a distasteful alternative?"

Diana's blue eyes darkened. "It wasn't an alternative. Your father was the son of one of the most powerful men in Great Britain. Along with that came certain responsibilities."

"Such as?"

"An arranged marriage to a textile heiress. The knowledge nothing could ever come of our feelings for one another didn't stop us from being together." Her voice dipped. "When I learned I was pregnant, I contacted my father and left Cambridge immediately. Your father never knew."

It was Rourke and Kate all over again, but different. "You didn't even give him a choice."

She shook her head. "I loved him too much to risk his doing something foolish. Besides, your grandfather had other plans. He worked everything out. Your mother, I mean, Barbara, left town for several months and when she returned, she had a baby."

Rourke stared at the woman who had birthed him. "But I only saw you a handful of times for the first eighteen years."

"Not because I wanted it that way." She walked to the credenza, fitted a small key in the lock, and opened the drawer. "I have drawers full of your schoolwork. Drawings, essays, math tests." She pulled out a handful and waved them at him. "I promised Barbara I wouldn't have contact with you until you went to college. I never would have told you, Rourke. I wanted you to believe she was your real mother, but she went and told that damn woman."

"You blackmailed Georgeanne."

"I told her if she kept quiet, I wouldn't press charges. It was a win-win situation, hardly blackmail."

"And Kate? Did you know she was pregnant?"

"Of course I did. Georgeanne contacted me all in a frenzy, afraid her daughter would leave her. We made a deal. I'd distract you and she'd pave the way for Clay Maden to step in."

Rourke stared at Diana as a slow queasiness filled his gut. They'd all had their hands in plotting against him and Kate, even Clay, the righteous one. "We never stood a chance."

Diana shrugged. "Look at you, Rourke. Could you have accomplished all of this with a baby and a wife from Podunk, New York? And no education? You should thank me for stepping in and directing you."

"Do you understand what you've done? I *loved* Kate and you took her away and now I've probably lost her for good and there's not a damn thing I can do about it. Have you ever loved someone so much you were willing to give him up because it was the right thing to do?"

"Yes," she said quietly, her eyes bright. "I have."

Chapter 34

"You read the letter."—Rourke Flannigan

Rourke sipped his bourbon and nodded at Miles. He wanted this birthday party like a vasectomy without anesthesia. Diana had taken an indefinite leave of absence, which was just as well because right now, he didn't know what he felt toward her. After all these years, to learn that the mother who raised him was really his aunt was too much to take in. If that weren't exhausting enough, Kate had clawed a hole in his heart with a ferociousness that made it hard to believe it could still beat. And Abbie and Julia were driving him crazy with their secrecy.

"...and I must say, Maxine might just be right about that." A quiet smile slipped over Miles Gregory's face. "Maxine is a very intelligent woman."

"I think she appreciates your intelligence too, Miles." The man beamed like a 100-watt bulb.

"Indeed."

"So, what are you going to do about this mutual admiration?"

"Do?"

You'd have thought he asked the man to strip and do a half pike into the pool. Rourke glanced across the room to where Maxine huddled with Abbie and Julia. "You have to do something, Miles. Surely you know that."

"Why?"

"Because of the mutual admiration. I place you in charge of the legal dealings of my entire company and yet you can't figure out a simple attraction principle? That worries me, Miles."

"I'm not very good with relationships." He pulled at his bow tie and cleared his throat. "They're too unpredictable."

"Tell me about it."

"What's the point of forming an alliance and sharing pieces of oneself and one's emotions that can only be used as arsenal?"

"I agree."

"It's totally illogical." Miles glanced in Maxine's direction and his expression softened.

"Totally."

"Relationships strip a person of rational decision-making." Maxine looked up and smiled at him.

"Yes, they do."

"But there is that 1 percent of time and circumstance that leads one to hope." Miles smiled back at Maxine and lifted his hand in acknowledgment.

"Hope?" *Hope didn't belong in the relationship equation.*

"Hope for a blissful union," Miles said, sounding like a love-struck puppy. "Of heart, mind," he sighed, "and body."

Rourke downed the rest of his drink and patted Miles on the back. "Go for it, Miles. Just make sure the union doesn't end in a bloody massacre."

***

"You sent it?" Julia whispered, eyeing Rourke from the corner of the room. Well-wishers had been circling him all night. But not the one they'd hoped for.

"I'm sorry, girls. I thought it would make a difference." Maxine shook her head. "If I'm going to get fired, at least I wanted to do it for a cause."

"You *are* doing it for a cause," Abbie said. "We all know Rourke and Mrs. Maden are crazy about each other, even if they're too stubborn to do something about it."

"True."

Julia squeezed Maxine's hand. "Just like you and Mr. Gregory are crazy about each other."

Maxine turned fuchsia. "Why would you say a thing like that?"

"We might be thirteen but we can spot true love when we see it, can't we, Julia?"

"Absolutely. We can spot phonies, too. Like Janice."

"Mr. Gregory has never been anything but polite and courteous. Like a brother."

Abbie snorted. "No brother looks at his sister like he wants to squeeze the life out of her."

"Abbie, please."

"Okay, okay. We can deal with your love life later. Right now, what about Mrs. Maden? How do you know she's not coming?"

"She didn't respond to the fax."

"Oh."

"Should I call her? Or Angie?" Julia asked.

"There's no point," Abbie said. "If your mom didn't believe those papers, she won't believe anything."

"But I think maybe they really were meant to be together."

Maxine sighed and squeezed both girls' hands. "Sometimes that's just not enough."

***

"Happy birthday, Rourke." Abbie leaned up and gave him a peck on the cheek.

"Thanks, kid." His niece was turning into a human being, imagine that.

"Happy birthday, Rourke." This from Julia, who kissed his other cheek.

He pulled them both into a bear hug and chuckled. "Kisses from my two best girls. It doesn't get much better than this." His heart lurched as he realized the truth of his words. Somewhere in the last several weeks, they'd embedded themselves in his heart in a way only a child could. They were his children now. Both of them. Who would have thought?

"We tried to plan a surprise for you," Abbie said, her words smothered in disappointment. "But it didn't work out."

"I'm too old for surprises," he said, wondering what they'd attempted. A magician? A juggler?

"I guess." Julia made no effort to hide the dejection in her voice.

He hated seeing them so disappointed. Was this how a parent felt? He tackled the beginnings of panic head-on. "Having the two of you here is the best present a guy could hope for."

"That is so lame," Abbie said but gave him a full-blown grin.

"Mr. Flannigan? Sir?"

He turned to see Maxine beelining in his direction. "Maxine?" She looked redder than the sundried tomato spread he'd eaten earlier. "What is it?"

Maxine clutched Abbie and Julia's arms and whispered in faint disbelief, "She came."

"Who came?"

"I knew it!" Abbie beamed.

Julia cheered. "Me, too!"

"Who are you talking about?" If Janice had found a way to crash this party—

"Look, Rourke," Maxine said, dispensing with the "Mr. Flannigan."

He followed her gaze and spotted a woman standing in the doorway wearing a black halter dress, her dark hair spilling over creamy shoulders in a glossy swirl of magnificence. "Kate," he breathed. She moved toward him, sidestepping couples, waiters, and tables, her gaze never leaving his. "Kate," he said again, not realizing he'd been holding his breath. The woman who had haunted him for fourteen years grew closer, squeezing the air from his lungs with each step. He tried to speak but the words wouldn't come.

When she stood a heartbeat away, she opened her beautiful mouth and said, "My mother told me she called you."

"She did." He did not want to talk about this now.

"She told me about your mother." She hesitated. "Your real mother."

"Right this second, that's the last thing on my mind." *She was so beautiful.*

Her blue eyes rimmed with tears. "It seems everyone was determined to keep us apart. My mother, yours, even Clay."

"It's in the past now." *The future is what I want. With you.*

"I'm so sorry I didn't trust you more."

"Shhh." He placed a finger on her lips. "It's okay."

She nodded. "Just one more thing."

"What?" His gaze slid over her face. She really did have the most incredible lips.

"Please don't fire Maxine."

She licked her lips and Rourke had to force himself not to reach out and kiss her. "Why would I fire Maxine?" *Who the hell cared about Maxine right now?*

"For sending me the reports."

"What reports?"

Her perfect skin turned a soft rose. "The reports from your detective. The ones about me."

Rourke froze. *Maxine had sent them to Kate?* "Look, there's a perfectly logical explanation for those."

"Oh, I hope not." She moved closer and lowered her voice. "I hope there's no logical explanation. I hope there's only one, very illogical, impractical, and totally implausible reason for those reports."

"Really?"

Those full, luscious lips tilted at the corners. "Yes. And I hope it's a perfect match for the illogical letters I wrote in my journal, the same journal you wrote your letter in."

"You read the letter." He'd been hurt and desperate when he'd written it. He'd sounded like a complete wimp. Was that why she was smiling?

"Several times."

He settled his gaze on the top of her head and tried to regain control. "It was a weak moment. I don't usually sound like a…" He couldn't even say the word *wimp*.

Kate touched his cheek and murmured, "It was a beautiful moment and I hope there will be more of those."

She sounded like she really meant it. Maybe being a wimp on occasion wasn't such a bad idea after all. He crushed Kate against his chest and swung her off her feet. "God, but I love you."

She buried her head against his chest and sighed. "I've always loved you. Even when I thought I'd never see you again."

"Marry me." He eased her to the ground and looked down at her. "Let's not waste one more hour apart."

"It's not that simple."

"Of course it is." They loved each other. After all these years they could finally admit it—to themselves and each other.

"No, it's not. There are a million problems."

"I'm a very good problem-solver." He smiled and rested his hands on her shoulders. "Stop frowning or you'll be more wrinkled than a prune."

"I'm serious, Rourke."

"So am I. Wrinkles are not my idea of attraction, though I'd love you even if you were shriveled."

Her eyes narrowed to a glittery blue. "But why, Rourke? Why would you love me when you can have anyone you want?" Those beautiful eyes filled with tears. "I don't want to be a novelty that gets used up and bought off. I'd rather lose you now than live through that."

"I asked you to marry me, Kate. I've never asked a woman that before."

"There are women who won't care if you're married or not when they come after you."

"I want you."

"I won't be thirty-three forever. I'll get old and very wrinkled."

"So will I."

She threw him a look that said she doubted it. "I could gain a hundred pounds and lose my hair."

The woman could be exasperating. "More to love and have you ever heard of wigs?" She was not getting out of this so easily, not when he almost had her.

"What about Julia?"

"What about Julia?" He glanced at his daughter who gave him the thumbs-up. "I think she'll be fine, especially when she finds out Abbie's part of the deal."

Kate's voice fell to a whisper and he had to lean in close to hear her next words. "I'm so scared. I've been living with your memory for so long; what if the real thing isn't what I thought it would be?"

He stroked her cheek and trailed his hand along her neck. "What if it's so much better than either of us thought it could be? I'm sure as hell not giving that up. Don't be afraid, Kate. I'm sure enough for both of us."

"Then yes," she breathed.

"Yes?"

"Yes, I will marry you." She rose up on tiptoe and kissed him softly on the mouth. Once. Twice. "And I will love you for the rest of my life."

Rourke pulled her to him and whispered against her lips, "Remind me to give Maxine a raise."

She kissed him. "And a bonus."

"A car, too," he said, smiling down at her. "How do you think she'd look in a Jag?"

"I think there's a whole side of Maxine we haven't seen yet."

Wait until he told her about Miles Gregory. "I think you're right." He kissed her once again and released her. "We are definitely going to finish this later tonight. Right now I'd like to introduce you to this roomful of gawkers."

She clasped his hand and smiled up at him. "Maybe even a toast? To us?"

"To the way we were," he said gently, loving the feel of her beside him. "To the way we will be for the rest of our lives. Together."

Epilogue

To file:

Clients: Abbie Flannigan and Julia Maden as approved by Ms. Maxine Simmons and Mr. Miles Gregory.

Subject: Rourke and Kate Flannigan

Date: July 27th, 2010

Mr. and Mrs. Flannigan checked into the Ritz Carlton on Central Park South at 4:15 p.m., July 23rd. At 6:50 p.m., Mr. and Mrs. Flannigan exited hotel and walked to Tavern on the Green where they proceeded to dine on lobster and filet mignon. They shared a bottle of Chardonnay 1991.

Couple remained at the restaurant until 9:30 p.m. at which time they made their way back to the hotel. Best estimation, lights out at 10:20 p.m.

Mr. and Mrs. Flannigan spent the next two days seeing the sights of New York City: Statue of Liberty, Guggenheim Art Museum, Good Morning America studio, and The Lion King. *Dining out included Chinese, Italian, Vietnamese, and various corner hot dog vendors. A bottle of Chardonnay 1991 accompanied each meal (with the exception of the hot dog vendors). One trip to Tiffany's where Mr. Flannigan purchased a string of pearls with matching earrings for Mrs. Flannigan Mr. Flannigan made two other purchases, one for his daughter and one for his niece. Said purchases will remain a secret until such time as Mr. Flannigan chooses to divulge their contents.*

Couple departed for France on July 26th. Honeymoon progressing in a satisfactory manner for all parties concerned. End of report.

The End

If you'd like to be notified of my new releases, please sign up at http://www.marycampisi.com.

Many thanks for choosing to spend your time reading The Way They Were. If you enjoyed it, please consider writing a review on the site where you purchased it. And now, I must head back to my characters and help them get in AND out of trouble!

One Last Thought

As with all of my books, *The Way They Were* underwent several revisions. I clipped and tweaked, added on, deleted, and pretty much drove myself crazy trying to get just the right feel, tone, and words for this story. But, there was one particular journal entry that didn't fit inside the book yet perfectly captured Kate's undying love for Rourke...

Journal Entry – May 4, 2007

Clay died twenty-two days ago. He fell thirty feet while on a job in Syracuse. This project was supposed to change things for us, give us a better life, more money, more time together, a new start...a granite countertop for the kitchen...all it got him was dead.

I'm bursting with guilt—guilt over not having loved him enough...guilt over loving you too much.

Why did such a good man have to die?

The company he was subcontracting for sent a floral arrangement to the funeral home—it covered half the wall. Literally. You'd have thought they were his closest friends. It's just guilt. The owner probably doesn't even know a man died on his job site.

But he's going to—I'm not through with Reese Construction yet.

My whole life has changed. What I thought I could count on has vanished, as quickly as you did fourteen years ago. And I find myself alone. Again.

Thank God for Julia.

If not for her, I would curl up and let the pain consume me.

Pain of loss.

Pain of guilt.

Pain of not loving enough.

Pain of loving too much.

Pain of loving the wrong man.

Clay loved me and in my own way, I loved him. But I don't think he ever really believed that. And now it's too late.

I've always loved you. Even though you'll never know.

This will be the last time I write in this journal. It is the only way I know to honor Clay's memory. It is the least I can do. But fear not, you live inside me, you always have— you always will.

About the Author

Mary Campisi writes emotion-packed books about second chances. Whether contemporary romances, women's fiction, or Regency historicals, her books all center on belief in the beauty of that second chance.

Mary should have known she'd become a writer when at age thirteen she began changing the ending to all the books she read. It took several years and a number of jobs, including registered nurse, receptionist in a swanky hair salon, accounts payable clerk, and practice manager in an OB/GYN office, for her to rediscover writing. Enter a mouse-less computer, a floppy disk, and a dream large enough to fill a zip drive. The rest of the story lives on in every book she writes.

When she's not working on her craft or following the lives of five adult children, Mary's digging in the dirt with her flowers and herbs, cooking, reading, walking her rescue lab mix, Cooper, or on the perfect day, riding off into the sunset with her very own 'hero' husband on his Ultra Limited aka Harley.

Mary has published with Kensington, Carina Press, and The Wild Rose Press.

website: www.marycampisi.com
e-mail: mary@marycampisi.com
twitter: https://twitter.com/#!/MaryCampisi
blog: http://www.marycampisi.com/blog/
facebook: http://www.facebook.com/marycampisibooks

Other Books by Mary Campisi:

Contemporary Romance:
Truth in Lies Series
Book One: A Family Affair
Book Two: A Family Affair: Spring
Book Three: A Family Affair: Summer
Book Four: A Family Affair: Fall
Book Five: A Family Affair: Christmas
Book Six: A Famiy Affair: Winter
Book Seven: A Family Affair: The Promise
Book Eight: A Family Affair: The Secret

That Second Chance Series
Book One: Pulling Home
Book Two: The Way They Were
Book Three: Simple Riches
Book Four: Paradise Found
Book Five: Not Your Everyday Housewife
Book Six: The Butterfly Garden

The Betrayed Trilogy
Book One: Pieces of You
Book Two: Secrets of You
Book Three: What's Left of Her: a novella
Boxed Set: The Betrayed Trilogy

Begin Again: Short stories from the heart
The Sweetest Deal

Regency Historical:
An Unlikely Husband Series

Book One - The Seduction of Sophie Seacrest
Book Two - A Taste of Seduction
Book Three - A Touch of Seduction, a novella
Book Four - A Scent of Seduction

The Model Wife Series
Book One: The Redemption of Madeline Munrove

Young Adult:
Pretending Normal

CPSIA information can be obtained
at www.ICGtesting.com
Printed in the USA
LVHW021541060519
616793LV00001B/59/P